A DARK SHAPE ROSE
FROM THE SHADOWS
AND HOVERED CLOSER.

"How are you?" queried O. M. Timm.

By the light of the gas jets, Frank Coughlin eyed the face under the black slouch hat. "I'm drinking my grandfather's scotch at my brother's wake."

"Ah, well. It's a terrible century when a man can be murdered for a parcel of...air."

Temple's eyes flickered. "The police say it was an accident."

"Well, the police work for the City, and the City works for big business." The landmark expert's goatee framed a private smile. "Cornerstone is immense. Of course, your safest route is to sell them this saloon—but then your brother will have died in vain. Seek historic designation, however, and his killer may be lured into the open."

Coughlin raised an eyebrow. "You mean, act as bait?"

"Hey, Frank," Temple cut in. "I don't like this..."

SHATTERED MASK

D. G. DEVON

BALLANTINE BOOKS • NEW YORK

Library of Congress Catalog Card Number: 83-90645

ISBN 0-345-29849-7

Manufactured in the United States of America

First Edition: November 1983

To my brother Bill
and
To Ave, Sam, and Sherry

Thanks to Mary Anne Page; Susan Blond; Sue Charney and Carole Fields of Sue Charney Models; Arthur Fox; Alan Haber of the New York City Landmarks Preservation Commission; Sally Lindberg; David Manning; Sue Radmer of The Information Exchange, The Municipal Art Society; and the Local History and Genealogy and Performing Arts Divisions of the New York Public Library.

"Houses live and die: there is a time for building
And a time for living and generation
And a time for the wind to break the loosened pane . . ."
—T. S. ELIOT

This is Temple Kent—or rather, a reasonable facsimile. If you'd like the real thing, leave a reasonable facsimile of yourself, and I'll call back when I reconstitute. The best message wins a free vacation for two in sunny St. Croix. Offer expires midnight, December thirty-first.

BEEP. "Hiya, Temple. Don't you sound pretty on a winter afternoon. It's your favorite saloon keeper, Kevin "Casey" Coughlin, looking for the handsome one in the family. If you should run across my baby brother Frankie, have him call me at the Saloon, okay? We got trouble."

BEEP. "I don't talk to robots."

BEEP. "Bill VanderPoel calling. In case you haven't been paying attention, it's next year already—but you know that. You're a real trouper for helping me with this landmarks do tonight. I hope it's not just because I'm your boss. If you don't have Frank in tow, I'll take you out to dinner afterward."

BEEP. "What happened to yesterday's tape? I had the most super animal noise all ready for you too. You'll have to hear it anyway, luv. A pterodactyl, by your booker, Annabel Fletcher. Here goes: *GRRRRRRRAAAAAAAAAAAAASSSSSKKKCH!* How was that? . . . Oh, don't forget, New York's hottest model is due at Jimmy Shelby's photo studio tomorrow at noon. Don't be tardy. Ta, Number One."

BEEP.

BEEP. "The name's Lewis Tedesco. Jimmy Shelby gave me your number. I'm casting girls for the next James Bond flick, and I think you'd be tee-riff. What do you think? Might be your big chance to find out if Hollywood's as bad as you've always hoped. Reach me at 495-0-double-0-7. . . . Do I win the prize?"

1

BEEP. "Frank, angel. You sure you need me at this high-class protest rally tonight? I may be tied up in court, so start the good deeds without me . . . Oh, and thanks for making my bed this morning. Later . . ."

BEEP. "Dammit to hell! Listen, it's Casey again. I *have* to reach Frankie double-quick! Tell him . . . Just tell him some big outfit's stealing our family home: The Saloon . . . the house . . . *everything*."

FRIDAY

One

A long-legged redhead hopped from a taxi in front of the Frick art collection, housed in one of Fifth Avenue's last surviving mansions. Temple Kent, armored in beauty, hurried across the icy night sidewalks and entered the stuffy museum. She was in her mid-twenties, barely single, and amused but excited to be partying with elders who thought she belonged in such elegant surroundings.

In the cloakroom, she stripped off her mismatched leather gloves—one yellow, one blue—and shoved them into the pockets of her ankle-length black cashmere coat. Beneath it was a dramatic black dinner dress that bared an opposing leg and shoulder, designed by Norma Kamali.

Shaking out her full mane of titian hair, Temple strolled through the turnstile with the air of a thoroughbred. She sauntered past the roped-off grand staircase leading to the upper floors, and paused in the hall to admire women by Vermeer, Ingres, Monet, and Renoir. Then she realized strangers were appraising her as though she, too, were an *objet d'art*. So Temple roamed away through the priceless collection, watchful for someone of her very own.

She poked her head into the preciously frippy Fragonard Room, where a series of feathery canvases charted the *Progress of Love*. Just then, a powerfully built man with coal-black hair filled the opposite doorway. His gray flannel suit and striped tie conveyed crisp authority. Prowling the room with the confidence of a jungle cat, he frowned at the French piss-elegance surrounding him. When the parquet floor let out a prissy squeak under his boots, the room suddenly seemed even wimpier. Somehow Temple felt the paintings must be watching him too.

Then he sighted her. She dropped her violet eyes to fish an apple out of her purse, crunched a bite, and looked up to find the man gazing at her openly with a crooked grin. He winked.

3

Her own mismatched lips skewed into a knowing smile. She lobbed the apple to him underhand before drifting across the gleaming floor to a small plaque on a stand.

In seconds, the man was beside her.

"Jean Honoré Fragonard," he said in a deep, velvety baritone.

"Pleased to meet you, John. My name's Temple Kent."

He glanced at her quizzically, then pointed to the plaque he was reading. "'Jean Honoré Fragonard, 1732–1806. The four large canvases representing the *Progress of Love* were completed in 1773 . . .'"

The man gazed around at the flowery paintings and spindly furniture before chomping into her apple. "This must be Liberace's idea of heaven," he mumbled with his mouth full.

Temple eyed the tight corsets, spilling bodices, and cumbersome hoop skirts of the pinched, pale girls on the walls. "I remember coming here as a kid and telling my dad that if this was love, I didn't want any part of it."

"You don't think it's romantic?"

"Ick. I feel like I'm drowning in cotton candy." She pointed to one of Fragonard's swains in satin breeches and a frilly lace collar. "How can you respect a man who wears face powder?"

He took another huge bite of apple. "Actually, these are very hot paintings."

"They are?"

"It's all in the symbolism." He dangled the core by its stem. "Want your apple back?"

When she reached for it, he reached too.

"Frank! What are you doing?"

"It's known in the trade as 'simple assault.'"

Temple gave him a quick kiss before squirming free. "Didn't you get enough last night?"

"Sure . . . But why are we here?"

"We're paying our dues. I like the idea of a fleeting beauty like me making a stand for permanence. And a little publicity wouldn't hurt your career either, you know."

"*Women's Wear* doesn't care about municipal judges."

"You said the mayor has you in line for a promotion. It's good for you to meet these people. Think of it as an audition. Smile a lot."

Coughlin made a face at her as they wandered into a cul-de-sac containing Boucher's *Four Seasons* paintings. Temple was studying *Winter* when she remembered Casey Coughlin's messages.

"Your brother called looking for you. Twice. It sounded pretty important."

Frank kept eyeing the three nudes in the pastoral painting called *Summer* on the opposite wall.

"It was something about the Saloon, Frank. He really sounded worried."

"I'll call him tonight," Frank murmured, not taking his eyes from the milky pink derriére of one of the *Summer* women.

"You like her?" Temple sniffed. "I'll buy you the postcard."

Coughlin's gold-flecked eyes danced with amusement as he patted her bottom through the clingy Kamali.

"Not here." She pushed his hand away nervously. "There are people around."

He glanced up and down the hallway. Grabbing her arm, he walked quickly to the forbidden grand staircase, raised the braided gold cord, and tugged her under. They darted up the carpeted marble steps.

"Frank!" She pulled him to a stop on the first landing, whispering fiercely. "We could get caught for trespassing!"

Coughlin grinned wickedly as he dragged her toward the privacy of the second-floor offices. "We could get caught for more than that," he promised.

"Pardon me. Would you stop what you're doing?"

A cultivated voice rolled out of the loudspeakers in the Garden Court, ricocheted through the entrance hall, and floated up the staircase.

A few seconds later, Temple's head popped out of a door on the second floor. When Frank joined her by the wrought-iron bannister, they peered down the cavernous stairwell like two children spying on a party of grownups.

"Ladies and gentlemen, would you join us please?"

"No," Coughlin muttered, turning back toward the office.

Temple began smoothing her dress. "Come on. Watching rich people give away money is fun."

"It's more fun up here," he insisted.

"True. But you know the first law of adulthood: Business before pleasure." Sitting sidesaddle on the thin wooden railing, she kicked up her feet and slid smoothly down to the landing.

"The name is Ogden Maldwyn Timm . . . That's two M's in

Timm. Lend me your ears, please . . . I'll ask for your money later."

Frank straightened his tie and walked down the steps behind her. Temple turned the corner and slid down to the South Hall floor.

"I greet you tonight as chairman of the Upper Times Square Landmarks League. Many of you also know me as a consultant to New York's Landmarks Preservation Commission, or as architecture columnist for the TriBeCa TriWeekly. *Some have even been so kind as to call me the dean of American architectural gadflies . . ."*

"C'mon, chicken—slide!"

"I can't, Temple. I'm a judge."

She looked left and right into the hall. "There's nobody coming," she stage-whispered.

"Promise?" Balancing on the polished railing, Coughlin let himself go, swooshing down so swiftly he nearly bowled over two blue-haired ladies as they rounded the corner. They glared at the embarrassed magistrate as though they intended to have a word with his mother.

"He's so sorry," Temple grinned, waltzing away into the courtyard at the center of the museum.

The Frick's Garden Court was a classic Ionic colonnade, laid out around a central fountain, with a vaulted glass canopy overhead. Two frog statuettes spouted thin arcs of water into the shallow pool, and flowers blossomed in the dead of winter.

At the north end of the court, a portly little man in a natty tweed suit stood at the microphone, leaning on a silver-tipped walking stick. His bald head was fringed with a ring of salt-and-pepper hair that matched a neat little goatee. He was directing his remarks to a cluster of reporters armed with notebooks and tape recorders.

"New York's landmark laws are more enlightened than those in other parts of the country, and yet the progress we've made thus far is just a drop in the bucket." The speaker leaned over and theatrically splashed his champagne into the fountain. *"As our largest newspaper commented recently: 'When you think about it, maybe you should think about it . . .'"*

Milling around the marble benches and sitting on the low steps were perhaps a hundred people feeling good about themselves. Fendi furs bristled against dark Armani suits. The latest Milanese booties scuffled across the stone floor.

"Consider the theater district: a chilling thought. Now that Times Square is a desirable area again, construction interests are trashing our theatrical heritage—and for what? The commonest commodity in the world, folks—air! Air rights to make way for buildings that look like toasters to satisfy their . . . edifice complexes."

When Coughlin caught up to her, Temple quietly pointed out some Best-Dressed types she recognized from the front rows of fashion shows, and a radical chic actress half-hidden behind a wall of retainers in Levi's.

"I bet they're all just waiting for Jackie O," he mumbled.

"There she is!"

"Where?" His head snapped around.

"Made ya look."

The man at the microphone was pointing to a map behind him, indicating a block in the north Forties, west of Broadway. *"A parcel of properties is now being assembled on this particular street by a mysterious real estate concern whose owners hide behind the name Cornerstone Equities. Obviously they have something to be ashamed of.*

"Unfortunately, among their targets are several buildings that merit protection. There is a row of Greek Revival brownstones—cut up into boarding houses now, but classics nonetheless . . ."

Frank reached for Temple's hand and twined their fingers contentedly.

"Then there's a mansion designed by James Renwick, the architect of Saint Patrick's Cathedral, the Smithsonian Institution, and Vassar College. Not only was it the first mansion built in this part of the city, it also became one of Prohibition's most notorious speakeasies—Petunia's."

Coughlin's eyes flickered. "Hey . . . I think he's talking about our Saloon."

"You mean this is about *your* block?"

"And finally, the Emerald Theater. Not a Broadway house, or even the vaudeville house it once was, this theater now shows revival films, leaving it completely undefended by the city's so-called unique zoning protection. Nevertheless, the Emerald is astonishing. At each corner of its neo-Renaissance facade, a pair of Corinthian peristyles rise to the roof. Where the columns meet the cornice line, attached sidewall sculptures of Comedy and Tragedy guard the approaches to the playhouse.

"Tonight we are indeed fortunate to have the owner of the Emerald in our midst.." Timm's cane pointed toward an elfin, white-haired man in a wheelchair, tucked among the marble pillars. *"Ladies and gentlemen, please welcome the distinguished Mr. Michael McQueeney."*

A hefty old woman rolled the invalid forward for an instant. The dapper gent wore a gray sharkskin suit, white shirt, and shiny navy tie. His thick prescription glasses were tinted magenta. He acknowledged the crowd with the merest flip of his wrist.

"His theater is living history, folks. The Marx Brothers broke in some of their greatest routines there. George Gershwin played the piano while Fanny Brice sang . . ."

"Frank? Haven't I seen that guy at the Saloon?"

Coughlin nodded, tugging her around the periphery of the crowd as Timm burbled on.

Frank leaned down by Michael McQueeney's vein-laced cheek. "I want you to meet someone, Uncle Mickey." He beckoned Temple closer. "Michael McQueeney, this is Temple Kent."

The old man smelled clean and fragrant, like a barbershop. When she took his hand, it seemed to lack all substance. "Pleased to meet you, sir."

McQueeney's eyes twinkled with life behind his tinted lenses. He spoke in a rough-hewn whisper that was surprisingly strong for such a fragile body.

"You're Irish, ain't ya?"

"Well . . ."

"No, no, no. Ya must be Irish—I can tell. And ya can call me Uncle Mickey."

Genially, McQueeney indicated the elderly woman behind his wheelchair. "This here's Dora Driscoll. I call her my pusher." A roguish chuckle brought color surging briefly into his pasty cheeks until he began wheezing into a white monogrammed handkerchief.

Dora Driscoll grinned with piercing crystal blue eyes. "I swear my Michael will kill himself with his own jokes someday." The old woman's handshake was so firm she could have been a masseuse. "Aren't you the prettiest thing, now?"

"You're the lady who always waves at me from the ticket booth of the theater."

"Ah, you're a lamb to notice. I always wave once I decide

I like the looks of a person." Dora winked. "It used to cause me the most terrible trouble with the gentlemen."

"Today, the fates of the Renwick mansion and the Emerald hang in the balance—just like the theater's huge, symmetrical masks of Comedy and Tragedy."

The old man tapped Temple's knee. "I call 'em Glee and Glum," he cackled. Then they turned to give O. M. Timm their undivided attention.

"A week from Monday, the Upper Times Square Landmarks League will try to rout the Philistines at the Emerald Theater. On that night, when all the other Broadway houses are dark, dozens of stars and celebrity amateurs will donate their night off to a satiric revue called A Comedy of Errors. *We're dedicating it to New York City's bureaucracy."* The landmarks expert smirked knowingly. *"We hope to raise two hundred and fifty thousand dollars—a salvation fund we'll use to survey every building in Upper Times Square, determining which of them deserve preservation.*

"Now I'd like to introduce our Honorary Executive Committee. You are all guests of the following friends of the League . . ."

One at a time, they stepped forward: a man bearing the name of a famous concert hall; the widow of a governor of New York State; the leftist actress and her chow dog; Tina Molineux, the owner of Temple's modeling agency; and Temple's exclusive employer, William VanderPoel, the trim, patrician chairman of the board of VanderPoel Cosmetics. He waved at her.

"This production is being underwritten by VanderPoel Cosmetics, and it was Bill VanderPoel himself who selected our hostess. You may not know her name, but I guarantee you the face is familiar. You've seen her on the cover of every magazine from Vogue *to* Sports Illustrated. *Ladies and gentlemen, I'd like to present the crown jewel of the Molineux Agency . . . the million-dollar face of the VanderPoel Narcissus line . . . Miss Temple Kent! Step forward. Don't be shy."*

As a hundred faces turned in Temple's direction, photographers rushed from the front of the room and began exploding flashbulbs in their faces. She glanced nervously at Frank. "Surprise. You think I should curtsy?"

Realizing he was losing the crowd's attention, O. M. Timm raised his voice and brandished a fist:

"This Landmarks League will rescue the Emerald, and we will not stop there in our quest for a more civilized world. We cannot escape the past, folks. In the end, we are all history, and our lives either do us honor . . . or betray us forever. So make history—not rubble! Power to the Preservationists!" To polite applause, the goateed man stepped away from his microphone, buttonholing several reporters.

McQueeney reached out a thin hand to tug Frank's sleeve. "I hope ya ain't becomin' one of these active citizens, Francis."

Coughlin grinned. "You're here too."

"That's a hundred and ten percent right. But I think I been suckered." The old man made a sour face. "This fella with the fancy stick is a big overreaction if ya ask me. Rushes in sayin' I got somethin' called a facade that's crumblin'. Hell, I can take care of my own business. I'm only goin' along with this play 'cause he says the rest of the block needs me. Only now I ain't so sure they want to be saved. Anybody wants to sell out to these real estate fellas, I'll back his right to do it. Could be we got a meddler here, just wants to see his name in the papers."

Suddenly, a champagne glass shattered on the stones. Angry voices exploded across the courtyard, where two men were engaged in a shoving match. One wore the collar of a Catholic priest.

"A devil, am I? Shame on you!" The clergyman's open hand cracked across his accuser's face.

The other man looked like Frank, only rounder. He had the same perpetually rumpled black hair, but a softer, red face.

"Jesus, it's Casey." Coughlin sprinted around the fountain with Temple at his heels, reaching his older brother just as the flushed saloon keeper raised a meaty fist.

Frank intercepted the blow in midair. "What are you trying to do—get eighty-sixed from heaven?"

Casey Coughlin glared at the priest hotly. Tugging his arm out of his younger brother's grasp, he lurched toward the coatroom.

When they caught up to him at the check window, Casey's bitter words echoed off the mirrored walls and parquet floor. "Who let *him* in? You know that turn-collar already applied to the archdiocese for permission to sell Saint Agnes? And now I find out he's representin' these builder sharks from Cornerstone! He had the nerve to pass me their offer for the Saloon. I tell you, they're closin' in on me from all sides."

Casey pounded his fist on the counter thunderously. "Christ, whose block is it anyway? Frankie, you remember when we were kids, all the years we spent watchin' the crowds line up at the old Garden for the fights and the circus? So what is it now? A parkin' lot!" He shook his head stubbornly. "Times may be changin', but not me. Not ever!"

Dora Driscoll was beside them now, sliding two plastic plaques across the counter, whispering, "Hush now, lad. You're attractin' entirely too much attention."

"I don't care." Casey lowered his voice nonetheless. "You know what that Father Dolan says? He says the Saloon can't be landmarked because of the new glass skylight I put over the dinin' room last summer. Christ, Frankie, I only thought it would perk up the place, you see?"

"It did, Casey—it's beautiful. Don't worry about it."

"Don't worry about it? All I do is worry about it."

"Why? No one can make you sell."

The older brother dropped his eyes and glanced around the floor nervously.

". . . Can they? Casey, the Saloon is doing okay, isn't it?"

"Sure, sure. You just don't know what's been goin' on."

Frank peered at his agitated brother closely. "Okay, what has been going on?"

Reluctantly, Casey passed him a folded piece of paper. Words had been snipped with pinking shears out of three newspaper headlines. Glued carelessly across the page, the jagged message couldn't have been more explicit:

SELL OR DIE!

Frank turned the threat over in his hands several times before passing it back. "Why didn't you tell me about this before? I grew up in that house too."

"Ah, I didn't want you involved. You got a career to worry about. Christ, Frankie, I guess I embarrassed you good out there, huh?"

"Stop talking like a jerk."

"I *am* a jerk. Temple, I didn't mean to bust up your party here."

As three coats were delivered across the counter, Frank

draped one around his brother's shoulders. "I want to hear more about this . . . pressure."

"Not now, okay? I gotta check out this priest first. I want to know what's in it for him. You come by the Saloon tomorrow night, I'll fill you in. Maybe it's time you knew more of the family secrets."

Frank raised a crooked smile. "Secrets?"

Casey's face mirrored his younger brother's. "Maybe you can help after all. I hear you got good connections. And bring Temple along if you want. I like the way you think around her."

Frank nodded. "'Night, Dora."

The old woman was juggling two coats. "God bless ye, kids."

Arms around each other's shoulders, the threesome swayed out of the Frick with Temple wedged snugly between the two brothers. The sidewalk was covered with a light dusting of virgin snow. They hailed Casey a taxi, rolled him in, and waved back when he made faces at them out the rear window.

Then Temple spied an empty Checker rounding the far corner. She began waving frantically at the yellow taxi—another endangered city landmark.

"Uh, Temple . . ." He nodded back to the sidewalk, where a battered but powerful red and black motorcycle leaned casually on its kickstand. "I drove tonight . . . Sorry."

"I thought you promised you wouldn't ride that thing in winter."

"In the snow, I said. It wasn't snowing when I left."

She followed him reluctantly, hoisting her skirts to straddle the chilly seat behind him. "Coughlin, there are certain times when the quest for cool is just too damned cold. Get it?"

"Don't worry. After the first ten blocks, you won't feel a thing." He kicked down savagely on the starter. "My place or yours?" he yelled over the thundering din.

"After all these months, you'd think we'd know the answer by now!" She gazed longingly as the warm, roomy Checker coasted by.

"Well?"

Temple wrapped her arms around the man's waist and held on tight.

"Surprise me!"

Two

Temple lay back against one end of her extra-large, lion-pawed bathtub as a bead of perspiration trickled ever-so-slowly down her chest. She was bathing by lavender candlelight, with "Winter" from a Rolling Stones album, shimmering around the dark, steamy room.

The naked man facing her in the bubblebath puffed a skinny New York joint and grinned lasciviously. The Rigaud flame on the ledge flickered, in his golden eyes. Over the sink, his red toothbrush spooned against her yellow one.

Under the suds, Temple's slippery limbs played over and inside his thighs. He hooked his feet behind the small of her back and tugged her closer.

"What's on your mind, Coughlin?"

Scooping up a mound of bubbles, Frank deftly sculpted a white meringue topping over each wet breast.

"Say, Temple?" The man examined her whip-tipped bosom. "You ever think of modeling for Dairy Queen?"

"Comedian," she muttered. Lunging suddenly, she smooshed both sundaes into his chest, before dunking his head. Several gallons of water sloshed onto the Spanish-tiled floor. When Frank surfaced with another mighty splash, she giggled at the soaked roach still hanging from his lips.

He began groping for her underwater, but Temple scrambled out of the tub in a flash of limbs, flushed pink and glistening as a saucy water nymph.

Coughlin cornered her against the chrome towel rack.

While his face nuzzled her neck, Temple caught sight of their mirrored nudes in the flickering candlelight. She admired the muscles flowing across his shoulders and down his back, and her own lithe form molded around him.

"We look like a Rodin," she sighed. Hugging him closer, she gently kissed the thin white scars that split his eyebrows like tiny sword cuts.

"You never told me how you got these."

"Didn't I?" He began sipping her lips lazily.

"Aren't you going to tell me?"

"Sure . . . in the dark . . . later." Frank carried her upstairs with her arms around his neck and her head nestling on his chest like a sleepy child's.

Temple's duplex loft on Great Jones Street was nicknamed Paradise for the sanctuary it provided, tucked away behind several dilapidated buildings in one of New York's most unsavory districts, NoHo. Built as a stable in 1873, its thick wooden beams and white-washed brick walls lulled visitors into another, more peaceful, time and place.

Frank crossed the pegged, broad-planked floor and knelt on a padded futon mattress under the loft's huge multiple skylights. He slid Temple slowly down the tops of his thighs until her bottom touched her mat. As he tipped her over backward, her arms were still around his neck, pulling him over her.

"I love how your lips turn dark in the night." He swept his hands over her curves, exploring her shape.

Her arms fell limp behind her as he continued stroking, until her breathing became tiny cries and she squirmed restlessly against him.

And he remembered the first night they'd done this together. How they'd flown into the city by seaplane one warm summer night, taxiing to his cottage in Greenwich Village. How they'd stayed outside in the walled back garden, drinking rum under the indigo sky, getting barefoot, and later barechested, and finally, far past midnight, barebottomed and wild in the long green grass. Rolling in the dew and the darkness so long that, next morning, she giggled and called him to the cottage doorway and pointed at the trampled lawn, saying, "Somebody tried to make snow angels without the snow."

Standing in his sunny doorway, laughing with nothing on but one of his Brooks Brothers shirts, while the morning breeze lapped at her bottom . . .

Temple's hand was looking for him now, sliding up his leg to pet him gently. And then more urgently.

"Frank . . ."

He sat back, staring down at the open woman. "I can't wait."

She tickled him forward with just one finger. "So don't."

Afterward, Temple lay on her back, combing gentle fingers through his coal-black hair.

"You awake?" she whispered.

He let out a low, affirmative growl.

"What's it like to have an older brother?"

"Well . . . he's my point man."

"What's a point man?"

"In the war, one guy would lead the way into dangerous territory. Casey does that for me. He gives me courage. You've got to love your point man."

"Sounds like how I felt about my dad."

"Sure. My dad wasn't the easiest guy to know, though, so Casey took up the slack."

Frank's eyebrows slid together. "The poor guy always had it rough. He spent most of his life in the Saloon pulling beers. You can imagine the women he meets. But if it hadn't been for him there in front of me, I wouldn't be where I am today. Hell, I wouldn't even have my apartment."

"Really? When I tell people you've got a West Village floor-through with a garden *and* a cottage out back for one sixty-three seventy-five a month, they foam at the mouth."

"That place wasn't always such a prize. When I set up my own practice, I was still living at home. I was dying for a place of my own—but I didn't know how to tell Casey. I was afraid he'd feel abandoned."

"Did he?"

"If he did, he never let me know it. He even went apartment hunting with me. When we first saw that yard, it was a weed-filled dump with a shack that had its roof caved in. There was an outhouse against the bakery wall, one dead tree, not a blade of grass . . ."

"Things have improved."

"Thanks to Casey. I wanted to turn it down but he wouldn't let me. We pulled up the paving stones and planted the garden, put in the lawn, the trees, the path. . . ."

"At the end of the renovation, I was up on the roof adjusting the TV antenna, when I slipped and fell. Man, I hit the ground so hard I thought I'd broken my back. But Casey came running out, scooped me up—and I must weigh one eighty—and he just cradled me in his arms like a baby. Know what he said? 'Channel Two's still got a ghost.'"

Temple laughed deep in Coughlin's chest.

"So I figure that since he rebuilt my house, I'm going to do the same for his. We've got great plans for that Saloon... First we're going to put back the wall that was knocked down between the bar and the dining room. Then we strip the ceiling to uncover the pressed tin, refinish that old bar, replace the wooden staircases, the boiler, the wiring, most of the plumbing... By the time we get done, Times Square should be spruced up enough to deserve another Twenty-one Club. 'Course, I'll have to rob a bank first. But I was the wild card he bet on—and it's time I paid off."

Temple snuggled closer. "I think my honey wants to be president, when he really wants to be a construction contractor."

Coughlin chuckled into her titian hair, one big hand palming the curve of her belly.

"What's so funny?"

"Nothing... You... All our fine houses." He raised his head and gazed down at her with a tender little smile. "You ready to move in with me yet?"

Temple smiled uneasily. "What, and lose a rent-stabilized paradise?" She sat up and plucked Frank's pink oxford cloth shirt from the floor, wriggled into it, and tied the tails in a loose knot before lying down again.

He spanked her lightly. "Cut the one-liners. I'm serious." His hands slid underneath the pink cotton. "I want to get so close to you, I become you."

Temple squirmed onto her side, watching him warily over one hip. "I can't keep up with you, Frank."

"Sure you can. Just hang on." Nestling in close behind her, he felt her stiffen. "Being with you is like being by the ocean," he murmured. "One steady pulse—and then all these crosscurrents."

Temple gazed sightlessly into the distance. "Watch out for the undertow," she whispered in a little voice.

SATURDAY

Three

Thanks for calling, but I'm out tonight. I know you have better things to do than wait twenty seconds to talk to a machine, hoping I'll get back to you before what you want isn't important anymore. By the same token, I hate listening to tapes full of hangups. Six of one, half a dozen of the—

BEEP.

BEEP. "My analyst says I've got a *lot* of hangups. One of them is smartass phone tapes."

BEEP.

BEEP. "Gracious how-de-dos from Shelby comma James. Your agency's tellin' all the mannequins to show at noon tomorrow, T-Kay, but I won't be ready to shoot till one. Don't cruise in any later than that, darlin'. This might be the last photo session I ever do. You curious why? Good. That's the way we like ya."

BEEP.

BEEP. "It's your mother. Listen, Sunshine, I won't be able to come down for Betsy's wedding Monday after all, so your presence is hereby requested to uphold the honor of the black-sheep wing of the family. There's a reception afterward at the Athletic Club. Oh, and don't let Grammy Clarke's senile act fool you; she's clear as a bell when she wants to be. You can bring Frank, too, if he doesn't mind getting the once-over from the whole clan. Have fun..."

BEEP. *"Bon soir,* Satin, it is me at last. Is my little girl grown up and married? I still dream about our island, where the peacocks cry in the night like you do making love...happy and sad all at once...And now I might fly to the States before long. Can you ever forgive me? I will call again soon. I miss you, little dream, especially when I fall asleep facing west...."

* * *

Oh, God. Him again.

Temple snapped off her answering machine and rewound the previous night's messages. Then she sat on the piano bench in front of an old Steinway that had been gathering dust in her living room for years. She sipped her morning coffee thoughtfully.

"Who's Satin?"

Temple spun around, startled to find Coughlin sitting up on the futon, yawning. She crossed her eyes and stuck out her tongue as she always did when he caught her face spotted with drying lotion and her hair in quick curlers.

"Who's Satin?" he mumbled again, rubbing the sleep out of his eyes.

At last she replied, "Me . . . That was Remy."

"Remy, huh?" Coughlin frowned. "Oh, right, your first older man . . . Mediterranean art gypsy . . . sable hair with a silver streak in it . . . He got you started collecting knives, right?"

Temple tipped her head at the baby grand. "He used to play me 'Satin Doll' on the piano. Always called me Satin."

"Cute. Who let him out of jail?"

Temple shrugged. "Old news. It's been years." She escaped into the kitchen calling, "Want some fresh coffee?"

By the time she reentered the living room, Coughlin had his pants on and was browsing contentedly through her red leather model's portfolio.

He paused at his favorite page—a beauty portrait of Temple winking, shot from slightly above by the great Richard Avedon.

She snatched it from his hands, replacing it with a mug of black coffee. "I don't know whether to frame this for you or burn it."

"Frame it! Why in the world would you burn it?"

"I don't want you getting used to me looking like that. Life isn't an Avedon beauty shot." She pointed to the spot of drying lotion on her nose.

Coughlin pulled her into his lap. "I like you this way as well as any other. I like you every way there is."

"Don't bet on it."

"I wish you would," he murmured gently.

Temple stared into his face a moment, then dropped her eyes. "You'll get tired of me."

"No I won't. What I'm tired of is all this 'my place or yours' nonsense. I want us together."

"You mean you want us to be a 'thing'?" she mocked faintly.

"We're already a 'thing.' I want to know what kind of thing it is."

She jumped skittishly off his lap. "Jesus, sometimes you're as possessive as Remy."

"You love it. . . . And didn't you love him once?"

"I was nuts about him, but he was taking over my life. I don't want the same thing to happen with you. You already know what you're doing with your life; I'm still figuring mine out. It's not a good time for me to be dependent on anybody, Frank."

"Who said dependent? You always pay for half of everything."

She brushed his hair out of his eyes. "What am I going to do with you?" She padded across the room to escape down the stairs.

Frank followed and sat on the top step, drinking his coffee as he listened to the little splashes in the sink below. When all was quiet, he called down, "What are you afraid of, Temple?"

A moment passed before her small voice crept up the stairs. "Happiness? Every time I let myself depend on it, it ends up deserting me."

"Who ever deserted you?"

"Remy did."

". . . I thought you said *you* left *him*."

"Only because I couldn't trust him anymore."

Coughlin gulped some more coffee. "Sounds like a perfect reason to me . . . Does that mean you can't trust me either?"

"Oh, I trust you completely." She appeared suddenly at the foot of the stairs. "It's myself I don't trust."

"Come again?"

"Sometimes it feels like you're getting too close—and I just feel like running away. The way you make love is so damn . . . personal."

He shook his head moodily. "I thought that was the whole idea."

"Well, I guess I need more time to get used to it."

Coughlin nodded glumly. "You want me to back off?"

An exasperated look clouded her face. "No!" Temple stared up at him and then made a decision. She vanished into her bedroom before returning up the steps to sit at Frank's feet.

"Token of my esteem," she said, placing her spare set of house keys on the man's knee.

He picked them up, weighing the small consolation in his palm. "Thanks," he muttered without enthusiasm. "I hope we pass the audition."

Four

"Chloris? There's a shoe on your head."

The slender brunette raised her distinctive hawk-wing eyebrows and smiled broadly at Temple. "It's my error, hon. Everybody's got one."

Dozens of models were milling around Jimmy Shelby's photo studio looking like a softball team from the loony bin. Consuela Forberg's pinstriped baseball shirt was buttoned on backward like a straitjacket. Another girl wore the full regalia of a hockey goalie. The *Comedy of Errors* ad set could have been captioned "How many mistakes can you find in this picture?"

Perched precariously on the stool by Shelby's lightbox was Countess Tina Molineux, president of the Molineux Model Agency. She dragged on a cigarette, nervously flicking her ashes into a wastebasket. She was polished and hard down to her copper-tipped fingernails, as elegant as she was, clearly, profane.

When one of her younger models strolled by, chewing loudly, Tina dug between the girl's painted lips to extract a fat wad of gum.

Temple drifted over and set down her bag, and the older woman looked up with a sigh of relief. "I thought you'd never get here," she said, trying to drop the sticky gum into the garbage.

"I'm right on time, Tina."

The agency head checked her watch, then glanced at the mob in the middle of Shelby's studio. "I'm glad somebody is."

Finally, she scraped the pink glob off on the edge of the light-box.

Jimmy Shelby's neurotic young assistant, Radie, crept up on black high-top Keds and propped a mockup of the newspaper ad behind the lightbox. A line drawing depicted the photo they'd shoot in the next few hours: a group of beautiful feminine baseball players cavorting for a team photo. One of them lay in front, smiling into the camera obliviously as the ball she'd just tossed in the air descended toward her skull. The copy read:

THE VANDERPOEL GROUP AND TEMPLE KENT

Invite you to

A COMEDY OF ERRORS
(not by Will Shakespeare)

A variety revue
For the benefit of the Upper Times Square
Landmarks League

STARRING

SURPRISE CELEBRITIES!
From stage, screen, tube, and tabloid!

And

An old-fashioned chorus line of fifty Molineux
Agency models

Monday Night
At 8:00

THE EMERALD THEATER

Tax Deductible Contributions: $1,000*/$500/$100

*$1,000 tickets include a private cast party at
Coughlin's Saloon

Executive Producer: Ogden Maldwyn Timm
Direction and Choreography: Logan

Tina Molineux eyed her most popular model. "Like it?"

"That thing makes me nervous. You know I can't act."

"No one expects you to, dear. You're *supposed* to make a

fool of yourself." The older woman smiled thinly. "Should do wonders for your humility."

"I don't see you risking your ego in public."

"Well, we can't all be stars, dear. As Will Rogers once said, 'Someone has to sit on the curb and clap as the parade goes by.'"

Temple made a face and strolled into Shelby's bedroom to change from her jeans and turtleneck into a Saint Louis Browns baseball uniform. The other models' scattered clothing made the photographer's retreat look like a girl's locker room. Preening before the mirrored wall was Temple's ice-blonde colleague, Nina Vartell.

"'Allo, Temple Kent," the French model cooed, tying and untying a stocking around her neck, first like a scarf, then like a bow tie.

"Hi, Nina." Temple nodded warily.

"I am so excited," the platinum-haired girl breathed. "Because of this show I will finally be discovered. I am sure."

Pulling out her beauty tools, Temple didn't bother to reply.

"I love the lights," Nina prattled on. "Flashbulb lights. Footlights. My name in lights. Mmmmm," she hummed tunelessly, "when the lights go on, I must turn to them."

"Sort of heliotropic, huh?"

Nina Vartell's eyes narrowed suspiciously. "What you call me?"

"Heliotropic. The tendency of living things, like plants, to turn toward the sun."

Nina sniffed and shook her head vigorously. "Who needs sunlight, eh? I need an audience—millions—all giving me their money."

"You ought to move to China," Temple suggested wryly. "Why settle for millions when you can have billions."

"Oooooh, yes!" Nina squealed. "There are so many fans there, *c'est vrai?*"

"Commies, Nina. Just your type. Heavy into sharing the wealth." Temple scooted around the perplexed mademoiselle and out of the room.

Back in the studio, Jimmy had dispensed with any semblance of his usual Tennessee charm and was simply dragging the women about like display mannequins. He raised their hands and baseball mitts over their heads as though they were shielding themselves from a towering pop fly. Several models were posed precariously on a high stepladder. When the lanky photographer was satisfied, he crooked his finger wordlessly at Temple.

Tossing her a catcher's mitt, he pointed to the floor. She lay comfortably on the grass-colored seamless paper at the feet of a model fielding a grounder with a pot holder instead of a glove. Then he knelt and held a gleaming white softball in front of Temple's face.

"You just lie there and get beanballed, darlin'." He was smirking.

"What are you looking so smug about?"

"Tell ya later," he drawled.

Jimmy backed away and shot them, this way and that, for an hour—a team of incompetents, tripping all over each other. Temple reclined on one elbow, mugging happily into the camera as Chloris dropped the ball, again and again, just shy of her head. Radie would load one box camera while Shelby shot with another.

They sweated under the hot lights until they looked as if they'd played a full nine innings. Finally Jimmy turned to the agency head. "That suit ya, Miz Molineux?"

"Very nice. Thank you, Jimmy. Rather like Norman Rockwell on LSD." Tina stubbed out another cigarette. "All right ladies—that's it! Those of you with work to do get hopping. The rest of you . . ." Tina was lost a moment, then recovered brightly, ". . . go lose some weight!"

As the models all stripped off their uniforms and pulled their weary bodies out of the room, Shelby wandered toward Tina and Temple. He leaned to whisper into the younger woman's ear: "Stick around darlin'."

Tina whirled out the door after a group of models like a mother hen chasing her chicks. Annabel winked, wrapped herself in a down coat, and followed the last gaggle of models out the door.

"Ta for now!"

Temple watched Radie gathering uniforms into a blue laundry bag in the suddenly empty room. When the girl left for the costumers, Temple asked, "What's on your mind, Shelby?"

"Do me a favor." He led her around behind his Hasselblad and pointed to the viewfinder. "Take a look through there and give me your advice."

He scooted around in front of the lens and grinned. "You gotta look at the little screen, T-Kay."

As Temple sighted through the camera, he began tilting his head significantly, first one way, then another. "Which profile you like best?"

"They're both adorable. What's up? You need a passport photo?"

"No, ma'am. You're lookin' at a fella who mighta grinned himself into a job on the money side of the camera."

She looked up and arched her eyebrows dubiously. "Oh, Shelby. You're *not* going to model are you?"

"Me? A prop?" The man looked wounded. "No offense, T-Kay, but no way. I'm auditionin' to be a TV news reporter."

"A . . . You?"

"An' why not? Carlotta says I have 'presence.'"

"Who's Carlotta?"

"Only Carlotta Robertson—owner and chairman of the board of Channel Three. She's lookin' for a new face to cover soft news: fashion, fads, style—all the disposable arts."

"But you're an artist yourself, Jimmy . . ."

"Not when I'm shootin' advertisin', I'm not. I can't take this grind anymore: Spendin' a week gettin' the exact shot I want, so today's boss can tell me it's very nice . . . just what he wanted . . . yesterday. Now he wants the sky green, the grass blue, and the girls hung up by their ankles. And I better do it fast, before that video game he calls a brain 'pings' with another bright idea. This commercial work is ruinin' my eye."

"But your private pictures are terrific . . ."

"Terrific ain't the point, darlin'. What sells is what's in fashion. I'm turnin' thirty, and it's time I thought about the future. I'm not hung up on some starvin' artist routine. But I gotta start protectin' my private eye, see?"

Temple nodded. "So you're on the air, just like that?"

"Amazin', ain't it? Carlotta sent me down to her husband, Henry—*he* works for *her*, runnin' the news operation. I've got two weeks to prove myself."

"Well, if that's what you want . . ."

"Yup, I figure I'll make all my buddies famous."

Temple clucked disapprovingly. "I had a teacher—a famous one—who said, 'Fame is a cocktail party after all the guests have left.' Who would you wish that on?"

"You, darlin'. Henry loved the benefit angle. Dotterin' ce-lebs, red-faced liberals, architectural masterpieces beleaguered by greedy developers. An' a beautiful dish to tell us all about it."

Temple chewed her lower lip and gazed out the window. "Wouldn't you rather interview someone who owns a building on the block and doesn't want to sell? Someone who's actually been threatened by Cornerstone?"

"I'd love it more'n honey on grits. Who is it?"

"I'd better ask first. I'll be seeing him tonight."

"Oh-oh. You cheatin' on the big guy already?"

"No. The big guy will be there too."

"That's m'girl. If you insist on hookin' up with a straight, he's just twisted enough to be my choice. Now when are you two gonna get down to some serious livin' in sin?"

Temple snapped, "Don't push me."

"Push?" Shelby looked startled. "What's holdin' you back, T-Kay? You're perfect together."

"I just don't want to be rushed," she muttered, retreating to the bedroom to find her clothes.

Temple was pulling on her sweater when Shelby poked an eye around the doorframe. "All clear?"

"I'm sorry. Lately, a week doesn't go by without a well-meaning aunt sending me a clip from the paper about someone I know getting married. The note always says something like 'Wasn't she in the class *behind* you, dear?'"

Shelby chuckled dryly. "Whenever a couple goes Reno, you oughta send the clips back like bad checks."

"You're a real pal, Shelby."

"Yeah? Then answer me a question. That property owner you were talkin' about wouldn't be the big guy's brother, would it? That little place in the theater district?"

"You have to let me talk to him first."

"Whatever you say. What was the name of that bar of his?"

Temple shrugged. "Coughlin's Saloon."

"Real clever."

"You don't need clever when you've got soul."

Five

Later that evening, Temple paused a moment outside a bookstore on Eighth Avenue to watch a sidewalk mime troupe plugging *The Mime Show*. Their painted faces mugged outrageously as they aped prostitutes, much to the amusement of a small clutch of sightseers.

When she came to a squat Catholic church named after Saint Agnes—the virgin martyr and patron saint of young girls—Temple turned the corner up a decaying block toward Coughlin's Saloon.

Past the parish house was an abandoned warehouse, its windows covered with tin. Next came Coughlin's Saloon and past that was a different sort of house of worship—the Emerald Theater. On this late winter night, only a few bulbs blinked and crackled on its uninviting marquee. The Emerald's placard advertised a double bill: *White Heat* and *Mr. Lucky*.

The Coughlin family business occupied a sandstone Victorian Gothic mansion with an attached one-story dining room, all well seasoned with grime. The high parlor windows, set into deep trapezoidal bays, sparkled with bold green and gold script: *Coughlin's Saloon*.

The Saloon's interior was murky with the soft glow of globed gas fixtures. A polished, dark mahogany bar ran almost the entire length of the room, fronted by a gleaming brass footrail. Behind it was the original license, #11, awarded to Frank's grandfather right after Prohibition. The mirror reflected a clock on the opposite wall, designed backward so customers could see the time without having to turn around.

Behind the bar, a husky, gray-haired man in a traditional long white apron delivered drinks to a couple of sophisticated theatergoers. The lady lifted a stick of celery out of her bloodred drink. "Excuse me, waiter. At the Polo Lounge, they make a Danish Mary with a frond of dill."

"That so?" The barman smiled. "Well, we don't fuss around with the cute little vegetables here, miss."

He laid the gentleman's bills into a wooden cigar box and distributed the change in a series of bowls. Coughlin's Saloon had never had a cash register.

Then the barman ambled down the boards, one finger running along the liquor bottles that glittered like royal crown jewels, and winked broadly at Temple.

"Good t'see ye, Red."

"Likewise, Pat."

He poured a stiff shot of Armagnac and soda and laid it at her elbow on a Courage lager coaster. Then he leaned his brawny forearms on the bar. "Them rich ones is always more trouble than they're worth. Gimme a bus driver or a laborer, now, he'll never stiff ye—but an heiress might. Have I thanked ye lately for gettin' me back to the honest side o'town, girl?"

"Only a half-dozen times so far. But, hey—once Casey's old bartender passed on, Patrick Xavier Duggan was the only man for the job. Frank had the same idea the same day."

"Now, don't go denyin' yer soft side, girl. The beautiful Mrs. Duggan says fast-talkin' yer way around yer feelin's instead o'stoppin' to taste 'em is the worst detour in the world."

"Yankee upbringing," Temple shrugged. "When am I going to meet the beautiful Mrs. Duggan?"

"Hard to say. She don't approve o'bars, ye know. Too many loose women."

As Pat moved off slowly, Temple sipped her drink and idly scanned the room.

Hand-lettered signs hung all around the walls:

WE TAKE BAD CHECKS
(AND MAKE YOU EAT THEM)

IF YOU'RE BROKE AND THIRSTY
THE HYDRANT IS OUT FRONT

Stuck around a pair of crossed Irish tricolor flags were portraits of John and Jackie Kennedy, the current Pope, a burly turn-of-the-century policeman with a handlebar moustache, and Britain's prime minister sporting a hand-drawn black eye.

WHEN THE BARTENDER IS BUSY
THAT'S WHEN YOU SHOULD BOTHER HIM

Suddenly a bugle blared from the men's room. Temple had snuck in there one night for a look. A battered old horn hung from the ceiling on a chain, and a plaque attached to it read:

IF YOU DON'T BLOW YOURSELF
BLOW THIS

Frank Coughlin strode into the bar, beating the cold off his chest and kissed Temple with cool lips. "Want some food?"

"Yessir."

The bartender drifted back to their end.

"Evening, Pat. Where's Casey?"

"Haven't laid eyes on the lad all day. Can I get ye the usual?" When they nodded, he leaned into an ornate brass tube—the antiquated intercom used as an alarm during Prohibition days. "Two chili-cheese, medium raw. Two potaters, burn 'em."

Frank took Temple's hand and led the way down three steps into the dining room annex, separated from the bar by wrought-iron pillars. Casey Coughlin took all his meals there and kept the room the way he liked it, with the tables large and spaced well apart.

Frank and Temple sat at Casey's regular table against the far wall, leaving the chair that faced the doorway empty. From his usual seat there, Casey could tip back against the wall to preside over the Saloon's long nights—on the lookout for old friends or any sign of trouble.

Overhead was the new glass skylight, the only change in the building's original design. At lunchtime, the crystal clear panes let sunlight pour into the room. At night, green spotlights on the townhouse roof shone on the stone dramatic masks hanging on the wall of the theater next door. To anyone looking up through the skylight, McQueeney's "Glee and Glum" provided godlike commentary on the activities below.

Temple's violet eyes focused over Frank's shoulder. At the next table, old Michael McQueeney sat in his wheelchair, sipping from a teacup. He was leafing through a pile of pink message slips, ignoring a worried man in overalls who hovered by the stairs.

"Hey you," Frank murmured into Temple's ear. "C'mere."

"Why?"

"Why not?" He reached under the seat of her chair and dragged her closer to him. Then his hand stayed under the table.

Temple realized Uncle Mickey was watching them over the top of his teacup. The old man caught her eye and winked.

Blushing, she muttered, "Move your hand."

Coughlin drew back, the merriment fading a bit from his eyes. "Is he cute?"

"Who?"

"Whoever you're looking at behind me."

"See for yourself. Here he comes now."

Uncle Mickey wheeled past them with a nod, the pink message slips piled in his lap.

"How come he's in here all the time?"

"I think Dora sends him over to get him out of her hair a couple hours a day. He's been using that table as an office ever since I can remember."

"Why?"

Frank shrugged. "Says he likes to be near people."

As Pat dropped off their food, Temple watched the old man slide a dime into the pay phone mounted on the back wall. While he made several calls, they nibbled on their dripping cheeseburgers. Then he wheeled himself back to the wall behind his regular table.

Shredding the message slips in an ashtray, McQueeney lit a wooden match with his thumbnail and set the scraps aflame. Only after he'd scattered the black ashes did he beckon to the long-faced fellow on the stairs.

Temple barely heard the old man's gravelly whisper as he peered at the supplicant and murmured, "Talk to me . . ."

"Temple, stop staring."

"What in the world is he up to?"

Frank was amused. "He's sort of a neighborhood patron. Lends money to people who can't pay interest, helps widows, buys shoes for orphans . . . No one goes needy on this block."

"I didn't think theaters made that kind of money around here unless they showed porno."

"The Emerald is just his hobby. Basically, he's a retired investor. All he really cares about is the neighborhood."

Temple licked her fingers. "So what's he to you?"

"Who do you think helped get me appointed a judge?"

"Really? He sounds all right to me."

"He is." Frank checked his watch. "I wonder where Casey is. Why don't I get some champagne so we can celebrate your acting debut?"

Moments after Frank had taken the stairs to the basement, Casey Coughlin slid into the empty chair against the wall. He was already talking as his fingers scrabbled at the buttons of his pea coat.

"You won't *believe* what's been going on around here! Father Dolan's carrying binders for something called Cornerstone Equities. I saw one of the offers they're making and it was huge! Then I tailed him up to West Eighty-eighth Street tonight and did some checking around, and I think—"

"Hold on, Casey. Frank will want to hear this from the top."

Casey drew the threatening note reading "SELL OR DIE!" from his coat and waved it in front of her. "Imagine that Judas, going up and down our block all day, telling everyone the Lord wants them to sell out and move. I have to give up my family home or be a sinner? That's no choice—and he's no man of God to ask me to make it!"

Temple nodded sympathetically as Pat brought Casey a foaming draught of beer. Immediately, the black-haired man drained half of it. Above them, windblown gravel clattered across the glass.

"Casey? I have a friend at WSAV News, if you think a little publicity might scare them away...?"

Lowering his mug to the table with a bang, Casey shook his head. "There's been too much publicity already. This stays in the neighborhood."

He tipped back against the wall, glancing up as a shadow flitted across the skylight. Casey sighed. "Nights like this, I begin to wish I had someone like you to come home to. I've spent so many years bottled up in this Saloon, I start to feel pickled. But then I remind myself this place doesn't only belong to the past..." He winked as Frank, whistling, skipped up the steps from the basement. "I'm counting on you and Frankie to—"

Suddenly the sky shattered. Wood and bone cracked as a

violent blow knocked Temple off her chair, bits of stone and glass spattering all around them like hail. A huge stone mask from the wall of the theater next door was crushing Casey Coughlin to the floor.

The tune on Frank's lips withered as he watched his brother's hands fight uselessly with the heavy face of Tragedy pinioning his chest. He raced over and heaved the table aside. Then he rolled away the granite sculpture.

Temple scrambled across the glass-strewn floor to cradle Casey's head in her hands.

A tray clattered as Pat ran for the telephone.

Casey clutched his brother's hand, gasping desperately in a voice as broken as his body. "Keep . . . bar . . ."

Then his grip loosened and his arm fell to the floor.

Old man McQueeney rolled his wheelchair closer, staring up in horror through the jagged hole in the new glass roof.

Only the mask of Comedy remained on the wall of the palace of dreams, grinning down through the greenish glow into the still face of Kevin "Casey" Coughlin.

Six

Temple leaned in the back doorway of Frank's West Village garden apartment, spilling light from the kitchen out into the cold winter night.

"Frank. Come inside."

"Not yet. Got to knock this wall down first."

Coughlin was barefoot in the grass and stone oasis he and his brother created out of rubble and weeds. The tails of his thin shirt hung out sloppily over his pants. He took a full windup, pushed off his right foot, and whipped a baseball into the darkness. It smacked sharply off the high brick wall of the bakery next door and dribbled back to his toes.

Temple shut the kitchen door behind her and wandered over to the sweating man, hugging herself in the cold.

"It's freezing, Frank. You've been out here for an hour."

"Feels all right to me." He plucked a near-empty bottle of scotch from the frozen lawn and took a long gulp. "Ever tell you how I learned to pitch? . . . From Casey. He was a helluva hitter in high school, and Dad was always too busy in the bar, so I had to pitch him batting practice out in the street. He always said, 'Never be afraid to throw it over the middle of the plate—you've got a whole team behind you.'" He passed the bottle to her.

"Some team," Frank grumbled. "He's been watching out for people on that block ever since my dad died. Even took over as the Democrats' block organizer. And the one time in his life he doesn't play ball, the whole world caves in on him."

"You think what happened tonight has something to do with that real estate business?"

Frank dropped his eyes, kneading the shredded horsehide in his strong hands without a word.

"Frank, wait until you see what the cops say tomorrow. Everybody knows that facade is crumbling. It could have been an act of God. Accidents do happen."

Coughlin whirled, his eyes gleaming brightly. "Not to *my* brother they don't. How *dare* He steal my only brother?" Frank snatched his bottle back, muttering, "Him or His pious flunky."

"The priest? You think he'd kill someone?"

Coughlin just grunted.

"Do you want to eat something?"

"No. I want to feel mean." Turning away from her, he gripped the hardball across its frayed, red-stitched seams and went back to his relentless pitching duel with the brick wall.

Temple sighed and crossed the yard to the small wooden cottage that was Frank's bedroom. She lit the fire in the grate, then turned down his bed, all the while listening to the thwack of the pounding baseball echoing around the enclosed courtyard.

Shivering in the cottage doorway, she watched him until the bells of Saint Luke In The Fields chimed their distinctive melody in the crisp, thin air.

"Aren't you tired yet, Frank?"

Coughlin rolled up his sleeves without looking at her and stared down into his red, stinging hands. Bullets of freezing rain began pelting the flagstones on the walk as he bent over to pick up the ball.

"Come inside, Frank. It's starting to rain."

He wound up and fired the ball with all his strength, but this time the pulped horsehide dropped dead at the base of the wall.

"Rain..." He sat down heavily. "My big brother's crying, he's so lonesome up there. But he was always good at making friends..."

Temple reached down and wiped the sweat from his brow. "Come to bed now."

Taking him by the hand, she led him into the fragrant pine-paneled bedroom. She sat him on the edge of the bed and began unfastening his belt buckle.

Frank mumbled, "You realize pretty soon I'll be older than he is? Year after year I'll be deserting him—turning forty, then fifty, then sixty—until I'm a whole generation older. But he'll still be here, a younger guy in an earlier time."

Temple slid off his pants before going to work on the buttons of his shirt.

"Who's going to be an uncle to my kids now?"

She walked to the bathroom, fetched two aspirins and a glass of water, and made him swallow them.

"Uk. That's horrible."

"You'll thank me in the morning." Rolling him under the covers, she took off her own clothes, snapped out the light, and climbed in beside him.

He laid his head on her chest, trembling silently in the dark.

"God, I'm tired."

"I know, honey." Temple began stroking his head, humming an old lullabye as she ran her fingers through the coal-black hair again and again.

When the trembling stopped and his breathing had relaxed into the ancient cadence of sleep, she was still humming sadly in the dark.

SUNDAY

Seven

The next afternoon, Temple's taxi slid onto St. James Place and pulled up to a hulking brown monolith: Number One Police Plaza, the Orwellian headquarters of the N.Y.P.D.

In the lobby, a guard behind a table full of communications gear eyed Temple dispassionately and refused to let her upstairs. Ignoring the brown leather benches, she drifted over to one of half a dozen bronze plaques listing New York City policemen killed in the line of duty. She was scanning them idly when she recognized Coughlin's voice.

". . . expected a lot more cooperation from you people."

Coming through the security gate, Frank was dogging a police official with danish crumbs all down the front of his pants. Temple hovered nearer but decided not to interrupt when she saw the peevish look in Coughlin's eyes.

"We're doing all we can, Your Honor. There are lab men on that roof right now, measuring the wind velocity along the wall."

"Wind velocity!"

"It's a very old facade, sir, and it was long overdue for inspection. This is a big vertical city, Judge Coughlin. We don't like to alarm the populace by publicizing it, but you'd be surprised how often this sort of accident happens. Just last month, a woman's skull was split open by a steel wrench that fell from the sixteenth floor of a construction site."

"Yeah, and sometimes people throw things on purpose. Remember that maniac who was tossing cinder blocks on people off the roof of the Palace Theater a few summers ago? Did you ever catch him?"

"Well . . . I don't recall. But if someone sincerely wanted to kill your brother, why choose such an inexact method?"

"I don't think killing him was a requirement. Even a near miss would have scared him. They just got . . . lucky." Coughlin sighed. "Listen—did you check for marks where the mask could have been pried off? Like crowbar scars, maybe?"

"We haven't been able to reach it yet. In fact, that's something else that makes your theory unlikely. Those masks are six feet below the roofline. That's a pretty long crowbar."

"Did you even look?"

The official smiled. "Your Honor, the best detectives combed every inch of that roof last night. There wasn't anything up there except a clothesline with an old lady's underthings."

Coughlin frowned. "Okay, so the murderer took whatever he used away with him. Anybody could have got up there, you know? Those fire stairs are never locked."

"So the owners told us. But it's hard to be inconspicuous walking out of a theater with a six-foot crowbar. Of course, if eyewitnesses come forward..."

"Great. Or maybe the killer will give us a call."

"There's always hope."

Coughlin glanced around in disgust, until his eyes fell on Temple in her black mourning dress.

"I hope I didn't keep you waiting," she said.

"You're just in time. C'mon." Nodding to the police official coolly, he strode off across the lobby.

"We'll stay in touch," the man called.

"Frank!" Temple followed him outside onto the red brick plaza. "Frank, what did they say in there?"

"That cop's been off the streets so long, he thinks you find Guardian Angels in church. He says they've tentatively classified the death as an accident."

Temple rested her hand lightly on his shoulder. "What about that threat Casey showed us?"

"They said it's interesting 'circumstantially,' but I shouldn't be optimistic... At least they held onto it."

"Well, that's a start. What did they say about the priest?"

Coughlin shook his head. "They already have an alibi. He was taking down the Christmas tree in the parish house with Dora."

"Your uncle's pusher?"

"His nurse, yeah. She runs the holiday cake sales every year."

"Scratch one suspect. What now?"

He smiled wryly. "They'd be happy to hear any suggestion I have to offer."

"What are you going to do?"

Coughlin started walking across the plaza toward the dazzling white Municipal Building. "I can probably twist a few arms at the D.A.'s office to give the cops a nudge. But first I want to find out who's behind this Cornerstone Equities."

"Are you sure you're up to it? Would you rather let me try?"

Coughlin shook his head. "I have to take the week off anyway to settle Kevin's affairs. In fact, I have to go to the office right now to get my docket together for the guy who's covering me."

They passed under the towering Greco-Roman arches framing the offices of New York City's bureaucracy, and stood facing west. Etched against a gray winter sky, the sleekly modern towers of the World Trade Center contrasted the Woolworth Building's neo-Gothic spire. Across Park Row the unexpectedly modest colonial lines of City Hall marked it as the oldest and most graceful of the government's buildings.

"This is what's left of my roots," Coughlin said, sweeping his hand across the shadowy intersection. "The Coughlin family started in America right here."

"On this very spot?"

"Yeah. This isn't genuine America—it's all landfill. In colonial days, there was a lake with an island in the middle where they executed people. Whoever located police headquarters here had a great sense of humor."

Temple's eyes flickered in his direction. "How come?"

"Before the Civil War, no cop would come *near* this place. The neighborhood was an Irish ghetto full of killers, pickpockets, hookers, wild gangs of twelve-year-old orphan girls, families living fifty to a cellar . . . By the time my family came during the famine, this was the filthiest, most degenerate place on earth."

"How do you know all this?"

"Uncle Mickey. People don't like to remember times like those—the memories disappear down the generations—but Mickey says it's remembering the desperate times that makes a man strive. C'mon—the office is this way." He touched her elbow and guided them north.

"Funny, I don't think of the Irish as newcomers. There are so many others."

Coughlin pointed down Chambers Street. "See that?" It was a grimy Palladian-style stone villa with a portico jutting inaccessibly high above the sidewalk.

"It looks abandoned. What is it?"

"Tweed Courthouse. Named for William Marcy Tweed, boss of the whole city over a century ago. He turned politics into a science. In a sense, everything I have came from him."

Temple hooked her arm through his. "A hero of yours?"

"He was the biggest crook in New York political history. Ran Tammany Hall. Ever heard of it?"

"Uh . . . sort of. What was it?"

"A political club. Back when the Irish came to this neighborhood, they were powerless. Immigrants who couldn't find jobs hung out in saloons, so Tammany used barkeepers as organizers to turn them into citizens as fast as they came off the boat."

"That was nice—but what for?"

"Citizens are voters, Temple. Before long there were more new Catholics than old Protestants in the city, and Tammany took control. There were always buildings like that courthouse going up, and Tammany's supporters got the jobs building them. Of course, there was a price for the job. You paid with your vote on election day."

"If they got you a job, maybe they deserved your vote."

Coughlin nodded. "They took care of their own. Do you know what rackets are?"

"Sure. Organized crime."

"Now. But originally 'rackets' were social gatherings. On holidays, Tammany threw parties for the faithful: boat rides, picnics, parades. All donated by local businessmen. The guys who collected the money were called racketeers. But pretty soon, the collections became extortion, and the racketeers became criminals. Trace the corruption of the word and you've got a map of how a good system went bad."

Temple stopped to buy herself a newspaper. "Well . . . how did it go bad?"

"Graft, mostly. Boss Tweed organized all the local vice— taxed saloons, whorehouses, gambling clubs—and gave the crooks protection in return."

"Sounds just like the Mafia."

"These are the guys who *taught* the Mafia. But at least their way poor people got a slice of the pie. If I'd been around then, they might have sent me to law school, so when I got out I'd write letters for illiterate people, stand up for them at city hall . . . It was underclass teamwork on a massive scale. Tweed was the biggest crook of all. That courthouse there was budgeted at a quarter of a million dollars, but it cost twelve million—and nine of that went to Tweed and his pals."

They walked in silence up Centre Street until it broadened into sunny Foley Square. Frank pointed to the Corinthian columns of the first building facing the square. "New York County Courthouse, built fifty years later to replace Tweed Courthouse. This one was budgeted at seven million dollars—and ended up costing thirty. And it had to be renovated before they even opened it."

"Why?"

Coughlin shot her a wry smile. "Among other things, some people thought it was inappropriate for judges to have a bar during Prohibition."

"So you're saying New York's courthouses are prime examples of corruption?"

"You're catching on. Construction is the graduate school of graft. And now there's Cornerstone."

Temple looked startled. "And you think *our* city government is—"

"The more things change, the more they stay the same." Coughlin shrugged. "The mayor's probably still polling to see which stand will get more votes. But historically, the odds are with the builders."

They crossed the street under the watchful, brooding criminal courts and the shell of the Tombs. Turning left up White Street, Frank held open the door of the judge's entrance in the rear of an unimposing modern structure that was the home of Civil Court.

"All those monumental palaces of justice and you get the one that looks like a Holiday Inn," Temple teased.

"At least it's a little cleaner . . ."

Frank flashed his I.D. card and signed the custodian's register.

The uniformed guard handed him a gray envelope. "Just come by messenger. Didn't know they worked Sundays. I woulda took it up if I knew you was expected."

"I wasn't. Thanks." He led the way between two metal

poles with Temple behind him—until the howl of a piercing siren split their ears.

The guard stared at her and began fidgeting nervously.

Coughlin looked back, furrowing his forehead. "Are you carrying?" he yelled over the din.

Sheepishly, Temple pulled an acid-edged boot knife out of her purse.

Coughlin shook his head as he reached back to turn off the metal detector. "What's this doing here, Freddie? I thought we only used them in courtrooms."

"Yessir, yeah. But we got some of them Liberation Army types gettin' tried next week so, y'know, better safe than sorry."

"Leave it on all weekend," Frank muttered. "Waste a little electricity."

He took Temple's elbow and led her to the elevator bank for his office. "I thought we talked about you giving up those blades. They're not ladylike."

"This is just an accessory. For decoration—like an ammunition belt."

"Uh-huh." The elevator doors slid open. "I'll be at least an hour. You sure you want to wait?"

Temple riffled the weighty Sunday *New York Times* in her arms. "Don't worry about me. This will keep me busy for hours."

Soon he was leading her down a long corridor. In his dingy office, a dozen pencils had been tossed into the soft acoustic tiles of the ceiling. As Frank plopped into the chair behind his desk, Temple made herself comfortable on the floor by his feet.

She was still on the *Book Review* when she realized he hadn't made a sound for several minutes. He was slumped on his elbows, resting his face in his hands.

"Frank?"

He didn't respond.

Temple got up and walked behind him to rub his shoulders. There, on the desk by his elbow, lay the ripped gray envelope. Directly in front of him was a torn magazine ad for Narcissus Cosmetics.

It was a familiar photo of Temple, kneeling over a reflecting pool of quicksilver. But glued over her head, in an assortment of letters clipped with pinking shears, was the warning:

SELL OR SHE'S NEXT

Eight

Pat plucked Temple's empty glass from the red-checkered tablecloth. "Another round, then?"

She glanced over to Frank, who was scanning a telegram the bartender had just delivered. Coughlin's scotch was nearly empty. So was the teacup in which Michael McQueeney drank his martini.

"Better bring them another," Temple sighed, smoothing her plain black dress.

Dora handed Pat the teacup, too, whispering, "Michael's had his fill. Bring him a Baptist special."

Coughlin's Saloon was closed to the public, but family friends and longtime political cronies had been drifting in and out all night, paying their respects in the murky dining room. A half-dozen waiters, several of them ex-pugilists, wove through the raucous din with huge platters of food. Overhead, the broken skylight had been hastily boarded up.

Frank flipped his yellow telegram onto the table. "It's from the mayor, in Albany: 'Both the governor and I share your grief,' he says."

McQueeney cackled softly. "Ya mean there's a tax on grief now too?"

Pat returned with their freshened drinks—including the old man's teacup baptized with straight ice water and garnished with an olive.

Temple sipped her Armagnac. "You don't suppose the mayor will mind a judge owning a saloon, do you?"

"Oh, doll-face," McQueeney cackled, "the saloons is where

politics began in this town. They was the first courthouses in New Amsterdam. The Dutchmen even paid their fines in drinks. In fact, I'm sentencin' myself to one right now." He picked up his "special" martini and took a slug as the two ladies exchanged amused glances.

Temple caught McQueeney's eye. "Did you know this place when it was a speakeasy?"

"The finest speak I ever seen—and they were everywhere. We had 'em disguised as soda parlors and synagogues. One was hid behind a coffin. Jack and Charlie's had walls that twirled around to hide the customers. But none of 'em compared to Petunia's."

Temple blinked. "Petunia's?"

"Coughlin's was a florist shop run by a bruiser by the name of Johnny Petunia. Six foot tall and five foot wide. He examined ya through a peephole next to the flower cooler, and if he liked your looks he buzzed ya through the electric door. Bat Masterson wrote his sports column on an old Underwood at this very table. The Vanderbilts and Whitneys'd be gamblin' and drinkin' with congressmen and senators . . ."

Temple interrupted. "What about the cops?"

"Our local boys? They figured drinkin' was a federal problem."

"And the Feds?"

The old man winked. "They was runnin' a speak of their own! Suppose I told ya that, once upon a time, a certain Captain Chapin decided to fire every one of his agents who was wearin' a diamond ring—and he lost half his force!"

He drained his glass and set it down with a thump. "Oh, Jesus, Mary, and Joseph, those were the days . . ."

"Good martini?" Dora asked.

"Pretty good," he replied, "but awful weak."

A well-built, uniformed police officer with a mean mouth and pretty eyes sauntered up to the table, cockily spinning his nightstick like a baton. He kept his hat on.

"Well, well, if it ain't one of New York's cheapest . . . er, finest," McQueeney needled. "Come to give us the third degree, Officer Falcone?" He winked at the other seated man.

"Not tonight," the darkly handsome patrolman muttered. He swung a chair around and squatted on it with his arms draped over its back, an intent expression etched on his street-wise face.

"Take a seat, sonny, and join us, why don't ya?"

Falcone blinked. Then he shifted his gaze to Coughlin. "I just wanted to let you know I'm on your team, Frankie. If it turns out this wasn't some accident, hey, you got my promise I'll personally hang the bastard out to dry—check?"

"Very good of you," Coughlin murmured. "Ummm, would you like a beer?"

"Can't," the cop barked, pounding one fist on the table so hard everyone's glasses jumped. "Gotta be walkin' these mean streets till dawn. Well, hell, a man's gotta do what a man's gotta do—check? You men hear anything funny, just whistle." He winked at Temple. "That goes for you, too, babe."

The cop stood, hitched up his service belt, and swaggered off, oblivious to the smirks and soft whistles behind his back.

"What's with him?" Temple asked.

"Ahh, he thinks he's Al Pacino," McQueeney smirked. "His life's one long audition for *Serpico*."

Dora shook her head irritably. "He's been tryin' to be an actor since before he made the force. Always sneakin' in the theaters when he should be out walkin' his beat. Hangin' round the stage doors, starin' at the showgirls."

"A theater groupie?" Temple asked.

"Just another mouse," McQueeney muttered, "lurkin' in doorways for his piece of cheese . . . That's what they used to call A.R."

"A.R.?" Temple asked.

"Arnold Rothstein. The J. P. Morgan of the underworld durin' Prohibition. When he gave ya a loan, he took out an insurance policy on your life for the same amount. That way, if you welshed on him and . . . ah, had an accident or somethin' . . . well, Arnold collected either way, y'see?"

"Let's have none o'that Rothstein," Dora snapped suddenly. "Any man who has the vice squad out framin' innocent women . . . any man who—"

"Ixnay," McQueeney muttered. His eyes flickered across the table.

"Michael, it was fifty years ago."

"That's a hundred and ten percent right. Let's leave it there."

Temple watched the old couple stare at each other a moment.

"Oh, yer a horrible buncha boys," Dora said, standing and tapping Temple on the shoulder. "Come on, then, dearie. This is no conversation for upstandin' women. Let's leave these hooligans to ruin their livers in peace."

The ladies carried their drinks to the bar, where Temple sat on a stool, tapping her feet restlessly on the hollow brass railing. As Dora nestled on the next perch, Temple asked, "What was that about?"

"Ah, Michael and I have dealt with all kinds over the years. Some were bad enough. But Rothstein was the worst."

"You two have been together a long time . . . ?"

"Forever and a day."

"And you've known Frank since when?"

"Since he was in his late ma's tummy. The Coughlins and McQueeneys go back to the days of the famine."

Temple glanced solicitously back to the table where McQueeney held court. Frank was just staring into his drink. "Is Mr. McQueeney actually Frank's uncle?"

"Francis hasn't told you 'bout the family yet? Shame on him, then. My Michael's granddad was Francis's great-great-granddad, come over from Ireland in 1843."

Dora sipped her Manhattan and continued. "Ah, but they were a pack o'lemon-tasters, them Coughlins. Just poor, shanty Irish like the rest of us, but didn't they put on airs now. All of them in Tammany or on the police by the turn of the century, always pretendin' to be the most upstandin' straight-necks y'ever did see. No wonder she couldn't stand livin' with 'em."

"Who?"

"Why, Michael's mother, Kathleen, who else? They managed to keep her penned up till she was on the wrong side o'thirty-five, but once she laid eyes on Black Jack Mc-Queeney, she was off to the races. Did ye ever love a scoundrel, dearie?"

"In Europe," Temple muttered. "It didn't work out."

"Well, every woman should, or she hasn't lived. But them Coughlins straight disowned her when she moved in with him and had the baby. And then poor Black Jack gettin' killed in a knife fight, what could she do but go live with her family. Oh, they were perfectly civil to her and the boy, ye understand—they just wouldn't acknowledge 'em in public. That awful Johnny Coughlin, older than my poor Michael by twenty-some years, never callin' him nothin' but 'bastard.' After the consumption carried his mother off, there was nobody for Michael, a'tall, y'see? Is it a wonder he run off before he was ten?"

"Where did he go?"

"Go? Why dearie, where was there to go? To the streets, o'course—livin' by his wits. We didn't have all the social programs in them days, y'know." Dora shook with chuckles. "I reckon Michael was a right little adventurer, too, workin' his way up in the saloons."

"Why saloons?"

"Where else would Tammany be conductin' their business?"

Temple cocked an eye. "What kind of business?"

"We called it politics, dearie—the only way to get in on things. Playin' his cards right, a lad like my Michael could end up ownin' a theater like the Emerald before he was thirty. Lordy, I wasn't a day over seventeen the night he picked me out of the chorus line . . ."

Temple watched the stout old woman push a loose strand of gray hair behind her ear.

"He was the kindest, most generous man, even then. Always slippin' Francis's dad pennies for candy, an' takin' him to the ballgames. It's sure Michael was a better father to him than that high-and-mighty copper ever was. For thirty years, I passed letters between 'em while Michael was away."

". . . For thirty years?"

Dora nodded sadly. "After the Crash, it was. He left me the Emerald, bless his sweet heart, and went off to the old country to make his fortune exportin' Irish whiskey. For thirty years I ran that projector—memorizin' our time together while my childbearin' years passed us by—until one day he walked right through that door, lookin' bold as brass. My, oh, my, wasn't that a day . . ."

As the older woman dreamed, Temple suddenly realized the bar had fallen silent. Looking over her shoulder, she followed everyone's gaze to the rear of the smoky room, where Father Dolan was leaning over Frank's crowded table.

"Pop him one, Frankie!" a drunken voice snickered.

Coughlin listened to the priest expressionlessly while old Michael McQueeney dozed at his side.

Temple whispered, "Should he be in here?"

"Ah, he's a kindly little man, and there's no harm to him. You should see the way he babies the runaways in the church shelter. He's been lookin' poverty in the eye so many long years, I'm thinkin' he's grown tired of it and wants to play with the big boys."

"You don't think trying to sell his church is kind of sacrilegious?"

Dora shrugged. "The Church is in business, too, ye know. It's not like that corner is Calvary."

Scraping chairs in the corner announced the party was breaking up. Strangers nodded respectfully to Temple on their way to the street. Frank was shaking the priest's hand as he walked him to the door.

"Lordy, look at the time—and we're the last here. I'd best be gettin' Michael off to bed or he'll wake up cussin' me. Now you keep a good watch on our Francis, girl."

Dora trundled the snoozing old man off into the night as Frank ambled wearily back to the bar.

Temple asked, "What was that with Dolan?"

"Condolences. And he wanted me to understand his point of view."

"Which is?"

Coughlin sighed, watching Pat dry the last glasses at the other end of the bar. "Church costs are going up. Contributions are going down. The endowment won't cover the maintenance he's been deferring for the last ten years. Fund raising doesn't bring in nearly enough . . . I have to admit he's got a problem.

"He thinks this Cornerstone thing is a miracle. They're offering a million-dollar installment to the diocese on signing, and a five percent tithe of all the office rents they collect for the next fifty years. That's regular money for missionary work with the runaways out on Eighth Avenue . . ."

"He really put the screws into you."

"That he did." Pat was fitting iron gratings into their slots over the front windows. "It's two A.M. Time to head home?"

In a far corner of the empty room, a dark shape rose from the shadows and hovered closer. A broad-brimmed slouch hat matching the figure's long black cape hid his face until he reached the gas jets by the bar.

"How are you?" queried O. M. Timm, saluting with his silver-tipped walking stick.

Nine

Frank ran his eyes over the dandified little man irritably. "I'm drinking my grandfather's scotch after my brother's wake. How are you?"

Timm winced sympathetically. "It's a terrible century when a man can be murdered for a parcel of . . . air."

Coughlin's eyes flickered. "Murdered?"

"You don't suspect so?"

"The police seem to think it was an accident."

Timm chuckled. "Well, the police work for the city, the city works for big business. And Cornerstone Equities gives every indication of being immense. They own a variety of properties around the city."

"And you think they . . ."

Timm shrugged. "Or someone with parallel interests."

"Such as?" Temple asked.

"Would it surprise you to learn that the offers being tendered along your block are conditional on *all* the owners going along? Some of these people are in desperate financial straits. If your brother were scuttling the deal for them, he'd be quite unpopular with a lot of people . . ."

They waited for him to continue.

"Of course, the future of this gin palace is in your hands now, Mr. Coughlin. Have you given it any thought?"

"No thought at all."

"I see. Well, you're sure to receive an offer equal to the one your brother turned down. But I'd like to persuade you to join Mr. McQueeney and myself on a more responsible course. Er . . . may I join you?"

Glancing at them hesitantly, the little man slid onto the stool next to Frank. Coughlin squinted at Timm as he swirled his cape off, folding it carefully inside-out and laid it on the stool next to him.

"Closin' time, Frankie!" Pat was pulling on his coat.

46

"I'll lock up. We're going to sit awhile."

The burly barman nodded, tossing Frank the keys. After a hard look in Timm's direction, Pat headed out the door.

Timm removed his hat with both hands, and placed it carefully on the stool before he resumed. "When I first asked Mr. McQueeney to seek landmark designation, he was humble enough to suggest the Emerald was just a run-down old music hall. The old fellow wouldn't agree until I threatened to denounce him in the newspapers if he didn't!" Timm chuckled. "My column doesn't pay very well, but it does give me a certain . . . persuasiveness. I'm afraid I wouldn't take no for an answer.

"I must admit I was less successful with your brother, though. He seemed very reluctant to make a public case. In fact, he wouldn't even discuss it until he assured himself I had Mr. McQueeney's blessing."

Frank shrugged. "People around here keep their problems to themselves. Do you really think this is worth all the trouble?"

"Apparently your brother did; he agreed to holding the cast party here after our show Monday night. I hope we can still count on that, Frank. May I call you Frank?"

"I'll let you know," Coughlin muttered.

"Landmarking is not only a duty, sir. It can also be quite profitable."

Coughlin squinted irritably. "That's not the way I hear it. I hear it cuts off an owner's options. Every repair and alteration has to be approved by the city, which can triple the cost. Who needs the grief?"

"Now, don't be selfish, sir. I know what it's like to take on the Philistines, but as a landmark this building with your family name on it would be nearly impossible to destroy. And designation would lend a certain cachet. You'd attract a much better crowd, so you could double your drink prices."

"Sure. And lose all our friends."

Timm shrugged. "If you really care about your community, you have no choice but to save its heritage. Quickly."

Coughlin slugged his drink and stared sullenly into the glass.

Timm's goatee framed a small, private smile. "Of course, your safest course is to sell to Cornerstone. But then your brother will have died in vain. Pick up the gauntlet, however, and his killer may be lured into the open."

Coughlin raised an eyebrow. "You mean act as bait?"

"Hey," Temple cut in. "I don't like this, Frank."

The judge scooped up a handful of peanuts and weighed them in his hand. "What do you have in mind?" he replied at last.

"I propose to build a case for landmarking. My work has been cited by the commission many times before. Designation should follow as a matter of course. Suppose you begin by telling me about the provenance of this building."

"Uh, what exactly . . . ?"

"Who built it, who bought it, who lived here, who renovated—"

"Oh." Frank popped some peanuts into his mouth and chewed thoughtfully. "Well, I don't know how it started out. It was a speak during Prohibition—the cops shut it down—and my grandfather bought it after repeal . . . around 1933, I guess. It's been in the family ever since."

Timm pulled out a small spiral notebook. "Your grandfather's name?"

"John Coughlin . . . Inspector John Coughlin."

"What did he inspect?"

"Criminals. He was chief inspector of Manhattan detectives."

Temple glanced at Frank. "Well, well. Live and learn."

"He solved some of the city's toughest cases: the Aspirin Gang, the Radio Burglar, the Bobbed-Hair Bandit . . ."

Temple grinned. "You're putting me on."

Coughlin raised his right hand. "The absolute truth—I swear. You can look it up. He was made commander of the detective division in 1920."

Timm stopped scribbling. "Why would a man with that kind of record retire to run a neighborhood saloon?"

"Disgusted with the work, my dad said. One night when he was young, Dad asked Inspector John if what the other kids were saying about him in the schoolyard was true. Grandad quit the force the next day."

"And was it? True, I mean."

Coughlin fixed the other man with a level stare. "I like to think he was as honest as the system allowed."

"Of course. Well, that's enough to get me started." Timm snapped his notebook shut and put it away. "Meanwhile, I suggest you use your influence to find out more about this Cornerstone Equities. It would help to know what kind of plans

Cornerstone Equities. It would help to know what kind of plans they've presented to the city, what kind of tax abatements they've been promised, who their contacts are."

"I know the routine." Frank stood up and reached behind the bar for his and Temple's coats.

"You may be in a dangerous position, Judge Coughlin, so please be careful."

Frank just nodded and snapped out the lights as they went outside. He pulled a steel fence across the door and snapped the heavy padlock shut.

On the sidewalk, Temple undertoned, "Where are we headed?"

Timm swirled his black cape up over his shoulders and hailed a taxi with his silver-tipped walking stick. "I'm heading downtown. Care to split the fare?"

Frank held the door open while the landmarks maven slid across the backseat. Then he shut it firmly behind him.

"Let's get rid of him, and I'll put you in a cab," Frank mumbled to Temple. "I'm going to stay here tonight. I'll come by for breakfast before the funeral."

Timm rolled down his window. "Aren't you coming?"

"You go on. We'll be in touch."

"Oh. Well, proceed with all due haste, sir. Don't forget—the enemy is right on your doorstep." Timm pointed ominously to the abandoned warehouse next door.

Stenciled on the tinned-up windows was a black logo—a chunky foundation stone, inscribed with the letters:

C/E

Ten

Today, we'll say much by saying little . . . at the sound of the tone.

BEEP. "It's Tina Molineux, dear. Annabel just told me what happened. If work will help, I'll get you more. If it won't, remember there's no job that can't be canceled. Call me at home if you want to talk."

BEEP. "Lewis Tedesco here, babe. I was flipping through *Glamour* on a checkout line, and I read that you like sushi. Well, I know a place where they make it with raw meat. If you've got the James Bond spirit, you'll join me. 495-0-double-0-7."

BEEP. "Guess who, Sunshine? Your mother. Just wanted to let you know you'd sent Betsy and Jonathan engraved Waterford crystal for their wedding present. You thoughtful girl, you . . . Is everything okay?"

BEEP. "Temple? It's Phoebe. Just my luck, I've got an hour between planes and you're not home. Why is it growing up means not seeing your real friends enough? Well . . . the news in a nutshell: This girl's in love. With a vice-president. Only problems are he's married, and I told him I'm an industrial spy. I thought it sounded more glamorous than investment banking. How's by you? Have an answer ready by spring, kiddo. They're calling my flight. It's Mozambique this time, if you can believe that."

BEEP. "It's Jimmy, T-Kay. I heard about the big guy's brother. Nothin' I can say, but if there's anythin' I can do—anythin' at all—you just let me know, okay?"

MONDAY

Eleven

Frank sprinkled a handful of dirt into the long, deep scar in the earth. It rattled forlornly on the wooden casket below.

"See you later," he murmured.

Kevin's grave lay at the feet of Kieran Coughlin (1910–1977) and his wife Annie Finn Coughlin, who in turn lay at the feet of Inspector John Coughlin and his wife Mary. This part of Calvary Cemetery in Queens, New York, was crowded with Coughlins.

Frank stared skyward a moment, fingering the black ribbon on his sleeve, and then stepped back unsteadily over the ground reserved for him. A few yards away, a dozen familiar faces respectfully avoided each other's gazes as they chanted along with the priest:

". . . and deliver us from evil. Amen."

As the clustered mourners scattered toward the caravan of cars on the drive, Frank and Temple walked over to Michael McQueeney. The man in the wheelchair was slipping hundred-dollar bills to two laborers leaning on shovels under a barren tree.

". . . know how hard the ground is this time of year," he concluded. "Oh, Francis. I'll just be a minute."

McQueeney motioned with his hand, and Dora pushed him up to the grave. After a moment of silence, he reached into his overcoat, pulled a Saint Christopher's medal from around his neck, and tossed it onto the coffin. Then Dora rolled him up a slight rise where he sat awhile by another marker, before wheeling around and heading for the last long limousine.

Temple drifted around to the far headstone and read the inscription: *Kathleen Coughlin McQueeney 1865–1907.*

By the time Temple reached the car, Dora was sliding her hands around the spindly old man.

"Can I help?" Temple asked.

"You'll just be dirtyin' that pretty suit, me darlin'." The old woman eyed Temple's Chanel, heaved McQueeney into her arms, and slid him straight into the backseat. "There, ye see? I'm used to it. In ye go now, bunny."

The four of them stared out the windows at the gray winter sky until the limousine slid over the Queensboro Bridge.

Michael McQueeney sighed. "It's a curse of old age to see the younger fellas goin' to their rest before ya. It's up to you to bury me now, Francis."

Coughlin rested his hand on his great-uncle's knee without saying a word.

"Y'aint in any sort of trouble, are ya, Francis?"

The younger man started. "Me? Why?"

"I just don't want ya inheritin' your brother's bad luck."

"What are you talking about, Uncle Mickey?"

The old man still gazed out the window. "There's some that think our Kevin's blind date with that chunk of rock wasn't exactly an accident."

Frank swallowed dryly. "You mean this guy Timm?"

McQueeney's eyes slid back into the car and examined his protégé's face closely. "A very knowledgeable individual, our pal Timm. He's told ya about our friends from Cornerstone? Now there's a pushy bunch of wiseacres. Not the kind of fellas to be patient with a saloon owner who's too stubborn to take their money and run. I'm thinkin' they bought our Kevin a whole block of enemies. . . . They want the Emerald, too, ya know."

"And?"

McQueeney smiled grimly. "I'm thinkin' of hirin' a bodyguard . . . What about you?"

Temple squirmed. "I thought the police didn't suspect any funny business."

"Oh, doll-face, open your eyes. Didn't ya notice that nice Officer Falcone payin' his last respects just now? The coppers have their eyes open, make no mistake."

Coughlin sighed and frowned out the window.

"Listen, fella, if you needed any help, you'd be comin' to me, wouldn't ya?"

Frank nodded silently.

"Ya need any money?"

"I don't know . . ."

"Well, don't be shy about askin'. God knows booze is a

rotten business. Your people worked hard to keep ya out of it. If ya want to stay out, Francis, I'll take it all off your hands for a good price. I promise ya—we'll keep this block Irish forever."

"I'll manage somehow."

"Just as ya like, just as ya like." McQueeney sighed. "But there's a nasty row comin' up. I've been smellin' it for months, and now it's started. If ya take my advice, you'll lay low on this one and let me take the risks for both of us from now on. I'm an old, old man, Francis—too old to lose much if things go wrong. But you're still a youngster, and you've got . . . all this." The old codger smiled and petted Temple's knee lightly through her black suit.

Coughlin glanced at her uncertainly as the limousine turned into their block, coasted past the warehouse with its black stone logos, and rolled to a stop in front of the Emerald Theater.

When Dora had McQueeney settled on the sidewalk, he gripped Frank's wrist with surprising strength. "I want a promise," Frankie."

"Anything, Uncle Mickey. What is it?"

The old man let go and shrank back into his wheelchair. "Promise me the next funeral in this family is goin' to be mine."

Twelve

Carrying two foil-wrapped hamburgers, Temple climbed the back staircase out of the Saloon's grimy kitchen in her stocking feet. Frank was still in the frayed, overstuffed family parlor, slumped in a straight-backed chair at a desk lit only by one feeble lamp.

"Delivery," she chirped, switching on the overhead light.

The gathering after the funeral had broken up quickly, and the Saloon was shuttered for the day. They had spent hours organizing Casey's belongings before Frank set to culling through his brother's papers. The day was dying early when Temple suggested some food.

She walked up behind Frank to place one of the silvery packages at his elbow. On the desk in front of him were the ledger books from the bar and a box of yellowing photographs. The one on top showed several people lined up in front of the bar.

Temple pointed to a black-haired boy with an enormous crooked grin. "Cute kid. That's you?"

"Hmm?" Frank rubbed his eyes and listlessly began unwrapping his dinner. "No, that's Casey." He pointed to another boy staring at Casey. "That's me, there."

"Really? You look taller."

Coughlin smiled. "I'm standing on a carton of beer. I was always trying to be as big as him."

She indicated a burly man in an apron, with a tough but fair face. "Your dad?"

"Yep." He took a bite of his burger, swallowing fast.

Standing behind the others was a dapper man with slicked-back hair and hooded, gleaming eyes. "This guy is definitely cool."

"That's Uncle Mickey. He sure is."

"No wonder Dora fell for him. I bet she still sees him that way. He sure has . . . shrunk."

"Everything shrinks," Frank muttered glumly.

Temple began leafing through the rest of the snapshots. "Is there a picture of your mother?"

"Down the hall."

"Can I see it?"

Rising wearily to his feet, Frank tossed his balled-up foil into a wastebasket and ambled slowly down the darkened passage. They turned into a middle bedroom. "This was mine and Casey's as kids."

Like most abandoned children's rooms, it was frozen in time, stocked with possessions that had outlived their usefulness. A City College banner was tacked to the wall over a narrow single bed. On the red-painted desk was a dusty Police Athletic League boxing trophy.

Temple plucked a hand-tinted photo of a beautiful woman off the bedside table. "This is your mother?" She took his face in her hands. "You have the same eyes."

"She died when I was fifteen." Coughlin pulled away and disappeared out the door.

Temple followed him back to the front room, where he stood glaring down at Casey's books.

"I always did hate math," Coughlin grumbled.

She perched on the arm of a chair. "Casey's paperwork all in order?"

"I got to the safety deposit box before it was sealed. The will seems okay. No papers are missing that I know of. But these damn books don't make a shred of sense."

"How come?"

"Casey kept them himself, so maybe I just need an accountant to decipher the arithmetic. But as far as I can see, this place is losing something like twenty-five thousand a year."

"Ouch. Is that a lot?"

"It is when the bar's been in the red for fourteen straight years. I never had any idea." Frank fingered the long ledgers tentatively. "The odd thing is he's always paid his bills on time. But he's never borrowed a cent from the bank. Never declared a loss on his tax forms. I just don't understand how he kept the place afloat all these years."

"Maybe he had another source of income. Like investments."

"No way. This building was his whole world. He must have been a magician to make this place work—and now he's taken his secrets with him."

He glanced at her despondently. "Sorry, but I better get back to work. If I don't figure this out . . . well, I may have to close the Saloon."

Temple squeezed his arm. Then she reached for her coat. "Think the folks next door would let me snoop around on their roof?"

"Oh, come off it," he muttered. "The cops were up there all weekend."

"I know. But they don't have a woman's eye. And I got threatened, too, remember?"

Frank sighed wearily. "It's not you they were threatening— it was me."

"What's the difference? It was Cornerstone who sent you my ad, wasn't it?"

"Probably," Frank shrugged. "Or the priest. Or one of the

landlords in those brownstones. Anyone with an interest in the block . . . Hell, for all I know it could have been the mayor."

Temple nodded. "Or even your Uncle Mickey."

The white scars over Coughlin's eyes flew up in surprise. "You've got to be kidding."

Temple shrugged. "I'm just wondering. He sure didn't waste any time making you an offer."

"That doesn't mean anything. He's had a standing offer to buy this place ever since I was a kid."

"Oh. Then he doesn't know about all the red ink?"

"How would I know? What if he does?"

"Stop acting so huffy. You have to admit he's not your garden-variety senior citizen. Even Dora says so."

Coughlin scowled impatiently. "I told you how it was down in Foley Square. The meek just got squashed deeper in the mud. Didn't Dora tell you how he kept our front window from being smashed by Mafia soldiers selling linen?"

"How did he do that if he's retired?"

"Respect. He still has a lot of connections. By the time he came back to America in the fifties, none of his old scams could work anymore—but he was sort of like a professor emeritus. He's been on the up-and-up for decades, you hear me? The man's a saint."

"If you say so," Temple said quietly.

He stalked up to her and jabbed the air in front of her face with his index finger. "Don't start getting brainstorms about things you don't understand, okay? A rich family like yours that's fallen on hard times isn't in the same boat with one that's been digging potatoes since Adam and Eve."

"Okay, okay. I just thought he was being a little opportunistic. If he already has one money-losing business, why would he want another one?"

"Loyalty. He wants to keep the bar in the family."

She reached up to smooth his troubled eyebrows. "Seems to me you're the one being loyal."

"You bet I am." He grabbed her thin wrist in his fist. "You wanted to know how I got these scars on my eyes? I'll tell you a story . . ." Letting go, he began pacing the room.

"When I was thirteen, I got caught shoplifting a Smokey Robinson album from Woolworth's. On a dare. They haul me down to the precinct, and lucky for me the desk sergeant recognizes me from the Saloon. Instead of calling my father—

who'd have let me rot in jail overnight to teach me a lesson—
he calls his old friend, Michael McQueeney.

"Mickey comes down to night court at three A.M. with a
lawyer. The judge is a Democrat, and after the three of them
have a little chat, he lets me go with a warning. I figure I'm
off scot-free.

"But on the way home, Uncle Mickey takes me down into
an empty subway station and backs me up against the wall.
Tells me I have a choice: Either he tells my father what happened, or I can let him decide what to do with me, right there.
Well, it would have killed my old man, so I tell him he should
decide. I figure he'll make me get a job and pay for the lawyer
or something.

"But Mickey has a little surprise for me. He tells me I can't
grow up to be a lawyer if I don't respect the rules. And then
he beats the *hell* out of me—yelling, 'Don't steal!'

"I mean, I hurt for a month. Had to tell my old man I got
mugged. It was years before I realized that was the biggest
favor anyone ever did me in my life."

"And you learned your lesson?"

"I'm a lawyer, aren't I? You don't forget the one who sets
you straight. So stop running down the only friend I have left
in this world—okay?"

"Not the only one."

He sized her up distantly. "Oh?" He turned away, staring
out the lace-curtained windows down at the empty street.

Temple felt adrift. "What are you doing now?"

"I told you. Back to the books. Don't you have a wedding
to go to?"

"I can get out of it. It's just a family thing."

"Just a family thing . . . Be glad you've got one."

"Frank . . ."

"Look!" He spun around suddenly. "I don't need a baby-
sitter. And I sure as hell don't need a reluctant girlfriend. Got
that?"

Temple stood perfectly still as his bitterness washed over
her. "I'm doing the best I can," she said gently.

He stared at her a moment. Finally, he sighed and pecked
her on the forehead. "I'm sorry . . . You don't know anything
about accounting, do you?"

She shook her head.

"Then you'll only distract me. Why don't you take off and have a little fun. It'll do us both good."

"Want me to come back later?"

"I dunno . . . Call me." Rolling his sleeves above his elbows, Frank was already ignoring her.

"What's the secret, brother?"

He sat down wearily, flipped a page, and gazed into the family ledgers that made no sense at all.

Thirteen

"Well, if it isn't the famous Temple Kent!" The man jumped to his feet, pulling out a chair for her at a table set with costly linen and silver. "Didn't I ask you to marry me in the fourth grade? I'm still waiting for an answer."

Douglas Clarke Eaton had gotten plumper and balder but still wore the same plaid bow tie and the navy blue blazer with egg stains on its sleeve. A perfect match in somebody's heaven— but not hers.

"You're sweet, Dougie, but I'm afraid I'm spoken for these days."

He lifted two side-by-side placecards. "Grammy Clarke is still hoping. You know, she doesn't approve of the Irish. I believe this seating arrangement is no accident."

The card in Dougie's right hand read *D10-1630*—Temple's identification number in the Clarke genealogy. The *D* indicated she was the daughter of 10-1630: her mother, who was a tenth-generation American, with 1629 older cousins. Grammy Clarke insisted on maintaining this elaborate family tree, and her trust funds always got their way.

Temple muttered, "God forbid we make do with social security numbers like normal people."

The New York Athletic Club was a massive monument to preppy physical culture on Central Park South. Here, men still had to don a jacket and tie just to enter under the awning with the red-winged shoe before stripping to play sports. Generations of former Ivy League jocks kept trim by wrestling or playing squash, until they graduated to the domino and billiard rooms. Ultimately, they retired to the dingy swimming pool upstairs, where wrinkly old chairmen of the board lay naked on hothouse chaises, blinking at their heirs.

Betsy Clarke's wedding reception was being held in the ninth-floor library, a huge room with a magnificent view of Central Park. The men's boxy suits and women's boxy dresses dated from the Eisenhower administration and might have all been designed by the same man at Brooks Brothers.

Dougie Eaton stole a glance at the neckline of Temple's clinging midnight-blue beaded sheath, made more modest for the occasion by a pearl-buttoned blue silk jacket, shot with threads of silver. "You know, every time I pass your name in the Social Register, I think of giving you a call."

"Really? I've been trying to get my name out of there for years. Think it would help if I married my Irishman?"

"What! Oh, you're kidding, aren't you?" He squeezed her arm hard enough to bruise it. "I never could fathom your sense of humor."

"It's not that deep, Dougie." She shifted her arm so that next time he'd hit a different spot.

"So how's life in the land of stocks and bonds?"

"Making me broker and broker," he cracked. Temple stared at him blankly. "Sorry. Old Wall Street joke."

Dougie Eaton flipped over the strawberry in the middle of his grapefruit. It was green. "I've got some nice little defense stocks you might want to consider..."

"Sorry. I don't like investing in things that explode."

A tall brunette in the matron-of-honor's dress approached them beaming a beatific smile. Gripped in her arms was a feisty infant, squirming to break free. She sat down on the other side of Temple. The place card there said her name was *11-1366*. Temple's older cousin Pamela was a born Clarke with a number all her own.

"Isn't it romantic?" she gushed.

"Heartwarming," Temple replied. "How's my god-kid, Toby?"

Pamela hugged her struggling son tighter. "I'm thinking of having the little monster stuffed."

Out on the dance floor, an elderly couple glided by to a Lester Lanin foxtrot, perfectly wedded to each other's arms.

Pamela wiggled her fingers at them. Her parents waved back.

"Mom's a little tipsy," the matron of honor confided. "Know what she told me? She and Dad still do it!"

"It?"

"You know. *It*. Twice a week!"

Temple watched the old couple's effortless movements. "You mean there's life after marriage after all?"

"Uh-huh," Pamela beamed. "So, were you two having a nice chat?"

"Sure were!" Dougie grinned.

"Swell," Temple agreed, nudging Pamela under the table. She rolled her eyes meaningfully.

"Umm . . . Keep me company in the ladies' room, Temple?"

"Thanks . . . I mean, sure. We're going to freshen up, okay, Dougie?"

"You two are pretty fresh already."

Pamela smiled weakly and lifted Toby into the paunchy man's lap. "If we're not back in ten minutes, you can sell the kid."

As they skirted the dance floor, a little boy in short pants chasing another barreled straight into Temple. He looked up in awe, suddenly overcome with shyness.

Temple sighed. "Why can't they stay this cute forever?"

"Don't you think Dougie's nice?"

"Mmm. So gallant—for a guy with cabbage-leaf hair."

"And mature."

"And boring."

Pamela nodded. "He's a Clarke, all right."

Swiping a bottle of champagne from the liquor table, they pushed into the ladies' room. Pamela's engagement ring sparkled next to her wedding band. She never took off her trophies. She'd bagged a banker and was radiantly fulfilled.

"So how's it going, Temmy? The word's out about your judge, you know. Where's the mystery man?"

Temple passed the bottle to her cousin. "Who wants to know? Grammy Clarke?"

"Everybody's dying to get a look at him. Grammy figures with Betsy getting married four years younger than you, you're long overdue."

"What is this, a contest?"

"Tell me about him." Pamela took a hit from the bottle.

"His name's Frank. Real smart. Real sure of himself."

"Nab him." Pamela wiped the rim and returned it.

"He's not the nabbing kind."

"But of course. Handsome?"

". . . Interesting looking."

"All the better."

"He's got these gold flecks in his eyes . . ."

"Oh, mama. If you've got one like that, how did you wind up next to Dougie tonight?"

"Grandmama." Temple sipped daintily, enjoying the fizz in her mouth before swallowing. "I'm making up for missing Thanksgiving."

"Grammy Clarke can be very insistent. Still, why not show off Frank too?"

"I just want to keep him to myself awhile. You know how it is: Your family knows you're seeing a guy, and suddenly everybody's treating you like a couple. I hate that feeling, when the momentum of an affair is pushing you along faster than your own emotions. I just don't need the pressure."

Pamela nodded. "They'd be all over him, all right. I thought maybe you were self-conscious about what he'd think of the family."

Temple lowered her eyes. "You always were the smart one."

"True. So true." Pamela took back the bottle. "You going to marry him?"

Temple looked into the mirror, avoiding her cousin's eyes. "Well, I dunno. After all these years solo, it's hard to think in terms of a permanent duet. Living alone gives me a mobility that's good for my career. And it helps me identify myself."

"I suppose." Pamela didn't seem much impressed. "Myself, I learn more from living with Paul than I ever could on my own. When you see yourself through the eyes of someone you love, it expands your awareness."

"Yeah, that happens to me with photographers."

Pamela laughed. "I said 'living with,' not play-acting. Be serious."

"Oh, well . . ." Temple took back the half-empty bottle; it was cold in her fingers. "It just seems like such a death—killing off all your options. No matter *who* he is."

"Options? Such as what?"

"I dunno." She rested the bottle by the sink. "I'll try anything—as long as I know I can get out of it."

"Real brave," Pamela said dryly. She hugged her younger cousin around the waist. "You're scared to death, aren't you? Well, listen up. Trying lots of men may seem like variety, but after awhile you'll realize you're running through the same maze of emotions over and over. Then there's only one way left to push yourself deeper into life—something you might think is boring, but really puts you through the most changes of all: *One* guy. Know why?"

Temple shook her head.

"Because ultimately, the interesting options are things you can't do with a rotating cast of characters. Like getting married, or buying a house together, or having kids."

"But how can I be sure he's the right one?" Temple wailed.

"It'll be obvious, Temmy. I knew pretty quickly with Paul. All I can tell you is the real thing is nothing like the rehearsals."

"Better or worse?"

"Well . . . different."

"You're not just trying to get me hitched, are you . . . Mom?"

Someone pounded on the ladies' room door. Dougie Eaton's well-rounded tenor pierced the grate. "I still want that dance, Temple."

"Just a moment, Dougie." Winking, she splashed a bit of champagne into her palm, then daubed it daintily behind her ears.

Pamela blasted herself with a breath freshener. "C'mere," she commanded. She gave her cousin's mouth a squirt too. "Now, behave yourself."

"Don't I always?"

"No. But maybe that's why you always end up enjoying these things in spite of yourself."

As they rejoined the wedding party, a syrupy version of "You'll Never Walk Alone" gushed over them. The laughter seemed louder. Eyes shone brighter. The hors d'oeuvres and liquor tables looked like the aftermath of an aerial bombing.

One of Temple's uncles looked up from an earnest conversation with a preteen niece in ankle socks. He eyed Temple's dress appreciatively and winked. "When are *you* getting married?"

Dougie Eaton was dandling Toby awkwardly on his knee.

The infant gurgled, then reached up and pulled the man's bow tie apart.

Temple giggled. "Kinda nice having a family, isn't it? Corny . . . but nice."

"Yes it is." Pamela eyed her smugly. "Think about starting one of your own."

Temple laughed. "You *are* on my mother's side."

Pamela's parents were cheek-to-cheek now, dancing with the sureness of blended memories. The old gent dipped suavely, cradling his wife deep in the crook of his arm. Pamela's mother's eyes were closed.

"How about that dance, Temple?" Dougie Eaton tightened the plaid bow knot around his throat.

"Let me make a phone call first, okay?"

"I'll be waiting."

"I know."

Out in the hall, Temple dropped a dime into the pay phone and dialed Casey Coughlin's apartment over the Saloon. The line was busy.

She retrieved her dime from the tray and turned reluctantly back toward the reception. At the buffet table, Dougie popped a deviled egg into his mouth before licking his fingers and wiping them dry on his blazer.

Temple stopped dead in her tracks, making a face. Then she spun around and fled down the stairs, away from the boy with the cabbage-leaf hair.

Fourteen

When Temple stepped out of her cab in front of Coughlin's Saloon, the Emerald late show was just letting out. Several moviegoers rushed the taxi. Others huddled by the theater's plate-glass doors as a blast of frigid air screamed past, warning of a snowstorm moving down from Canada. Temple hoped her relatives had appreciated her decision to sacrifice warmth for style on such a brutal night.

Then a ghost floated down through the night, a white shape swooping out of the green glare of the Saloon's spotlights. When it fell limp on the sidewalk at Temple's feet, she bent to pick it up: a lady's white slip.

Looking up, she saw spectral shadows flickering across the Emerald's rooftop. It was certainly an odd hour for Dora to be taking in her wash.

As Temple ducked into the flocked red velvet lobby, the marquee lights dimmed out behind her. She trotted up the elegant staircase, curving past staggering frescoed Maxfield Parrish landscapes to the mezzanine landing.

Ignoring the corridor that led to Michael McQueeney's private suite high above the audience, she took the nearer path to the roof, a fire stair by the projectionist's booth.

She pushed the crash bar on the big fire door and emerged onto a flat expanse of tarpaper. Up here, the arctic winds knifed at her more sharply; goose pimples crawled up her legs and back. Clutching her thin jacket closed, she wedged a book of matches inscribed *Betsy and Jonathan* into the door to keep it from locking behind her. Then she circled the stairway enclosure.

But there was no one else on the rooftop. The only shadows were those cast by the empty, scarecrowlike clothes pole.

Temple pinned the slip to the clothesline, then walked to the brilliantly spotlit side of the roof. Looking over the balustrade, she saw the boarded-up skylight, and the lone stone face, laughing into the glacial winds off the Hudson. The mask of Comedy was out of reach, all right—a good six feet down from the nearest spot on the roof. Where Tragedy had been, there was only a raw scar on the wall.

The skeletal clothes pole shuddered and reeled. Temple eyed it as it spun this way and that in the gusting wind. It was taller than she was—well over six feet.

She sprinted toward the aluminum tree, folded its metal arms down against the central pole, then lifted the whole thing neatly out of its slot in the roof.

The end of the hollow pipe was crushed—there were burrs and gouges in the soft metal, as if it had been used in a manner the manufacturer hadn't intended.

Could it reach?

Hoisting the cold contraption over one shoulder, she staggered awkwardly across the roof again. She hooked an arm under one metal limb, anchored her weight on the low balustrade, and poked the long pipe down.

Its crushed end scraped the scar on the wall easily. When Temple fitted it snugly behind the remaining mask, she felt little surprise or satisfaction—only a dully unsettling sense of finality.

Suddenly a loud crash echoed behind her: the door slamming!

She ran around the enclosure to the fire exit, but there was no handle on this side, and it was shut tight. Betsy's wedding matches lay crushed on the ground.

Temple's fingers scrabbled uselessly at the edge of the door. It wouldn't budge. When she pressed an ear against it, all she got was a stab of pain in the thin cartilage—and silence.

Loud banging brought no response from the old couple below.

Quickly, she edged down the rear fire escape until she found herself stranded three stories above the ground. It was frozen with ice or age, and made horrible little creaking noises that drove her quickly back up the rusty steps and across the roof.

The street out front was dark and deserted now, the Saloon still shuttered in mourning, the theater closed for the night. What had O. M. Timm called Mondays? "Dark night"—the one night of the week when the entire theater district shut down.

"HELP!!"

She yelled—and kept on yelling—hoping someone might hear. Fifteen minutes later, an answer drifted by on the chilling wind:

"Aw, shut the fuck up!"

Temple's extremities were going numb. Her throat constricted as the glands in her neck began to swell. Desperately, she huddled behind the stairs enclosure. Even with her jacket up over her ears, the wind rumbled past like fast traffic.

Soon, she had to shut her eyes against the stinging air. The green lights of Coughlin's Saloon were so bright she could see blood shadows moving in her eyelids. Dimly, she wondered what images would appear as the night grew colder and clawed deeper into her with its hoary touch.

Time passed. Interminable minutes that could have been hours. And then the lights clicked off. She opened her eyes into a shroud of darkness, recalling Coughlin's lights were on an automatic timer—it was 2 A.M.

Five hours till daylight?

Wrapping and rewrapping her thin silk jacket, Temple vowed that if she could model bikinis in the dead of winter, this trial would be a snap.

Or at least, she'd die pretty.

A door slam.

An engine coughing.

Temple's eyes flickered open in the thick darkness as the engine coughed again, struggling for life in the cold.

She tried to stand, but her legs wouldn't hold her. They weren't even there. In her mind she saw him adjusting his white crash helmet, swinging his strong leg over the soft leather seat.

She crawled on her knees to the front of the roof and pulled herself over the balustrade as the motorcyclist twisted his accelerator and bent to jiggle the choke.

"Fra-ank?" Her voice croaked faintly in her swollen throat, as though it were afraid of disturbing him. Frozen with frustration, Temple watched as he shoved his bike off its kickstand.

She pulled off one blue heel and tossed it feebly down to the sidewalk—but Coughlin rolled right by it. He hadn't seen.

Desperately, Temple yanked off her other shoe and used every bit of her strength to heave it wildly into the street in front of him. Last chance . . .

This time he braked abruptly. He stared in disbelief at the blue silk heel, then craned his neck to peer up at the sky. Even when he looked her straight in the face, he didn't seem to register what he was seeing. Temple waved, her mismatched lips giving him a trembling smile.

Instantly, Frank cut his engine and hopped off the bike. He rattled the Emerald's plate-glass door, then backed off to stare up again.

Cupping his hands around his mouth, he yelled: "I'm calling them on the telephone! Stay right there! You hear me, Temple? Don't try a thing! I'll be back in a minute!"

. . . But he wasn't back in a minute.

Or even in many minutes . . .

At some point, Temple's aching arms simply gave way, dumping her rudely onto the rough tarpaper.

There was no point in moving. The cold was relentless—it followed her everywhere. It would freeze her beauty, and her discovery.

Another victim of the wind, they'd say. Just like Casey . . .

Dimly, she heard the deep grumble of an engine working hard, like a garbage truck chewing its cud.

Suddenly Coughlin's handsome head popped over the top of the balustrade.

"How did you get up here?" she mumbled drowsily.

"I flew. Hurry up, I'm tired of flapping my arms."

It was a hallucination, of course. Frank—for all his many virtues—couldn't fly.

When she merely stared at him, he stepped onto the rooftop and gathered her into his arms.

Then the hallucination stepped carefully up on the balustrade—and off into thin air.

But they didn't fall. Instead, stars burst in her eyes; the street was bathed in red and blue lights. Parked with its wheels up on the sidewalk, a red fire truck was carefully lifting them down in its cherry-picker.

Snuggling closer, Temple tried to do up the top of Coughlin's shirt, but her fingers were too dead to manipulate the button. "How did you get them out at this time of night?"

He kissed her on the forehead. "Told 'em my kitten was stuck up in a tree."

As soon as they stepped onto the sidewalk, an old fireman winked and wrapped Temple up in a blanket. Then a younger fireman held a paper cup of steaming coffee to her lips. It burned going down.

"Thanks, fellas," Coughlin was saying. "You're all drinking free this month."

The young fireman smiled shyly at Temple. "Meow," he whispered.

She buried her face into Coughlin's chest . . . and purred.

TUESDAY

Fifteen

At eleven o'clock the next morning, Temple emerged alone from the IRT subway into a windy circle at the bottom of Manhattan. To her right was the elegant Beaux Arts U.S. Custom House. Before her, the tiny oval called Bowling Green.

Glancing at her watch, Temple realized she was nearly late for her meeting with O. M. Timm. She hurried past a dry fountain, crossed at Beaver Street, and entered the massive curved building at 26 Broadway. In the high-ceilinged marble lobby, she found him under a clock decorated with the signs of the zodiac. The landmarks maven wore a wide-brimmed lambskin fedora and a knee-length woolen cape fastened with a pearly cameo beneath his salt-and-pepper beard.

"What is this place?" she asked.

"Originally it was the Standard Oil Building—home of the world's first push-button elevator. It also has one of the city's most interesting setback towers. Did you notice it from the green?"

"Sure did. I love the smoking urn on top."

"It's a disguised steam vent. Obviously you have the proper instincts for urban appreciation: Always look up. Up, up, up!"

The elevator lifted them quickly into the tower, where Timm led her through a maze of windowless pea-green corridors. Finally, he paused before an unmarked green glass door. Unlocking it, he ushered her into his private hutch.

Crowding the little room were dusty file cabinets, tin ceiling plates, doorknobs, moldings, masonry, stained glass, a crowded umbrella stand, and even an ornate bidet. Through a grimy little window, Temple could barely discern the best harbor in the world, the Statue of Liberty, and the immigration buildings of Ellis Island.

Unable to find a place to sit, she pulled off her Scandinavian goose-down coat and folded it over her arms. She sneezed three times in rapid succession. "Isn't it time you had a rummage sale?"

"Not at all. I think of myself as an urban archeologist." Timm knocked several old books and magazines to the floor and kicked aside a black tool bag so Temple could shoe-horn herself into a green-slatted folding chair. He leaned his ample behind against a radiator. "That chair was once in a third-base box at Ebbets Field."

"You were a Dodgers fan?"

"No," he chuckled, "but I love a lost cause. Some things should never change."

"If things never changed, there wouldn't be any history."

A feminine giggle leaked through a connecting door to the next office. Timm pursed his lips irritably. "Pardon my neighbor. Mr. Stoessel fights unemployment by hiring working girls."

"You mean hookers?"

Timm shot her an owlish smile. "It can be somewhat distracting."

Temple glanced around until the giggles faded next door. "So you . . . what, plunder old buildings?"

"I rescue things with character before they are demolished."

"You turn lost causes into antiques? Great racket."

"It has its rewards, but money isn't one of them. What I make selling salvage doesn't nearly cover my expenses. Good deeds never come cheap."

"You certainly attracted a well-heeled crowd at the Frick."

"Dilettantes, I'm afraid. You see, I attended St. Paul's on scholarship, so many of my school chums now own or control landmarks. Meanwhile, their wives have little to do but charitable work. It's a difficult situation: I'm encouraged by the wives and barely tolerated by my peers, who can't understand why condominiums don't belong between the spires of St. Patrick's."

Timm shifted uncomfortably as a jet of vapor from the radiator's steam valve sprayed under his thigh. "I'll let you in on a dirty little secret: The old rich are no longer wealthy enough to protect themselves from the new rich. The landmarks cause needs public donations if we're to have an effect. If only we could get a media star like Mrs. Onassis involved Monday night . . . Er, you wouldn't know her, would you?"

"No, but I beat her daughter in field hockey once."

"Too bad. You see, my hope is that our little pageant can

be publicized in a substantive way. During this campaign, we must go everywhere together."

"What about Frank?"

"Mr. Coughlin will have to understand. After all, we're doing this for him. You'll love doing interviews."

"Actually, I'd prefer not to."

Timm looked alarmed. "Please? I've already arranged one with my own paper."

"The *TriWeekly?* That's only read by downtown trendies."

"Yes, but trendies have influence . . . and, er, donate money."

The radiator squirted again. Timm rose to rustle through some papers. "I've put together a fact sheet you might study before the interview."

"I'll go over it tonight."

"I am afraid it has to be done this afternoon. The next issue closes tonight and space is being held for you."

"I guess that'll be okay." Temple sniffled. "Where and when?"

"I've arranged for you to meet Sasheen Lopez at Pink's at six P.M. . . . . Perhaps you could return the favor?"

"Favor?"

"Bill VanderPoel tells me you know a television reporter who plans to cover our festivities." Timm beamed at the model. "I am available any time."

"You mean for an interview?"

"By all means. See what you can arrange, hmm?" He glanced at his watch. "Does Judge Coughlin know the way? No, of course not. Why don't you call your reporter friend while I direct him here."

Temple dialed Shelby at the TV station and filled him in.

The southerner drawled, "This the fancy twit with the walkin' stick? Why, sure! Thanks for steerin' him my way, darlin'."

"You didn't need me. As long as you work for Channel Three, this guy doesn't care if you're the janitor. Make sure you do it in his office on Broadway and Beaver Street."

"Where in hell's Beaver Street?"

"Wall Street area. This place is like the attic of a museum."

"I'm an uptown boy now, T-Kay. I'll get the bends goin' all the way down there. I like streets with numbers."

"You're a reporter, kiddo. Your gig is to suffer. Say, you ever heard of Sasheen Lopez?"

"Mmm . . . *TriBeCa* columnist?"

"Yeah."

"Achin'ly hip. Mostly writes about her friends. Dresses like a sloth. I've seen her slothin' round the clubs."

"Should I let her interview me?"

"Prob'ly. She's good ink. But tread careful-like."

"Why?"

"Trust me. Women are irrational on the subject of models."

"Aww, Shelby. That's not fair."

"Neither is a face like yours, darlin'. Signin' off . . ."

Sixteen

O. M. Timm trotted through the door in front of Coughlin. Frank was unshaven and haggard, wearing a frayed shirt, jeans, scuffed loafers, and an old camel's-hair coat. He might have slept, but he hadn't rested.

"I was just asking Judge Coughlin if he'd let me borrow you for the ballet tomorrow night. Everyone will be there."

Temple glanced over the little man's shoulder. "What about that dinner party, honey?" She winked broadly. "Remember?"

Frank looked around for a chair distractedly, finally resting his foot on the lip of the bidet. "I must have forgotten. I'm not in the mood, anyway. You two go ahead."

O. M. Timm beamed. "It's settled then. Hallelujah. In the meantime, Your Honor . . ." He clapped his hands. "What's new?"

Frank sighed wearily. "I've been tracing Cornerstone Equities all morning—or trying to."

"What do you mean?" Temple wiped her nose.

"They've got a logo, a post-office box, and an out-of-state phone number with an answering machine—no message, just BEEP. So I checked with an old friend of my dad's in the city register's office, where ownership records are supposed to be filed."

Temple cocked an eye. "Supposed to be?"

"Yeah. See in theory, they'd have the most recent records. But owners transfer titles back and forth between all sorts of management and holding companies, partnerships, decoys..."

"The most recent records have to exist somewhere."

"Right. Somewhere. But the deeds are only updated every six months. That's enough time for a dozen more transfers. The papers chase the changes, see? They don't always catch up. And if Cornerstone has a friend somewhere in the administration..." Frank let the sentence hang.

Temple pulled a handkerchief from his pocket and wiped her nose. "What about the last deed to the warehouse that's on file?"

"It was a corporate name—CORNERCO, INC. So I went to the secretary of state's office to find out who the officers were. And that led to some very strange information."

"Well?"

"... They're all dead. Then I tracked down a lawyer who had a vague memory of transferring all of CORNERCO's assets to a holding company in Delaware."

"Why Delaware?"

"Delaware is a favorite haven of the rich." Timm smiled wryly. "The state's disclosure laws are almost useless."

"Great," Temple grumbled, offering Frank his handkerchief back.

He waved it away. "It gets worse. Even though Cornerstone is an out-of-state corporation, they still have to pay property taxes. So I called the city tax collector. The last payment was made in cash—over the counter—and if there was ever any record of who made it, it's disappeared."

Timm offered another resigned smile. "The tax people don't care who pays, as long as someone does."

"Then who's making these offers?" Temple demanded.

Frank shook his head. "Somebody's out there... somewhere. They sit on an empty warehouse all these years, then suddenly they want to buy the whole damn block. But they haven't filed a single plan. It's a ghost company..."

O. M. Timm cleared his throat. "Ghosts can be materialized."

"How?"

"Once we declare for landmark status, Cornerstone will have

to step forward to challenge us—unless they're not willing to risk exposure, in which case you should win by default."

Frank scratched his stubbly chin. "I'd rather find out who killed my brother."

"Come, come. It's a marvelous structure deserving your attention."

"Yeah, and it's losing twenty-five thousand dollars a year."

"At least there's your Uncle Mickey's offer," Temple muttered.

Timm raised an eyebrow. "Offer?"

"If I wanted to sell," Frank grumbled. "Which I don't."

"I'm sure you have the means at your disposal, sir."

"On a municipal judge's salary? We're talking three hundred thousand just to bring the building up to code. More, when you realize the landmarks people would have to be satisfied too."

"Oh, come now, Judge Coughlin. You can confide in me." Timm examined him craftily. "Don't you have some... undeclared resources?"

Frank's eyes narrowed. "Like what?"

"The more I discover about your inheritance, sir, the more intriguing it becomes."

Temple leaned forward in her chair, resting her chin in her hands. "What have you found out?"

O. M. Timm rustled some papers and began reading from a manila folder. "The house was built in 1870 for a robber baron named Jim Fisk. He was truly an outsized man by today's standards—an infamous rake. He wore admirals' and militia captains' uniforms, scarlet-lined capes, and countless rings and diamond sparklers. He also cultivated a Robin Hood image by giving freely to old ladies and news dealers in the streets. Fisk's greatest coups came in concert with his partner, Jay Gould. They plundered the treasury of the Erie Railroad. . . ."

"How could they get away with that?"

Frank glanced at her wryly. "They didn't have government regulations in those days. These are the guys the laws were invented for."

"Just so, Judge Coughlin. These two were also hooked up so neatly with Tammany Hall that Boss Tweed let Gould manipulate the city treasury to control interest rates. They were quite a team: Gould had the intelligence, Fisk the image, and

Tweed ran the game . . . And then they went after the biggest mark of all: President Ulysses S. Grant."

Coughlin leaned back, folding his arms across his chest. This was his kind of dirt.

"Have you ever heard of Black Friday?" Timm continued. "In the late 1860s, Gould and Fisk decided to corner the gold market so they could manipulate prices. To do this, though, they had to neutralize the vast holdings of the American government.

"First, they persuaded the president's brother-in-law to lure Grant to a meeting on Gould's yacht. Grant had a taste for alcohol, you know, and when he admired the solid mahogany bar aboard, Gould offered to donate it to the White House—among other gifts. Evidently, the president didn't take the bait, but bribes *were* paid to his First Lady and his secretary. Before long, the plan seemed to be working.

"Gould had accumulated a great many gold futures—that is, he'd bought rights to the substance at current prices for delivery some time in the future. In fact, it was widely suspected people owed him twice the limited supply. Then, on Thursday, September 23, 1869, rumors suddenly spread that Gould was about to demand settlement of these debts. Naturally, this set off a mad scramble among his debtors as they tried to buy enough gold to meet their obligations—which was impossible, of course—and prices soared.

"That night, however, President Grant seems to have double-crossed them. He released the government's gold, and the next day—Black Friday—prices tumbled, causing a nationwide depression."

Frank whistled softly. "So they were wiped out?"

"So one might assume. But some think Fisk and Gould knew what was coming all along, and sold out just in time. It's estimated they split a fortune of eleven million. Whether or not anyone warned them of President Grant's intentions . . ." Timm turned his palms up and shrugged.

Coughlin raised his eyebrows. "That's a hell of a yarn."

"It's a true story," O. M. Timm said. "It's history."

"But what does all this have to do with the Saloon?"

"Examine the context, Judge Coughlin. That very year, Fisk fell in love with an actress named Josie Mansfield. The girl was just sixteen years old. When Jay Gould built a mansion on Fifth Avenue at Forty-eighth Street, Fisk decided it was time he moved his mistress north as well—a touch 'above' polite society. He built a mansion as a gambling club—your house, Judge Coughlin—with an apartment upstairs for the Mansfield girl. She was going to be the hostess, and she decorated it all through 1870. But she never moved in . . . and the club never opened."

Temple leaned forward in her chair. "Why not?"

"L'amour," Timm intoned, relishing his tale. "Josie indulged herself in an affair with another of Fisk's associates, named Stokes. When Fisk finally saw through the haze of his infatuation, he cut her off—and she sued him for breach of promise! Then he accused them of blackmail, and they countersued for libel . . . Josie was ruining him.

"Unhappily for Fisk, 1870 and '71 also brought the downfall of the Tweed ring. So the Fisk/Stokes trial promised to be a sensation. It had everything: sin, betrayal, greed, corruption . . .

"But on the night Josie began testifying, Stokes shot and killed Fisk with a Colt revolver in the lobby of the Grand Central Hotel. He spent six years in Sing Sing and died a broken man. Fisk, on the other hand, lay in state while the public wept for him."

"And Josie?"

Timm shrugged. "It seems she left for Boston, where polite society ignored her. Eventually she disappeared. Such a waste: she was barely nineteen . . ."

Coughlin's foot slid off the porcelain bidet with a thud. "I still don't see what all this has to do with me."

"Patience, sir. Through a number of deed and title transfers, the Fisk mansion came under direct control of various Tammany bosses, who passed the gambling club on to their successors. In 1924, ownership devolved to one George McManus, a gambler and bookmaker who ran a floating card game."

Temple grinned. "Like in *Guys and Dolls?*"

Timm nodded. "It wouldn't surprise me if someone lost the bar to him on a wager."

Coughlin nodded absently, checking his watch. "I've got a meeting at two o'clock," he warned.

Timm hurried on. "McManus ran the club as a speakeasy for several years. But the records show another transfer—in 1928." He studied Coughlin over the top of his file. "McManus deeded the bar to a police inspector—your grandfather."

An awkward silence filled the room.

"This transfer took place at the height of Prohibition, you see?"

A bar of sunlight glinted dangerously in Frank Coughlin's gold-flecked eyes. "So?" he murmured, suddenly alert.

"So how did a high police official come to own an operating speakeasy in 1928—not 1933, as you cavalierly led me to believe?"

"I don't know," Frank snapped. "I wasn't there."

"Ah, of course not. Well, perhaps you'd know how he could afford such a magnificent palace on a police salary?"

"It was the Depression. My dad said Gramps bought it cheap after the Crash."

O. M. Timm shook his head. "The Crash came in 1929, Judge Coughlin—a year later." He smiled cryptically. "Isn't there anything you'd like to tell me?"

"What the hell are you getting at?"

Timm sighed. "I was afraid you wouldn't want to talk about the, er . . . gold."

Frank and Temple stared at the round little man as though he'd just popped out of a spaceship.

"Gold?" they exclaimed in unison.

"President U. S. Grant's bribe money." O. M. Timm was beaming smugly. "Thanks to my contacts with certain private archives, I've been able to examine some Erie papers. They suggest Fisk and Gould set aside a sizable fortune for the old general. If he double-crossed them, of course, it would never have been delivered.

"Maybe it was frittered away on other bribes—by Gould up in Albany, or by Fisk in his lawsuits. Remember, this crew was notorious for traveling around with trunks full of cash. But I have a theory that it was kept in Fisk's gambling house. *Your* house, Judge Coughlin. It might be hidden there still."

"That's ridiculous."

"Is it? Josie Mansfield certainly didn't think so—and she was sleeping with the man. She sued to gain control of the mansion after his death. And lost."

Coughlin shook the idea around in his head. "And all those politicians who owned it just let a pile of gold lie there all this time?"

"Oh, no. They wouldn't have had a clue." O. M. Timm licked his lips carefully. "There are a great many papers in this world that the public has no access to. And never will. The ones I saw were sealed for a century—until 1972."

Frank glanced at his watch again. "That's quite a story, but I'm afraid you've got an overactive imagination."

"Really? Forgive me, but you've already lied about the date your family took over the bar and—"

"I didn't lie," Coughlin snapped. "I just didn't know."

"All right, sir, whatever you say. Just don't do it again, hmm? Everything is recorded somewhere. It won't do to play fast and loose with the truth."

Temple scrunched her eyebrows at him. "Let me get this straight. You think Frank's grandfather got his hands on the lost gold?"

"Perhaps."

"And you think Frank has it now?"

Timm's chuckle was infuriating. "Perhaps."

"I'll tell you what," Coughlin grumbled. "When you can prove there's buried treasure in my basement, you let me know and I'll pay for the shovels. Until then, stick to your landmarks. We'll all be better off." He draped Temple's coat around her shoulders and yanked her to her feet. "Now if you don't mind, I have a district attorney waiting for me." He pulled open the green glass door.

Quickly, the little man reached around him to flip it closed again. "I think you better hear me out, Your Honor. This property transfer from a criminal to a constable—well, it looks peculiar and will have to be explained."

"It's ancient history, Timm."

"Exactly. That *is* our concern after all. Perhaps you'd better find out what happened back in 1928."

"Swell. Maybe I should dig up Gramps and ask him."

"You may end up wishing you could. Consider your position, Judge Coughlin, and how it could be distorted. It isn't the facts that matter so much as the nuances."

Frank spoke with glacial coldness. "What's wrong with trying to save my own home?"

"Why, nothing—by itself. But you must admit a fortune in hidden gold suddenly constitutes a compelling motive for, er...fratricide."

Frank's eyes glazed over dangerously. "Who would dare imply—"

"Any interested party," Timm observed quietly. "Cornerstone, if they wanted you out of the way. The police, if they needed to find a culprit. Why, even myself, if I thought you weren't committing your full resources to preserving that lovely mansion. Whoever you spurn will seek to cast you in the worst possible light, Judge Coughlin. It's time to choose sides."

The two men stared at each other, neither one blinking.

Finally, O. M. Timm shrugged. "Perhaps you'd better poke around for that gold, hmm? And think about who your friends are. Carefully. In the meantime, I'll see if I can locate the Mansfield girl's records and—"

Coughlin wrenched open the glass door again and stalked out into the corridor.

The urban archeologist gave Temple a crafty look. "Please look into my questions . . . one of you? I assure you, even a judge can be made to seem a villain."

Temple studied the man a moment, then followed Frank around the corner. She caught up with him just in time to see him punch the elevator call button with a closed fist.

Temple paused on the windy sidewalk. "Aren't there laws against extortion?"

Frank nodded. "I'll see you later, okay?"

"I've got a couple of hours to kill."

He shook his head, staring sullenly across Bowling Green to the sea. "I'm going to see if an assistant D.A. I know can light a fire under the cops."

"Can't I come? It's good to have corroboration."

"Yeah, it's great. But in a court, when you're incriminating someone—not when you're asking a favor from a friend. David's an old law-school buddy. I might have to do some fancy footwork, and it's better I do this dance alone. I'll call you later." Frank began striding north, up Broadway.

Temple had to trot to keep up. "You trying to get rid of me or something?"

He halted with a sigh. "Look. It would be a big help if you stuck with this guy Timm. I don't have time for it, but you can be my eyes and ears. Let me know what he's up to. Anyway, don't you have lines to learn or something?"

"They say they want it rough. Don't forget, I'm the one who found that clothes pole."

Frank eyed her thoughtfully.

"Besides," she grinned, "I want to see you in action."

"You promise to behave?"

Temple raised two fingers. "Scout's honor."

A fifteen-minute walk brought them to One Hogan Place, at the top of Foley Square. The assistant D.A. was Frank's age and size, but the resemblance ended there. David wore a rumpled gray suit, thin black socks, black oxfords, and a G.O.P. elephant tie.

His office was as small as his self-image was large. The paneled room was lined with framed credentials and citations. As they pulled up chairs, David shot a flirtatious glance at Temple that fell to the carpet like a broken arrow.

"Frank, I want you to know that, personally, I would kill for you. But the boss specifically wants me to remind you that the code bars disclosures about investigations-in-progress."

"Sure, I know." Coughlin summoned an easy grin. "How about a general overview?"

"No movement at all, I'm afraid. The investigation is dead in the water. I called downtown to see what I could stir up, but . . . nothing." His fingers dropped into a magnetized pile of diamond-shaped metal chips swirling in the desk toy.

"That's the same picture they showed me Sunday—only the paint hadn't dried yet."

"It has now, ol' buddy." David pushed the diamond chips up into a wall.

"Well, I've got some new information that might help things along. Temple thinks she found the murder weapon last night."

She nodded. "The clothes pole on the roof."

"And there's something else that might be useful. It was messengered to my office." Frank pulled the ad threatening Temple's life from his jacket pocket and slid it across the desk.

David studied it a moment, his fingers swirling new spirals in his desk toy. Then he stood abruptly and excused himself.

Temple grinned. "That ought to stir things up."

"We'll see." Coughlin slouched in his straight-backed chair. "It doesn't matter what we have. They have to care enough to push the cops."

"Do you think somebody tried to, uh . . . hurt me on purpose last night?"

"I don't know." He mulled it over. "You ought to be safe enough—unless you spooked them by snooping around. I haven't turned down Cornerstone; they haven't even made me an offer yet. Until then, they probably want you available . . . and vulnerable."

The prosecutor bustled in again. "I've had copies made and sent the original downtown. But no guarantees, you understand?"

"Can't you at least guarantee they'll try?"

David settled into his swivel chair and tipped back, resting his black oxfords on the desk. "Look at it from the police point of view, Frank. No witnesses. Vague accusations against powerful, unidentified interests . . ."

Coughlin nodded to his friend across the desk. "I know you're doing all you can. Would you mind if I made a suggestion?"

"Shoot."

"Look into a company called Cornerstone Equities. I can't pin them down in any city records."

"Our record keeping is pretty slack, too, Frank. It's fiscal-restraint time all over town. I've got a case load you wouldn't believe, and a boss who makes Attila the Hun look like Walt Disney."

"My heart bleeds," Temple muttered.

"What?" The D.A.'s head jerked toward her.

Frank glanced at her irritably. "She didn't say anything."

"I'd like to hear what she has to say."

Temple looked nervously at Coughlin but took the plunge anyway. "People get killed in New York all the time, right?"

"Right." David's finger began building a tower of magnetic chips.

"How many cases get solved? Not necessarily with convictions. Just solved."

The man behind the desk shrugged. "Some."

"And how many get swept under the carpet due to fiscal . . . restraint?"

Frank jerked around in his chair. "You're not being fair, Temple. David's just doing his job."

The prosecutor plucked a bunch of diamonds from his magnetic tower and let them sprinkle back to the pile. Then he picked up a pencil and scribbled a note on a pad.

"I'll look into it in my off hours."

"Off hours?" Frank's eyebrows knitted together in alarm.

"Best I can do." The assistant D.A. dropped his pencil and stood to end the meeting.

Coughlin rose, too, but his shoulders were sagging. "Just don't let them close the case, David." His voice slid into an unfamiliar pleading tone. "Not until you're really satisfied. That's all I ask."

"I'll do everything I can, Frank—but you know I can't speak for the boys in blue. Their enthusiasm is tied to their budget. They give priority to the high-percentage cases."

He patted Frank's back. "I did speak to the commissioner this morning. He suggested that, with your connections, you might have a chat with the mayor to see what he can do about getting them the funds to operate properly ... 'With justice for all,' I think he said."

"That's blackmail!" Temple snapped.

Coughlin looked stricken. "It's really just politics."

"So what you're saying is, the police only investigate crimes that are convenient?"

David shrugged. "They do have plenty to choose from."

Temple's violet gaze burned into his face until the embarrassed young prosecutor flushed. "Can I ask you one more question? Aren't you ashamed of yourself?"

"Frequently," the official replied.

She reached out and knocked over his little tower of magnetic chips.

Coughlin cringed. He grabbed her arm to lead her out.

"I'll do the best I can, ol' buddy. But try to see the mayor. That's the best shot." David returned to his desk, his fingers drawn to the shifting, magnetized diamonds.

In the privacy of the elevator, Temple fumed. "I hate seeing you be like that."

"You asked to come along." He punched LOBBY. "Like what?"

"...Mousy."

Coughlin peered at her a moment, chewing his lips as they began to fall. "You think it's just a question of nerve? Sure, I could have yelled at him. Or made a few rapier cracks. Hell, I could have punched him in the nose—that would be pretty impressive. But it wouldn't have gotten the job done. If you want results, you horse-trade. Get it?"

"No wonder I don't like politics. It's ... weaselly."

Frank just sighed.

"You were getting the runaround from an old school buddy."

"He was giving me all he could, Temple. He just doesn't have the clout. If you listened more closely instead of opening your big mouth, you might have heard him say that. Instead, you embarrassed the guy."

"He embarrassed himself."

"Well, I can't argue with that..." They rode down in silence.

When they reached the lobby, Temple asked, "What are you going to do now?"

"Keep after Cornerstone, I guess. They might be hidden, but their contact man isn't. Father Dolan's next on my list."

"What about the mayor? This David seems to think..."

"Yeah. But, God, I hate asking for favors."

"Why?"

"They're the currency of politics. The more you ask, the more you owe."

Temple nodded. "What about me? Want me to check out the questions Timm asked?"

"What questions?"

"About how your grandfather got the bar. I could ask Uncle Mickey—he knew him, and he was there at the time."

Frank shook his head. "I'll take care of Uncle Mickey myself. If there's something fishy about my family, I ought to know it first, right?" In the tiny lobby, several people stepped warily away from the irritable voice. "Besides, he's an old man who deserves his privacy. You leave him alone."

"Whatever you say. But don't forget to ask him what he knows about the gold."

"Oh, come on. He'd laugh in my face."

"Frank! First you can't figure out how Kevin kept the Saloon solvent. Then you hear there might be gold around. Let's ask the man, for godsake."

"Look, I know how to talk to my own uncle, Temple." His face tipped down, the crooked mouth faintly sour. "And you're not ready to be part of this family—remember?"

As they hit the sidewalk, Temple ducked under a blast of chilly air. "I just thought he might have some answers."

"Not to the questions you'd be asking. He's not the enemy, you know."

She stepped in front of him and spoked softly. "Neither am I, Frank. I'm the girl you sleep with, remember? You saved my life last summer."

He avoided her eyes.

"Look, I know this is your turf. If you think your connections will help you—fine. Just remember, all those Davids you're dealing with have been trading away their loyalties for years. They might not have much sympathy left."

"Nobody bucks the system for another guy's idea of what's right."

"Well, I'm not in the damn system."

Coughlin sighed. "Temple, I couldn't bear for you to get hurt solving my problems."

"Don't be so egocentric! This is all happening to me, too, you know. I have a right to enjoy the buildings these jerks are tearing down. I have a right to believe in neighborhoods staying together and people like Casey being safe in their own homes. Sometimes it seems like the whole world is being shoved around by bullies—and I'm sick of it. I have a right to make myself count . . ."

Frank nodded and looked away. "I'm not very good company today, am I?"

"Lucky for you I'm a patient girl. Want me to buy you lunch?"

"No, thanks. I've got some thinking to do."

"Good. You do that, then come spend the night with me."

"Well . . . I might be busy."

"Oh?" Temple fixed her eyes on the traffic. "Something not for me?"

Coughlin grunted. "Yeah, Brooke Shields is coming over and she's shy about spectators." He made a face. "I just want to wake up in my own bed. With my own thoughts. Okay?"

"Oh, c'mon. I'll cook you dinner." Temple patted him fondly on the rear.

"Cut it out!" Coughlin whirled, batting her hand away sharply.

"Frank!" She stared at her stinging hand as though it had betrayed her. "That hurt!"

"Sorry. . . . I must be a little upset."

"A little? Maybe I'd better leave you alone for a while."

"Oh, let's not break up today. I'm too busy to think about it right now."

The wind ripped across their faces. "Sometimes I can't tell when you're kidding."

"Likewise." Coughlin stared her down recklessly. "Can I go now?"

Slowly, Temple nodded.

He turned away and disappeared into the chilling afternoon—alone with his worries at last.

Seventeen

"Want some drugs? You can put them on your credit card."

Temple glanced away from the bartender, surveying the all-pink, downtown designer restaurant. "This place is too chic for me," she muttered.

She returned her attention to a column in the centerfold of the *TriBeCa TriWeekly* in her lap.

A few minutes later, a tiny woman in a fuchsia leather dress with over-pronounced shoulders came threading her way through the empty tables. She stopped in front of Temple.

"Hi! I'm Sasheen Lopez." Her angular face was striking under black crew-cut hair, but more glamorous than truly pretty. The journalist had gone a bit heavy on her blusher but was otherwise perfectly dressed for Pink's.

Temple closed her paper. She was in a quilted green coat decorated with a snarling hand-painted tiger and the legend: *"Watch my flaps."* "Hi, I just read your piece on baby alligators." The corners of her mouth twitched slightly. "Are they really that much fun to take a bath with?"

Sasheen grinned and crushed her cigarette into the ashtray on the bar. "That's Ed the Editor's idea of how to sell papers. He says for every serious column I write, I have to do one that's totally frivolous."

"Which kind of column am I?"

"Didn't Om tell you?" Lopez began unpacking her bag.

". . . Om?"

"O. M. Timm. At the office, we all call him Om. He says

your benefit is going to preserve the superstructure of Western civilization. That's serious column stuff."

"Great, but I'm just the lead mannequin. You should talk to him if you want to know about architecture."

"Can you imagine a photo layout of Om? He has hair sticking out of his ears. And frankly, I think Ed the Editor has a crush on you."

"Which ad?"

"Rapunzel Shampoo. The one where you're on the sailboat with your hands tucked into your bikini bottom. He says the smile on your face drives him nuts."

Temple laughed. "That's just good acting. We shot that in November at the Seventy-ninth Street Boat Basin, and I hid my fingertips because they were turning blue."

"I won't tell him. Okay if I turn this on?"

Temple nodded, reached for her bullshot, and watched Sasheen snap on her black-jacketed Sony TC-55 tape recorder.

"I need some personal background first, okay? Models always seem to appear out of nowhere . . ."

"Not me. I had parents—a full set."

"Where were you born?"

"Paris."

"But you're American, aren't you?"

Temple nodded. "My father was a doctor—he was studying a French surgery technique at the Sorbonne. Met Mom at Cafe Flor."

"She's French?"

"Nope—she was working as a runway model at Chanel. They moved into a tiny apartment in the sixteenth arrondissement, got married, and had me. When I was six, the family moved back to Boston—Wellesley, actually—when Dad got an appointment to Mass General."

"'Moved back'? Who was from Boston?"

"Mom's family had been in that area for centuries."

"Came over on the *Mayflower?*"

"Heavens, no," Temple laughed. "That was just the servants. Mom's people came on their own boat after the crops were planted."

"Great quotes. I don't even care if they're true." Lighting another cigarette, Sasheen sucked in deep quick drags until her face was wreathed in a pale blue cloud. ". . . So that's how come you're listed in the Social Register?"

"You have been doing your homework." Temple made a face. "That's Mom's fault. Every time I try to get deleted, she sends in an update on me. What can you do with a proud mother?"

"How come your father isn't listed too?"

"He died when I was fourteen."

"I'm sorry." She didn't mean it. Sasheen glanced at the tiny spinning wheels of her recorder. "What happened to him?"

"He smoked two packs of Gauloise a day for twenty-five years. Mom told him they made him look like Belmondo."

Sasheen took a last long pull from her cigarette and stubbed it out in the ashtray. Temple reached into her purse for a violet pastille.

"Were you always a pretty kid?"

"Well . . . I suppose."

"Why be modest, right?"

"What am I supposed to say? Boys started following me around when I was ten. At twelve, they were throwing snowballs at me. When I was sixteen, I started dating their older brothers."

Sasheen reached for another cigarette and then put it away. "Being pretty must make life a lot easier," she sighed.

Temple shrugged. "It's a mixed blessing. You have to be that much more defensive, even just meeting people's eyes in the street. Not everyone wants the attention."

"I know what you mean . . . I guess. Maybe I shouldn't tell you this, but the other day I was having lunch with a publicist in Le Gillon, and I said I was planning to write about you. He told me there's graffiti about you in the men's room. It says . . . 'Temple Kent gives good—'"

"Headlines," Temple snapped. "And I know what it said before I altered it too."

"*You* changed it?"

Temple nodded. "When I heard about it, I wanted to see if I recognized the handwriting—but I didn't."

Sasheen glanced at a three-by-five card tucked into the cellophane of her Kools.

"I understand you dropped out of Wellesley after one year. Why is that?"

"The required reading got too dull. And the bills were tough on Mom."

"How did you get into modeling?"

"I'd been posing for art classes. A friend of mine showed Eileen Ford some pictures he'd taken. She invited me to New York."

"Didn't you feel guilty about dropping out to model?"

"Guilty?"

"Your mother wasn't disappointed?"

"Not at all. She thought it was entirely practical. My freshman roommate teaches poetry now—for about nine thousand a year—and she's papering her cabin in the woods with rejection slips from the *New Yorker*. Going to college doesn't necessarily save your life."

"Okay, okay. So you came to New York. How old were you?"

"Nineteen. Eileen put me up in Saint Margaret's Residence for Women. They had ten o'clock curfews."

"Sounds wholesome . . ."

"Oh, it was disgusting. I lasted about a month there before I discovered I liked the hours at Max's Kansas City better."

"Oh-oh. Rock stars."

"A party every night until four A.M. Five hours later I'd be modeling wedding gowns for *Bride's Magazine*. It got so I couldn't stand wearing white, and I started blowing my morning appointments."

"Eileen's not the type to appreciate that, right?"

"I think she was pretty disappointed in me, but I was getting tired of virgin's gowns and kitchen smocks. I played the happy homemaker until I felt like I was trapped in a loveless marriage. So I dropped out for a few years."

"And did what?"

"Grew up. Tried to, anyway."

"Back in Wellesley?"

"Uh-uh. Europe."

"How did you support yourself over there. More modeling?"

"No, I. . . . A friend took care of me. He . . ." Temple reached over and snapped off the Sony. "Look, I'd rather not talk about that, okay? Next question?"

". . . Okay." Sasheen's hand drifted over the recorder. Its tiny wheels started spinning again. "So you were what? Early twenties when you came back?"

The bartender came out of the bathroom sniffling and rubbing his nose.

"That's late to restart a modeling career, isn't it?"

"I'm a late bloomer."

"Hmmm." Sasheen checked her index card. "Do you have a boyfriend?"

"I generally call him a man. It's good for his self-image."

"What's his name?"

"I should have known how personal this would get from the things you did with those alligators."

"Do you live together?"

Temple frowned. She watched the white spokes of the cassette's tiny wheels twirling silently. "Next question, please."

"Okay . . . Do you want to have kids?"

"Not by myself."

"So you want to get married?"

"I think I want another drink. You?" Temple signaled the bartender for another bullshot. Sasheen ordered a Lillet and resumed the interrogation.

"What's the best way to pick you up?"

"Gently."

"Has a man ever ripped off your clothes?"

"Well, this gay guy stole one of my shirts once . . ."

Sasheen smiled.

The bartender delivered their fresh drinks, giving Temple a conspiratorial smile as she blew her nose. She ignored him, stirring her drink with a pink swizzle stick.

"Tell me, Temple, have you always wanted to be an actress?"

"No, in fact, never. I tend to freeze in front of large groups of expectant *Homo sapiens*."

"What about a singing career?"

"Not me. I can't carry a tune in a bucket. The other day I was walking down the Bowery singing to myself, and a bum looked up from under his pile of old boxes and said, 'Don't worry, honey, I can't sing either.' When I'm done posing, I'll disappear back into the real world where people are functional instead of decorative."

"Don't you want to be a star? I thought every model did . . ."

"Not really. I've never understood the compulsion to be in the spotlight. It's the audience that's privileged: The performers are working for them. All this nonsense about celebrity is the tail wagging the dog."

"Still, this role is a great opportunity to get discovered."

"I'm not sure I want to be discovered. Robert Redford says

that once you're famous, instead of being able to observe people, suddenly they're all looking at you, and not behaving naturally. It feels as if you're slowly going blind."

Sasheen scratched her head. "Why are you doing this show then?"

"My boss asked me to. I've been concentrating on myself so much the past few years I thought it would be nice to show a little civic spirit."

"Do you know a lot about landmarks?"

"No more than the next person. I read Ada Louise Huxtable in the *Times* if the photo catches my eye, but mostly I just like knowing they're there. This country's landscape changes too quickly. It's nice to know something has been respected and left alone."

"Are you nervous about Monday night?"

"No. Petrified."

"I'm sure you'll do beautifully."

"I hope not. I'm supposed to act totally inept. Must be typecasting. We're just trying to have fun and raise money for a good cause."

"And get a little more famous," Sasheen persisted.

"I'm not famous."

"Well, you're pretty well rumored. Didn't you have something to do with putting that phony modeling agency out of business last summer?"

"Oh . . . did I?"

"I heard you did."

"I heard I spent the night with a senator in Maryland once. That doesn't make it true."

"You didn't spend the night with a senator?"

Temple smiled. "I've never been to Maryland."

"Still, people think you fixed those cousins—"

A sharp click drew Sasheen's eyes to her Sony. Its white wheels were no longer moving.

"Oh, dear." Temple smiled sweetly. "You've run out of tape."

"It doesn't matter. I've got all I need. We'll probably end up as a sidebar to Om's piece anyway."

"He's writing about the show too?"

Sasheen nodded grimly. "He's been trying to make the front page for years—it's sort of an office joke—but it looks like he's finally got something. A nice juicy scandal. He was the hit of the editorial meeting. Asked for a cover, a day's extension on his deadline, and a *lot* more space, when all he was assigned was a puff piece."

"Oh . . . and there's a scandal about the show? What am I getting involved in?"

Lopez shrugged at the pink ceiling. "You never can tell with Om. He came back from the library this afternoon all hopped up about some dead actress who lived upstate with the Sisters of St. Joseph."

"And she's the scandal?"

Sasheen nodded. "Her, some old tycoon, a crooked cop, and a city judge who's playing coy about how he came to own this old bar."

Temple lifted her drink and eyed the reporter over the rim. "What do you suppose Timm's after?"

"A reputation," Sasheen sneered. "Why?"

"Oh . . . just curious to see what's knocking your column into a sidebar."

"I see . . . Well, graft, conspiracy, conflict-of-interest, all the usual yellow-press dirt. He's got half the research staff pulling cards downtown. If he gets anything on the judge, Om will tear him apart. He's been waiting for a chance like this for years."

"Do you think he will? Get anything?"

Sasheen shrugged. "Your guess is as good as mine. You'll just have to plunk down seventy-five cents and read all about it on Friday." She drained her aperitif, the ice clacking against her teeth. "Thanks for the interview, Temple. I have to run if I'm going to make my deadline."

"Sure." Temple bit her lower lip thoughtfully.

"Now don't worry, hotshot. It'll only help sell tickets if Om gets his cover story. Just remember—any press is good press— as long as they spell your name right."

Temple nodded, rattling her ice as the other woman hoisted her bag over her shoulder and weaved across the room.

When the bartender arrived, she realized Sasheen Lopez had stuck her with the pale pink check.

Eighteen

Temple dropped a coin into the pay phone at Pink's and dialed Frank in the West Village. The line was busy.

Unable to find a cab in the biting-cold evening, she hurried diagonally uptown on foot. When she reached Abingdon Square, she ducked into the phone booth across from the White Horse Tavern where the poet Dylan Thomas had drunk himself to death. This time Coughlin's phone started ringing.

"Hello?" It was the soft, unfamiliar voice of a woman.

Temple's reply stuck in her throat. She held her breath, paralyzed by uncertainty.

"Anybody there?" the other woman purled again. "Well, if you're going to be so shy, I'm hanging up." The line went dead.

It was beginning to snow as Temple looked down Hudson Street, intending to flag a cab and head home. Somehow, though, she found herself walking west instead. She climbed the steps to Frank's door, hesitated at the bell, and peeked into the living room.

There, by the amber glow of a cosy fire, Frank was polishing off a bottle of red wine over the remains of his dinner. Across from him, an attractive, comfortable-looking redheaded woman rose and began clearing the dishes. Frank drained his glass and stared into the embers.

When the woman returned from the kitchen, she placed her hands on his broad shoulders and began kneading them familiarly.

He reached up and patted one of her hands.

She bent down, whispering into his ear.

Coughlin nodded and got to his feet. He draped his arm around the redhead's shoulders and let her guide him toward the cottage out back. The lights flicked out.

Temple backed away from the darkened house uncertainly.

Across the street, snowflakes fluttered through the streetlight's glow like a rain of feathers. Somewhere down the block, a giggle was muffled in the softening air.

She began trudging out of his neighborhood, feeling forlorn and windswept as a little match-girl. Once she found Bleecker, she allowed her thoughts to wander, trusting her feet to follow the traffic east. Past the precious antique shops of the West Village. Across Seventh Avenue, through the snappy health-food and leather emporiums of the trendy strip. And then over Sixth, into the tacky, touristy remains of the folk era's cafe culture.

Leaving the bright lights behind, she glided by the monolithic dorms of New York University and finally plunged across lower Broadway into the murky netherworld that was NoHo.

By day, this wasteland of broken sidewalks was merely pathetic, dented and hollow as the inside of a garbage can. But after dark, with the seedy light-manufacturing shops shuttered for the night—or for the last fifty years—the occasional working streetlight shone on a no-man's landscape as lifeless as the dark side of the moon.

Then, at the corner of Lafayette Street, three dark shapes emerged from the unlit hole in the ground that led down to the IRT subway. Temple veered off the curb and crossed to the other side of the street.

In the corner of her eye, she saw one man lift a bottle-shaped paper bag to his lips, tilt it up, and then pass it to his sidekick.

"*Ojos a la derecha!*" The third man nudged them until all three were peering across the street.

A long, lazy wolf-whistle curved sinuously into the night air.

"Hey, honny—why you out in the dark without a man? You lookin' for company? Everybody need company in the dark, you know?"

Resisting a sudden impulse to run, Temple walked on, briskly but evenly.

One of them sniggered.

"C'mon baby, you workin' or what?" A thin, ratlike giggle scurried along behind her. "I got two dollars—no lie."

Temple fingered the knife in her pocket and kept on marching. She rounded the corner, heading north up Lafayette, past a dark gauntlet of closed liquor stores and auto repair shops.

"Hey, bitch! Man's talkin' to you! You too proud for us?"

At the intersection of Bond Street, a glittering object flew over Temple's head and smashed on the cobblestones a few steps ahead of her. Their bottle of Thunderbird. They'd be getting bolder now, like dogs smelling fear.

Temple grabbed two garbage-can tops, spun around, and began beating them together like cymbals:

CRASH! "'Hear the loud alarum bells—'"

CRASH! "'Brazen bells!'" She smashed the two lids furiously, reciting the words of a one-time Bond Street resident— Edgar Allan Poe—in a menacing singsong voice.

CRASH! "'In the startled ear of night'"*CRASH!*—"'How they scream out their affright! Too much horrified to speak, they can only'"—*CRASH!*—"'shriek!'"

The men slowed, eyeing each other doubtfully.

CRASH! "'. . . the bells, bells, bells, bells, bells'"—she began inching closer to them, brandishing her lids. "'In the clamor and the clangor of the bells!'"

CRASH!

CRASH!

The three men froze in their tracks and goggled at her.

One of them muttered "*Loco*" and backed away.

They glanced at each other nervously, whispered together, and slunk off around the corner.

"Creeps," Temple muttered. Sprinting across the cobblestones, through the light of a sputtering vapor lamp, she raced into the familiar shadows of Great Jones Street.

She attacked Paradise's heavy street door with her keys, slipped inside, and banged it shut behind her. Leaning against the cold metal, Temple gasped for breath a moment before she realized her legs were trembling.

Sniffling, she slipped to the floor. Then she punched her fist into the sheet metal so hard, it skinned her knuckles.

"Men!"

Nineteen

This is Temple talking. While you were out, the Earth was invaded by extraterrestrials. If you'd like to participate in the New Order, leave your name, number, and blood type at the tone.

BEEP. "Oh, Temple, what a cute tape. Thanks so much for the lovely wedding gift. Jonathan and I are off to Scotland tomorrow. I'll call when we get back, okay? Let's have lunch at the Woman's Exchange."

BEEP. "Cheers, Temple. Annabel here. The principals in our little production will be getting together tomorrow morning at eleven in Mr. McQueeney's suite at the Emerald Theater. That means you. Ta, for now."

BEEP. "Ilona Harris from Avedon, Temple. Richard will be happy to blow up that winking shot you want—just drop off the print you have. Call first, and he'll try to find time to say hello."

BEEP. "Hey, darlin'. Your Timm creature is quite a character. I take it he doesn't know he's gay? Listen, I know Frank's upset, but he's playin' hide an' seek with my camera crew. Help me get him on film, and maybe a lot of other people will get upset, too—know what I mean?"

BEEP. "O. M. Timm here. The research I'm turning up is quite promising. Have you or Judge Coughlin made any progress in answering my questions? They're positively looming. Let's discuss it at the ballet tomorrow night, hmm?"

WEDNESDAY

Twenty

She was wondering what Frank had had for breakfast—and who'd made it for him.

"Temple, are you paying attention?"

She put down her coffee cup and turned away from the window. The *Comedy of Errors* organizational brunch was winding down in Michael McQueeney's private apartment, high atop the Emerald Theater. Temple fingered the lapel of her Harris tweed jacket.

"Sorry, I was thinking about . . . food."

Logan, the skinny, one-named choreographer, quivered hyperkinetically. "I said we'll want you to wear something skimpy Monday night, not like this Villager outfit you've got on now."

"Haven't you noticed it's winter out there?"

"Yes, peaches, but it's ultrasummer under those hot lights. Wear something teeny-tiny—you'll be glad you did."

Uncle Mickey winked behind his magenta glasses. "And so will I."

The old man's hideaway was frozen in time. Scattered about the walls were original Ziegfeld posters, a sketch of Josephine Baker, and autographed photos of Jimmy Cagney and George Raft, mixing with dozens of forgotten politicians. Three dusty black Bakelite dial phones rested on the desk. Behind it was a large, wilting, green, orange, and white flag from the St. Patrick's Day parade of 1959. Against the far wall were glass display boxes containing what appeared to be an ugly gun collection. A tarnished silver shovel leaned in one corner, a souvenir of some long-forgotten ground-breaking ceremony. In this lair, high above Times Square, Michael McQueeney was surrounded by memories.

Ogden Timm stretched and yawned, chucking the anxious Logan on the arm. "My faith in you knows no bounds, you know."

"I don't need faith," Logan snapped. "I need celebrities." The reindeer on his sweater fidgeted across his thin chest.

William VanderPoel rose to his feet, running his hand through steel-gray brush-cut hair. "Thank you for coming, everyone. If you'll just keep on panicking, Logan, I'm sure we'll be well prepared by Monday."

As the committee filed out, Uncle Mickey's frail fingers clutched Temple's wrist. "Would ya mind keepin' me company till Dora gets back from shoppin'?"

The door was swinging shut. "Not at all." She replaced her coat on the blue silk sofa.

McQueeney began leafing through the oversized, board-covered Molineux Models catalogue. "Like a big box of yum-yums ya buy at the movies," he cackled, turning to Temple's page to see if the genuine article measured up. "How come you're wearin' such a gloomy puss today? . . . Talk to me."

"Oh . . . just tired, I guess."

"I'd say Francis does pretty well for himself. I never bother payin' attention to his girls until they last six months, but you're gettin' to be a regular fixture around here. Time I got to know ya. You're Irish, ain't ya?"

Temple had to smile. "You'll convince me yet."

The old man tore out Temple's page and slid it across the desk. "How about givin' an old man an autograph? You're goin' up on the wall."

Temple signed the sheet quickly. Then she pulled out her acid-edged boot knife to trim off the ragged edge.

"Nice blade," Uncle Mickey murmured.

"Thanks. Keith Richards gave it to me."

"Oh, yeah?" The old man nodded. "Who's he?"

"Uh, he's a Rolling Stone . . . a musician."

"Ya don't say." Uncle Mickey didn't seem much impressed. "Ya want to see somethin' with history?" He crooked his finger and wheeled across the room to the display cases of carefully mounted firearms. There were pistols of all shapes and sizes, most of their barrels plugged with lead. In a case by itself was a heavy Thompson submachine gun.

The old man selected a little pearl-handled revolver, weighing it reverently. "My first gun. Lefty Louie give it to me when I was twelve years old after he used it to bump off Beansy Rosenthal."

Temple examined the gleaming weapon. "This is quite a museum you've got here."

"Well, me and the Emerald have seen better days." He tapped his useless legs. "They wrote my obituary at the *Times* already."

"You couldn't be *that* old."

"Let's just say I was born with the century—and I'm hopin' to die with it too."

He peered at her intently. "Tell me the truth now. Ya use the cocaine?"

Temple shook her head. "It's overrated. Too expensive, too aggravating, and too damn chic."

"Chic!" McQueeney rolled the word around his mouth like a dirty penny. "My old man was killed by some coked-up Hudson Duster when I was still in diapers."

"Really? What are Hudson . . ."

"A gang. They was all over. The Gaslighters, the Plug Uglies, the Roach Guards, the Shirttails—they left their shirts hangin' out like Chinamen . . ."

Temple giggled. "They sound like punk rock groups."

"They're the original punks. They ran this city since before the War Between the States. Ya either had to run with a gang or join the police—I picked the gangs myself . . . We used to mug the cops for their pretty blue overcoats and give 'em to our girls. Back then it was all wide open."

Temple raised an eyebrow. "How wide?"

"Suppose I told ya even the cops bought their jobs? Three hundred bucks made you a patrolman. For fifteen hundred, you got promoted to sergeant. The captain of a good district paid the bosses fifteen grand a year, but a'course he was the bagman, so . . ."

"It's hard to believe it was that brazen."

"Oh, the bluenoses would try a little cleanup every couple years. The Americans hated the Irish, ya see—so anytime they talked about public morals, they was talkin' code for immigrant-hatin'. The only jobs with a future was against their laws."

Temple cupped her chin in one hand. "So what was your angle—if you don't mind my asking."

"Don't mind at all. Fact, it's a pleasure to meet a kid wants to hear an old man's stories." McQueeney smirked. "As the senator once said: 'I seen my opportunities, and I took 'em.'

By Prohibition, I was working for a guy name of George McManus, used to run a floatin' poker game."

"McManus?"

Uncle Mickey's eyes twinkled. "Name is familiar? It should be. He owned the Saloon before the Coughlins. I was dealin' his game in a garage one night when a guy put up a marker for that whole buildin'. I can still remember him: a full house, kings over aces. Cripes, I was holdin' four jacks, so I covered with my personal bankroll—and I took him! And then the boss changes the rules on me. Says it's *his* Saloon 'cause I was workin' his game. Now don't ya call that cheatin'?"

"I don't know. What were the rules?"

"Simple," the old man growled. "He had a gun and I didn't."

Temple smiled ruefully. "How did you get the Emerald?"

The old man's eyes turned soft and dreamy. "I fell for a showgirl. Dora, see? I just couldn't help it."

"That's all right. I'm sort of a showgirl myself."

McQueeney nodded gravely. "I went to these variety shows here all the time. One night, I spot this twist in the chorus line and I'm kayoed. She whispers in my ear that, if I can, I should make money offa somethin' I love. What a yo-yo. But I love her, I guess, and I love the life. When I hear this very playhouse is up for sale, I go to my boss—McManus—and I ask him for a loan. I figure he owes me, right? He tells me this place is a stupid investment and to take a hike!" McQueeney spat into his white handkerchief.

"But you got the money anyway?"

"Naturally. But I had to go outside the family to find it— and that got me tied up with people I did not want to be tied up with."

"Who's that?"

The old man glanced at her slyly. "He's dead a long time."

"It's so romantic. Borrowing money to buy a theater for the woman you love."

"Ahh, spare us the applesauce." McQueeney shook his head. "It was good business as much as good romancin'. In '27 and '28, my Emerald had the prettiest chorus line on Broadway— and Dora the prettiest among 'em. I was makin' tons of dough. Openin' nights I was turnin' down five hundred clams for front boxes. But ya know where the best seat in the house is? Right here."

Wheezing slightly, the old gent rolled his wheelchair around in front of his desk. "Close the drapes over there, will ya, kid? Go on, go on—I ain't gonna bite ya."

Temple crossed to the window and did as she was told.

"Now come over here and pull up this ring for me."

Temple joined him in the dim light and looked down to where he was pointing. Set into the floor was a trapdoor with a large brass ring embedded in it.

She hooked a finger into the ring and slowly lifted up the trap. As she did so, ghostly light flooded the room. It molded McQueeney's face in chiaroscuro, giving him, for a moment, the gleaming black hair and hooded bright eyes of the slick young man in the family photo from Frank's boyhood.

A blast of automatic weapons fire shattered the silence.

Temple peered down through the hole, feeling like Pandora looking into her magic box. They were directly over the movie audience, with a perfect bird's-eye view of the screen, where a man was bleeding to death in black and white.

Temple shut the trap and went to the window for the drapes.

"Cripes, wasn't that a time! Drinkin' all night, breakin' the Volstead law with the big bosses themselves. We stayed up watchin' the dawn come in fresh from Ireland, winkin' off the tiptop windows of the tallest buildin's and then slidin' down into the street. This town had sparkle! And ya know what we'd say? We'd say, 'It's a great life—if ya don't weaken'. And we thought we never would . . ."

Temple sighed prettily. "It still is, Uncle Mickey."

"For you I'm happy. And for Francis. But for me . . ." The watery old eyes slid to her sadly. "I'm afraid I been weakenin', kid."

A faraway look drifted into his face. "But there was a time I thought I was livin' in the grandest place on earth, the land of opportunity for the Irish: the Emerald City. We had a system, see: Those that needed to be good could play at bein' American, and those as was willin' to be not-so-good could live on their wits.

"With the system, a fella knew where he stood—the racket boys and the pols all workin' together as partners to the benefit of all. When the machine was hummin' around election time, oh, cripes, it was sweet to see the deals flyin' and the fortunes bein' made. You could practically *smell* the chances in the air. Everybody playin' by the rules of the fellas who pulled the strings—and if ya played it right, you could be pullin' a string yourself some day.

"Like the Wizard of Oz?"

The old face turned toward her dreamily. "That's a hundred and ten percent right, Temple Kent. Like the Wizard of Oz in the Emerald City. A young fella's dreams die hard in a town like this, ya know. Once in a while, even when he's old, that same dream comes back like a long-lost love and seduces a fella the same old way. And one more time, he's young . . ."

McQueeney sighed as his reverie abandoned him. "But for me, it just didn't come in the cards. Life deals 'em funny and sometimes . . ." the old man shrugged ". . . sometimes ya fold."

Twenty-one

Temple gazed into the careworn old face. "What happened, Uncle Mickey?"

"Ahh, you don't want to be hearin' an old man's gripin'."

"Yes, I do. I'm going to be old myself some day."

He bounced his hands on his rubber wheels resignedly. "They changed the rules on me, is what . . . Back in the good old days, a fella could make a real fortune—and keep it. But I was just thirteen when they passed the Infernal Revenue, and that ruined that. And then the Prohibition come along, and that was the beginnin' of the end. . . ."

"I thought that's when you bought the Emerald."

McQueeney nodded. "But that's also when bootleggin' got so profitable everybody wanted in—the Italian boys especially. It's them guys who started the system breakin' down."

"You mean like Al Capone?"

McQueeney gave her a sour glance. "There's exactly the kinda guy I'm talkin' about. It's when the Italians started cuttin' in that things got nasty. Once the business wasn't Irish anymore, there was no respect. Soon ya didn't know who to trust anymore."

The old man daubed his lips with his hankie. "I was brought up to figure if ya had to kill a fella, it was like admittin' ya wasn't sharp enough to outfox him. But these gang wars—

cripes!—everyone was droppin' like flappers' undies. No finesse is what I'm gettin' at. No class at all.

"And now, instead of politicians ownin' the gangs, the gangs started ownin' the politicians. No one was carin' for the system, only for themselves. This ruined everything."

Temple studied a blue vein that had started throbbing on the old man's forehead. "How come they got away with it?"

"For my money, it was all because of that Arnold Rothstein. Here was a guy so smart they called him The Brain—but he had no morals at all. Even fixed the World Series for godsake!"

"You mean the Chicago . . . uh . . ."

"Black Sox." McQueeney nodded. "But they never proved a thing against Rothstein."

"This is the one you called the J. P. Morgan of the underworld?"

"That's him. He gambled plenty, especially if the fix was in, but mostly he dealt in money. Money was all he cared for, all he was loyal to. This made him a fella to be reckoned with.

"Now, in Prohibition—with reformers in charge—the Tammany fellas who ran the city found themselves on one side of the street, and the fellas who ran the booze was on the other. Like they was enemies or somethin'. It just wasn't natural. What Rothstein did, he found a way of conductin' business at the corners—but he still looked straight."

"And he wasn't?"

McQueeney chuckled. "Kid, this is the fella who put the 'organized' into organized crime. He was the first guy to make it run like a business. When Rothstein died, a lot of powerful fellas got very nervous—especially since he did not exactly die a natural death. Which is how the Coughlin family comes to run that Saloon next door."

Temple blinked. "The . . . what? Wait . . . When was this?"

"Hmm, 1928, I think. But I'm borin' ya with ancient history. I wonder when Dora—"

"No, no, no. Tell me what happened!"

McQueeney grinned. "Nobody knows for sure . . . One night Rothstein went to a poker game and came out with a hole in his gut. He died without spillin' who nailed him. When the coppers searched the place, they found the usual whiskey bottles, dirty glasses, butts in the ashtray—some with lipstick on 'em—and a coat in the closet embroidered with a fella's name in the linin'."

McQueeney rolled closer and tapped her on the knee. "The name was George McManus."

"Your boss? The one who stole the Saloon?"

Uncle Mickey nodded. "A maid even eyeballed him. And the coppers found a motive: Rothstein wouldn't pay off his gambling losses because his money was all tied up in heroin."

"I didn't know they had heroin back then."

"It was the comin' thing—and Rothstein was bringin' it. No morals, see? The fella deserved to die."

Temple nodded. "So they sent McManus off to jail? And the Coughlins bought the Saloon?"

McQueeney's old eyes twinkled. "That's the way it goes in the fairy-tales. But you're dead wrong both times. McManus was never convicted, ya see. Somethin' about evidence and witnesses disappearin'. Fact is, that case is *still* unsolved legal-wise. Marked 'open' in police files. You ever want to tease the cops, you call 'em and ask 'em about the Arnold Rothstein case—and watch 'em go mum."

The old man snickered, beaming with the pleasure of inside knowledge. "'Course, right away I knew the fix was in. But this was Tammany's last big cover-up." McQueeney laid a thin white finger on the tip of his nose. "One thing that never fails me is my sniffer here. When there's trouble, it itches—and back then I was scratchin' it all the time."

"How come?"

"Ya see, Arnold Rothstein was the pin that held the seesaw between the gangs and the pols in balance. When he died, all hell was bound to break loose. Right away, reformers like Dewey and La Guardia started makin' headlines pickin' over the bones of Tammany."

McQueeney made a sour face. "I kinda like what Mayor Jimmy Walker said: 'Reformers are people who ride through sewers in glass-bottom boats.' What these characters didn't understand was, once ya crippled Tammany, who was gonna control the gangs? Bein' an Irish Robin Hood was one thing, but these young kids comin' up was just plain hoods. They didn't have no style, or no good examples to live up to. Ya know, the Westies in Hell's Kitchen today are just animals.

"My Emerald City was dyin' all around me, and thanks to my sniffer, I smelt it before I ended up with lead poisonin' myself. The old country was suddenly lookin' very safe in 1928. New York was just lookin' like a good place to die."

The old man's voice had sunk into a tired whisper. "So I went to Ireland."

Temple smiled impatiently. "You didn't tell me how the Coughlins got the Saloon."

"Well, it ain't so very hard to puzzle out if ya use your noodle. McManus got off because the coppers botched the evidence. Now, who do ya think the inspector in charge of Manhattan detectives was in 1928?... One guess."

Uncle Mickey watched her with amusement as the Coughlin family skeleton rattled out of the shadows.

"... Not Frank's grandfather?"

"It's right there in the record books, plain as day." McQueeney chuckled quietly. "Looks kind of funny, though, when you put it next to the fact he took over McManus's Saloon in 1928."

"Wait a minute." Temple shook her head. "McManus sold his bar to the cop who investigated him?"

"Well, I didn't say he sold it. I figure it was more like a thank-you present to the cop who *didn't* investigate him." Uncle Mickey grinned. "Now do ya get it?"

Temple muttered, "I'd rather not."

"Inspector John made some pretty big pals that year. They let him resign from the force real quiet-like, because he knew every hushed-up scandal in town—havin' done most of the hushin' himself." McQueeney smirked. "Some people thought he should have got a medal."

The whole room dimmed gloomily as a thick gray cloud blanketed the winter sun. Finally, Temple asked, "Does Frank know about all this?"

"He does now. But he didn't till yesterday. He was up to see me for a little advice, ya see."

"Did Casey know?"

"I never told nobody till yesterday afternoon."

"Why?"

McQueeney shrugged. "No one asked me. And I ain't one to force a man to know more'n he needs to."

"But you decided Frank needs to know now. What about Mr. Timm?"

"Francis was meetin' him this mornin'. But it wouldn't surprise me if he bent a couple of details. That story hangs over the Coughlins like a curse, ya see? He'll go a long way, that Francis—if the curse don't pull him down too."

"What do you mean 'pull him down'?"

"He's playin' a dangerous game, Temple. He's not only riskin' his neck for that pile of rocks, he's buckin' his bosses. And there's no future in that. If he ain't a team player . . . he's gone."

"What if he got the public on his side?"

"The public be damned. It's got nothin' to do with 'em. This fella's an appointed judge—he ain't runnin' for election. All the bosses gotta do is mutter to the newspapers how it's no good a judge rubs shoulders with certain unions a barkeeper has to. Especially a judge with a crooked family history. When they dismiss him, they look like reformers, see?"

"God, is that cynical!"

"It's the rules, Temple, and Francis knows 'em as well as I do. Confidentially, I ain't so sure myself which way the boy will go when the chips are down. He might have to go with the sell-out after all."

"I don't think so. Not after the way Casey died."

The old man shrugged. "It ain't that I don't trust the boy—it's just logical. If I was in his spot, I might not be tellin' ya all my plans. Ya might not end up on the side ya think you're on."

The old man scratched his nose lightly. "There's somethin' I didn't tell ya about my nose for trouble: Lately I'm scratchin' it all the time. When I say Francis ought to let me handle this, it's the same hunch workin' that sent me back to Ireland in the old days. I think the fix is in."

Temple smiled weakly. "At least we don't have to worry about gangsters anymore."

"Oh, no?" McQueeney met her eyes slyly. "What do you think big business is? They're a few steps away from where they was in the old days—but use your noodle, kid. What do ya think this Cornerstone is?"

There was a loud bump at the front of the apartment.

Slowly the apartment door creaked open.

Dora pushed into the room, awkwardly juggling three bags of groceries. A can of peas fell and rolled across the floor.

McQueeney grinned. "Hiya, sweets."

"And what are ye doin' up when ye should be nappin', Michael McQueeney? Get yerself off to bed and stop botherin' the child."

He winked at Temple from his wheelchair. "This dame is always tryin' to get me into the sack."

"Ah, don't be wicked, now. You know what the doc said about gettin' yer rest."

"Nappin' in the daytime is against my religion," he grumbled.

"Just get in there and put yer head down, old man. You'll sleep." Dora nodded to Temple. "He's like a baby that way. Tell him to sleep and he sleeps." She wheeled him away through another door.

After a moment, Temple called, "I'll be running along now."

"I'll have a word with ye first," the old woman answered as she returned.

"This is quite a layout you've got here."

"Ah, ye should have seen it in the old days. We entertained here, between shows, and had our suppers sent up from the speak next door." She nodded at an abandoned dumbwaiter on the wall connecting to Coughlin's Saloon. "And then, when the men were havin' their cigars, we'd all go down to the basement where Michael had his shootin' range. Some o'them guns in the cases there have the most awful histories."

"He was showing me. Did he ever use the, uh, machine gun?"

"Oh, Lordy no!" Dora began chuckling. "Has he been boastin' about the bad old days? Don't believe all ye hear, bunny. Those big guns were just comin' into style when Michael got out o'the rackets. Though I'll wager he didn't say that."

"Not really."

"There's an old Irish sayin', Temple: 'A wise man knows enough to quit when he's ahead.' The closest my Michael got to Prohibition was exportin' whiskey from Ireland—after it was legal again."

"But he made it sound like—"

"Ah, ye've heard him talkin' his gangster talk and nobody's had sense enough to set ye straight. Michael likes pretendin' he's a real bad one—but ye don't get respect like he has by killin' and maimin'. Come Monday night, he'll be shakin' hands with half the city council. Did he talk a'tall about Francis?"

"He was just telling stories."

"That's an Irishman for ye—never gettin' around to what he thinks the trouble is. Not enough blessed sense to talk to a woman about her man." The old girl picked up her sewing basket and started rocking. "I was wonderin' if yer Francis is likely to be as smart as my Michael was—quittin' while he's ahead, I mean. Or is he goin' to mess with Cornerstone?"

"I don't know. Sounds to me as if he's in a squeeze between the good guys and the bad guys—and he loses either way. Unless he gets some answers."

Dora nodded without looking up from her sewing. "Are ye doin' anythin' to help him?"

"I tried the other night and, uh, got trapped on your roof."

The old woman looked up quickly. "I heard about that."

"Frank called you, but nobody answered. I nearly froze to death." Temple felt like an idiot. "He had to get a fire engine to help me down."

"Oh, bunny, what a shame! It's the sleepin' pills, ye see, to keep us from wakin' up in the middle o'the night. It's been years since we was gettin' calls at that hour."

Temple watched her begin mending one of Michael Mc-Queeney's shirts. "Maybe I should just help Mr. Timm dig up history."

"I don't know. If Francis isn't wantin' yer help, could be he has his reasons. Ye know, there's more important things ye could be doin' for him."

"Like what?"

"Ye said yerself the man's in a squeeze. That Saloon's becomin' an albatross around his neck. Instead of helpin' him get that handsome neck broke, a woman who loved him would pull him out of this mess altogether."

"What do you mean?"

"Prepare his heart to let it go. The lad's got a career with a shinin' bright future, and he's riskin' it all to cling to the past. That's a bad bargain, Temple, and ye know it."

"I don't see what's wrong with wanting to keep the bar in the family."

"Why nothin', dearie . . . unless it kills him. Michael is family, too, ye know. He could save it for the boy without it costin' anyone his career. Francis can't. It's the only solution, girl. Or do ye want him left with nothin' to get him through old age but that losin' proposition next door?"

"Well . . . Why does Uncle Mickey want a loser, then?"

"Partly it prides him to know he can get his own godson out of a jam. But confidentially, I've a feelin' he wouldn't mind thumbin' his nose at the politicians one last time neither. He needs the challenge or there's nothin' for him but dyin'."

Temple chewed on her lower lip. "I just can't see Frank letting me sway him."

The old woman's hand fell on Temple's shoulder. "Any silly girl knows how to catch a man—but takin' care o'his best interests when he don't know what they are himself, *that's* the sign of a woman." Dora cocked an eye. "Unless ye don't really care enough to make the effort."

"I care . . . What effort?"

"This is where the road gets hard, girl. If yer only along for the fun, it's time ye got off. But if ye are a real woman . . . then this is where ye prove it. You show Francis the way, and he'll follow. But if ye don't move him quick, he'll sit on a barstool the rest of his days, wonderin' where it all went wrong . . ."

Dora put down the mended shirt, raised the needle and thread to her mouth, and snapped it off with her teeth.

Twenty-two

Temple bounded down the marble steps of the Emerald Theater, straight into the path of Frank Coughlin.

"Oh . . . It's you."

He arched his white-slit eyebrows. "Someone else you'd prefer?"

Temple shrugged and avoided his eyes.

He looked puzzled. "Late meeting?"

"Mm. We were figuring out whether to panic or not."

"That's what Tina Molineux told me. When she left two hours ago."

"Your uncle likes to talk."

"Uh-huh. What was he rambling on about this time?"

"Well . . . Your grandfather mostly. Did you know he covered up the biggest murder in city history?"

"Mickey told you that? Well, that's how he likes his listeners—impressionable."

"Face it, Frank: Inspector John was playing with a marked deck."

"You can't believe everything you hear, Temple."

"You mean a saint would lie?"

"Saints can have selective memories. Uncle Mickey had plenty of reasons for hating Gramps—including some my dad wouldn't even tell me. I don't know particularly whose word to trust."

"I'll tell you who *not* to trust . . ."

Just then, O. M. Timm pushed out the door of Coughlin's Saloon and strolled over to them.

"You're lucky I'm not with the health department," he sighed, cleaning his hands with a white linen hankie.

"Mr. Timm and I have been on a treasure hunt. Tapping on walls. Looking for loose boards." Coughlin smirked at the round man. "Give up?"

"Well, that oaf who works for you refused to let me look behind the bar."

"That's okay. I've got a structural engineer coming in Saturday to check the place over for repairs. We'll go over it with a fine-tooth comb—okay?"

"Mmm, I suppose. Well, young lady, are you looking forward to the ballet tonight?"

"Oh, Frankie! May I have a word with you please?" It was Father Dolan marching toward them, waving a piece of paper.

Frank nodded curtly, glanced at Timm, and then back at the priest. "Have you two, uh . . ."

"We've met," Father Dolan snapped. "Unfortunately."

O. M. Timm leaned on his walking stick, eyeing the legal sheet in the holy man's hand. "Well, sir, you're looking particularly . . . secular today."

The adversaries frosted each other while Frank glanced at them both.

Temple tapped her foot impatiently.

"Listen," Father Dolan blurted at last. "Cornerstone is raising its offer to you. They'll pay a million for the house—cash. The cashier's check is as good as signed."

"Thirty pieces of silver," Timm muttered.

Frank shook his head. "Uh, Father, this isn't the best time . . ."

"It's the only time, I'm afraid. Have you been around the corner to the Minnesota Strip lately? Do you realize how many teenagers are ruining their lives out there every day? Cornerstone is going to donate the money and space to build a new runaway center. But they won't do a thing until we all hop aboard."

"Why do they need *my* place?"

Dolan shrugged. "It's the plan. Frankie, the fate of those children is in your hands. If you don't help them now, they'll be dying on your doorstep soon..."

"Oh, please." O. M. Timm chuckled and began applauding. "Such feeble dramatics."

"Or soliciting your customers!" the priest insisted. "If your family had helped this parish before things reached this state, we might not be having this kind of trouble. But no, you support a convent way upstate while we're starving just down the block!"

O. M. Timm touched Frank's arm lightly. "You gave money to a convent?"

"None of your business."

Father Dolan sniffed. "Fifty years of devoted service to the Sisters of St. Joseph."

"...St. Joseph?" O. M. Timm was staring at the priest, a little smile flickering over his lips.

"A teaching order. They're well enough off already."

"Quite. Er, Judge, have you any thoughts on why your family's charity is sown so far from home?"

"No idea."

"Frankie! If you'll just examine this offer—"

"Praise the Lord, and examine this *divine* offer..." O. M. Timm drew himself up haughtily. "Really, sir, if you're going to entertain such nonsense, I'll be on my way!"

"What?" Frank watched, astonished, as the rotund little man stalked off in a huff. "What's his problem?"

"Never mind him. If the lady will excuse us, this offer has—"

"I'm sorry, Father. I'll only deal with the principals."

"Oh." The priest bit his lip. "Afraid I can't help you there. They contact me by mail."

"Really? Tell me how that works...." Frank looped one arm around the priest's shoulders and walked him away.

Temple watched the two men shuffle off.

"Frank?"

He ignored her. Possibly they were already out of earshot. *"Frank!"*

Passing by on the sidewalk, a mime from *The Mime Show* mimicked her disappointed face. Turning her back on him irritably, Temple's gaze swung up and down the street until she spotted O. M. Timm's black fur fedora bustling through the crowds on Broadway.

She glanced over her shoulder one last time, and then hurried after him.

Twenty-three

Timm was an accomplished pedestrian. He led her east through midtown, turned south on Vanderbilt Avenue past the Yale Club, and in through the exposed iron arches of Grand Central Station.

Temple lurked at the top of the stairs, pressing her back against marble walls until the corpulent man descended to the awesome concourse. As he lined up to buy a ticket, she watched from a bakery doorway. Timm scanned the giant information board in the dusty light floating through clerestory windows near the roofline. Then he hurriedly crossed the cavernous room, disappearing into another vaulted passage.

Temple scampered after him, turning down a ramp filled with cigar smoke just in time to see Timm pass jauntily into a train gate. A red and gold sign read:

Amtrak's TICONDEROGA

4:30 PM
Newburgh
Poughkeepsie

Kingston
Albany
Saratoga
Plattsburgh
Montreal

She was scooting across the waiting room toward a bank of pay phones when a garbled tenor cut through the early commuter din:

"Last call for the Ti-con-de-roh!-ga . . . Boooo-ard!"

Temple glanced hesitantly at the blue phone box. Then she joined the late passengers racing for the long silver train.

There was no sign of Timm on the murky platform. She boarded the last car of the train and cautiously picked her way through the smoke-filled cafe car, on the alert for a telltale slouch hat or ring of salt-and-pepper hair.

She'd just reached the front of the car when it lurched into motion. Temple weaved through the next coach, where, again, there was no sign of Timm.

Peering through the door to the third car, though, Temple spied a silver-tipped cane protruding into the aisle. She retreated to the previous coach and took a seat.

"Tickets! All tickets!"

Temple glanced up casually at the man in the dark blue polyester uniform and squared-off blue cap.

"Take your feet down, please . . . Ticket?"

"Uh . . . how much to the end of the line?"

"Fifty-nine dollars to Montreal."

Temple made a face as she turned over her American Express card. Transaction completed, she fished a rumpled *Washington Post* from the seat-pocket before her and settled in for the ride.

Outside Newburgh, Temple crept cautiously between the cars to see if Timm was detraining. Her eyes widened as the balding man came weaving down the aisle, flicking his silver-tipped cane before him. Of course—she was between him and the cafe car. Quickly, Temple yanked at the door of the lavatory and pushed into the tiny room.

"Occupied," came a startled voice inside. A tall man with his back to her craned his head, regarding Temple with embarrassment as she squeezed in next to him.

"Oh, uh . . . don't mind me." Temple smiled weakly, a blush rising in her cheeks. When the door outside slammed, she peeked to watch Timm's back lurching away through her car.

The man inside finished his business, turned, and straightened his handsome tweed suit. He was a fox. "I feel like I'm lost inside a dirty joke."

Temple couldn't smother her abashed grin. "Do you know the punch line?"

"No . . . but my wife might. She's in the first seat out the door."

"I'm really sorry."

"Quite all right. It keeps her attentive." As he squeezed out around her, Temple peeked down the aisle again. Timm was already heading back in her direction, juggling a microwaved sandwich, plastic cup, and a miniature bottle of Chablis. She closed herself in, listened for the crash of two sliding doors, and waited for a sixty count before heading toward her seat.

The tweedy fellow's wife gave her a hard stare, putting her hand on her husband's knee.

Timm stayed glued to his seat through Poughkeepsie, Kingston, and Albany. But when the conductor called, *"Station stop— Sa-ra-tohhh!-gaaa,"* he roused himself.

Temple trailed him off the train to a taxi stand. As his cab pulled away, she hopped into the next one in line.

"Where to lady?"

"See that taxi in front of us? It's my husband, going to meet another woman. Can you follow him without getting spotted?"

The driver spun his head around and checked her out from top to bottom. "That nerd is your husband?"

He faced forward again, shaking his head. "I'll never understand women if I live to be a hundred . . ."

Twenty-four

Temple was leaning on the counter of the Grand Union Motel office, idly scanning a brochure.

"Yeah?" A pasty-faced clerk materialized behind the desk.

"Room for one, please."

"Cash or charge?"

When she flipped her gold AmEx card at him, he twirled

the register around, handing her a pen from his clear plastic pocket protector.

Temple kept the felt-tip and pretended to write a note on motel paper. Then she handed the folded message to the night clerk. "Could you see that O. M. Timm gets this? He checked in earlier." As the blank paper slid into Timm's box, she noted the room number: 108.

Temple's room was across the motor court and around a corner. To keep an eye on Timm's lighted curtains, she had to wait in the concessions room with the laundry and soda machines. She dropped a dime in the pay phone there, charged the call to Paradise, and listened to it ring at Coughlin's apartment in the city. There was no answer.

Stuck without a book, she read the motel's brochure until she had it practically memorized. It pictured the original Civil War era Grand Union Motel, with an ornate, quarter-mile-long front porch and acres of marble and mahogany fittings. Temple wondered if O. M. Timm thought he'd be checking into the once proud resort, instead of the disappointing motel that had taken its place.

The leaflet went on to boast of Saratoga's famous racecourse, the local mineral water, and the legendary Casino, once a gambling establishment more notorious than Lucky Luciano's Chicago Club or even Arnold Rothstein's place, Brook.

When the landmarks expert finally switched off his light more than two hours later, Temple sighed and headed around the corner to her own room.

Leaving a wakeup call for 5:30 A.M., she undressed, washed in moments, slid into the big, cold bed, and snapped off the light.

Dialing in the dark, she tried Coughlin again—and again there was no answer. She slammed the phone down irritably and rolled over into her pillows.

Traffic headlights cast moving shadows across walls hung with cheap prints of Saratoga in its heyday.

Questions raced through Temple's mind like thoroughbreds circling the gingerbread flat track.

Like—What was Timm doing in Saratoga on the very night he'd bullied her into joining him at the ballet?

And what was she doing—or undoing—by following him? Did new surprises lurk at the Casino?

Would the ghost of Inspector John haunt Frank forever?

And where was Frank in the dead of night?

Unable to sleep, Temple sat up in bed and clicked on the light. She rummaged in the bedside table for something to read, but found only a local phone book and a Gideons' Bible. The original best-seller.

Flipping open the front cover, her fingers froze before turning the pages. This Bible hadn't been left by the Gideons after all. Stamped on the flyleaf were the words:

Sisters of St. Joseph
Saratoga, New York

THURSDAY

Twenty-five

Temple's rented black Lynx purred quietly in neutral. She waited behind its fogged-up windows, chewing a stale danish and sipping machine coffee from a pointed plastic cup.

O. M. Timm finally emerged at 10:10, taxiing out of town on Union Avenue. Cruising past the antique, spire-topped racecourse, they were soon deep in the country, where dense woods alternated with the lawns of great estates.

Finally, Timm's taxi turned into a gravel drive. He hopped out lightly, rang the bell of the stately Victorian mansion, and was admitted by an elderly nun in a black and white habit. Temple pulled into the drive and parked in the small lot beside the portico.

In the broad yard between the residence and the school next door, a dozen girls were playing in the snow under the watchful eyes of two nuns.

When Temple reached the heavy oak door, she tested the large brass latch. It was unlocked. She opened the door just enough to peek into the reception hall. There was no one in sight. The mansion's interior was austerely quiet as only an imposed silence can be. Polished hardwood floors and maple bannisters and mouldings gleamed with no-nonsense propriety.

Quickly, she slipped inside, listening a moment for the familiar reedy voice. There was a faint murmur behind the parlor door to her right.

A few steps down the hall was another parlor, separated from the first by sliding maple doors.

"May I help you?"

Temple spun around, startled by the nearness of the old nun's voice.

"Oh, excuse me," she whispered bashfully. "Er, the gentleman who just came in is—is he ahead of me?"

"Ahead of you?"

115

"Yes, for—oh, I'm sorry. Whom did he come to see?"

"Why, Mother Superior. And you were looking for . . . ?"

"Yes, yes . . . Well. May I wait in here?" Temple nodded her way into the parlor next to Timm's.

"Ahh . . . certainly." The old nun looked puzzled. "I only heard one bell. Are you expected?"

"No, no. I'll wait. It's, er, personal."

The other woman smiled tentatively and padded off as quietly as she'd come.

Temple wandered casually across the room until she was sure she was alone, then knelt by the keyhole of the connecting doors. The voice in the other parlor was unmistakable.

" . . . for seeing me on such short notice."

"Not at all, Mr. Halpern. You've come a long way. Can I offer you a glass of water?"

"Have you any tea?"

"I'm sorry. We don't take stimulants here."

"Oh, er . . . forgive me. Water would be lovely."

Temple peered through the hole as the stern, bespectacled Mother Superior poured him his water. "Now, how can I help the landmarks commission?"

"The truth is, Mother Superior, I've come on a mission of mercy. It concerns New York's cultural heritage, but also the salvation of a good man's soul."

The old woman nodded. "Pray continue."

"It all began some months ago, when a saloon owner asked me to look into the provenance of his building with regard to possible landmark designation. I realize my friend was in an ungodly business, but I'm persuaded he was a decent man, and the architecture, well . . ."

The nun touched her fingers together into a steeple. "It's not our duty here to pass judgment on the lives of others."

"Just so. Well, it's a magnificent edifice, and I'd barely persuaded him to file with the commission when he, er . . . died suddenly. I'm afraid his younger brother isn't made of the same moral fiber. He's discovered some discouraging financial shortages at the saloon; he's being offered a sinful amount of money by developers who would raze the structure; and he's being beguiled by temptations of the flesh as well."

"How do you mean?"

Timm sighed. "It seems he's involved with a most unsavory

sort of woman. Shallow, greedy, sneaky, and . . . well, frankly, she's a fashion model."

The senior nun pursed her lips. "We had one of those here a few years ago. She didn't work out."

"Ah. Then you know the sort of woman I mean. She wants him to grab the money and run from his responsibilities. He's a good fellow, they tell me, but I'm afraid he is quite consumed by lust. Unfortunately, I'm in no position to compete with this lascivious woman for his . . . favor. You understand."

"I certainly do. But I don't see how I can help you."

"Well, there's been a rather interesting development. In reviewing his books, the younger man discovered his late brother was donating fairly substantial sums to the Church. Er, to this very convent, in fact. It puzzles him that his brother should bankrupt himself by sending you contributions he could ill afford. Naturally, I'm most anxious to trace the source of these monies because they would allow us to maintain the building as a landmark rather than sell it. And, er, he'd be able to continue his brother's contributions to you, of course."

"How intriguing. Well, I'd be happy to check our records and call him about it. What did you say the name was?"

"Umm . . . frankly, Mother Superior, I think that would be a mistake just now. Unhappily, my friend died a rather violent death, and it's left his brother terribly . . . distraught. The deceased was seen to engage in some fisticuffs with the parish priest recently, and that, combined with the inexplicable donations to you, well—I know it sounds senseless—but I'm afraid the surviving brother suspects the Church of some form of extortion."

"Really!" The righteous woman frowned.

"I know, I know." Timm shook his head. "Still, I'm afraid he has no faith at all in his Church these days. And this comes at a time when he's struggling with such terrible temptation, this beguiling creature who whispers into his ear every night as they lie naked in the dark, entwined in their—"

"*Please*, sir," Mother Superior interrupted. "A terrible moral crisis, I quite agree. And you're sure the poor soul won't listen to the voice of God's messenger on Earth?"

Timm shook his head. "I'm afraid this situation calls for a secular solution, Mother Superior. I'm convinced that if I can find some reasonable explanation for those donations, clearly absolving the Church—and locate the source of my deceased friend's funds quickly—we can restore the brother to the path of righteousness. The landmark will be saved, the hussy will be denied—and, er . . . there will be no need for the donations to your worthy order to cease. I confess, we need a miracle. I'm hoping to find one here. If you—"

Suddenly the door behind Temple creaked open. The elderly nun in the hallway was peering at her on her knees by the door.

"Are you all right?"

"Oh . . . I think so," Temple mumbled, lowering her eyes to the floor. "I've just lost a contact lens and I'm having trouble . . . oh, here it is." She pretended to cradle the invisible object in her hand.

The nun nodded tentatively. "I'll be down the hall if you need anything." She shut the door behind her.

". . . can I help?" Mother Superior was saying.

"Tell me, ma'am, is the name Helen Josie Mansfield Reade familiar to you?"

"No . . . I don't think so. Is she this fellow's . . . model?"

Timm chuckled. "No, no, she's an adventuress from a distant era—a woman of pleasure for whom a wealthy man built the mansion in question back in the nineteenth century. When the man died, she sailed to Paris and married a lawyer named Reade. They returned to New York, but were divorced five years later, and Mrs. Reade dropped from sight.

"In 1899, she suffered a paralytic stroke, lost the power of speech, and moved to North Dakota, where she recovered slowly. She was discovered there in 1909 by a salesman who recognized what remained of her legendary beauty. Dreading the limelight, she told the papers she would 'seek shelter behind the walls of a convent.'"

There was a long pause before Timm resumed his recitation. "She was neither seen nor heard from again for two decades— until she returned to Paris, where she died two years later. Two maids and an acquaintance were her only mourners."

"How very interesting, Mr. Halpern," the Mother Superior murmured. "But why bring this cautionary tale to me?"

O. M. Timm smiled. "I have reason to believe, Mother Superior, that Josie Mansfield Reade spent her missing years— from 1909 to 1929—within these very walls."

"My goodness!"

"You see the coincidence, of course. The elderly mistress of a notorious robber baron is booted out of her mansion a century ago, and spends twenty years a recluse in a remote convent. And now we discover an unrelated family, which has owned her mansion since the time of her death, has been sending regular donations to the very same convent. This simply can't be chance."

"Well . . . I suppose not. But I'm not sure I understand."

Timm shook his head. "Neither do I—so far—but there has to be some connection. And if there is, it may benefit all of us. Did you say there might be, er . . . records? The name was Helen Josephine Mansfield Reade."

The Mother Superior went out the door to the parlor.

Temple stood to get her circulation flowing again, leaning unsteadily on a wooden chair until she heard the senior nun return. She bent back to the keyhole.

". . . seems as though you were thinking in the right direction. Take a look at these."

"Hmmm." Timm skimmed through two yellowing sheets of paper. "Yes . . . yes, these may do the trick. Too soon to know, of course. Er, do you mind if I take these documents back to the city to see where they lead?"

"Not at all. Sister Rose will call you a taxi if you like."

They rose and walked to the door. Too late for Temple to escape.

"Please let me know how everything turns out, Mr. Halpern."

"Of course," said O. M. Timm.

Twenty-six

Temple straightened up and smoothed yesterday's plaid skirt. After a moment, the double doors swung open, and Mother Superior was smiling at her vaguely.

"Good afternoon. Sister Rose says you wanted to see me?"

Around the corner, the hall floor creaked as O. M. Timm paced, impatiently waiting for his cab.

Temple mumbled something inaudible.

"Speak up, young lady. You're not in church."

"It's very personal," Temple whispered, glancing at the hall uncomfortably.

"So many secrets this afternoon." The other woman eyed her speculatively, then shut the double doors. "Is that better?"

Temple nodded and smiled.

Mother Superior waited. She raised an eyebrow.

"It's . . . it's about my daughter," Temple began. If Timm's taxi had to come all the way out from town . . .

"Yes?"

"Well . . . We've just moved into this area, my husband and I, and I'm concerned about getting her into the right school. This is a teaching order, isn't it? She's about to turn four . . . I'd like to have your advice."

"I see. That's a bit young for kindergarten, but our preschool program might suit her until fall. She's well behaved?"

"Oh, yes—she's an angel."

"A most unusual child, then."

"Oh, well." Temple smiled. "Just the usual girlish problems."

Mother Superior frowned. "Such as?"

"Oh . . . you know. She doesn't understand why she can't have hamburgers on Fridays." Temple chuckled uncomfortably.

"And why can't she?"

"Well . . . It's Friday . . . fish day."

A horn in the driveway at last. Footsteps in the hall, and then the slam of the heavy oaken door behind O. M. Timm.

"Miss?"

". . . Yes?" Temple glanced up to find Mother Superior examining her critically.

"It is miss, then, isn't it? I see you're not wearing a wedding band."

Temple glanced at the birthstone on her left hand, then smiled weakly. "I'm afraid I lost it. Down the disposal."

The holy woman leaned over. "I don't think so. You aren't even Catholic. Didn't you know eating meat on Fridays hasn't been a mortal sin for years?"

"Oh . . ."

"I think I know who you are, young woman. Perhaps you'd better leave before this becomes any more unpleasant."

Temple felt herself beginning to flush. "You don't understand, Mother Superior. That man told you some awful things that just aren't true."

"He told me you were a sneak. Obviously, he was right."

"But even the name he gave you was a phony."

"You will leave these premises this instant, or I shall be forced to call the police."

Crossing the driveway, Temple flinched as the heavy oak door thudded shut behind her.

"Forgive me, Father, for I have sinned . . ." Temple stomped a chunk of ice with relish. ". . . but all in a good cause."

Twenty-seven

Tack-tack-tack-tack . . .

Temple peered into the gloomy lobby of the former Standard Oil Building at the bottom of Manhattan. Hawklike winds swirling off the harbor froze her wet fingers with spray and drizzle.

She tapped her keys against the glass door again.

Tack-tack-tack . . .

Temple was as cold as she was tired—and twice as dirty. She had come straight from Grand Central Station, and the amenities of the ladies' room there left much to be desired.

Tack-tack-tack-tack . . .

Yawning deeply, Temple considered giving up. Going home and making a hot chocolate. Sinking back into bed.

A wash of reflected light illuminated the vaulted lobby. She heard footsteps.

Turning the corner from the elevators, a security guard squinted at her through two sets of glass doors. Grudgingly, he entered the vestibule and challenged her in a muffled voice: "Yeah?"

"Is Mr. Stoessel here yet?" Temple simpered. "I'm supposed to meet him tonight."

The night watchman's face split into a knowing grin. He

let her in with a flourish. "Not yet, missy. But if he's expectin' you, he won't be long." The man winked. "Mrs. Stoessel came by a coupla hours ago lookin' for him. I told her he signed out for the night."

"Oh . . . good work."

"You go right on up. I'll watch out for him." He winked again. "He's a generous man, Mr. Stoessel—right?"

Temple studied the watchman's eager face. Then she rolled her bookbag off her shoulder and reached in.

"No, no, no, missy," the guard said in a rush. "No need for you to bother with that. Mr. Stoessel takes care of me just fine . . . just *fine*. You take the elevator over there. He gave you the key, did he?"

Temple feigned a brief search of her bag, then dangled her own keys in front of him. "Got it right here."

Returning the man's wink, she stepped quickly into the elevator, and rode up to O. M. Timm's floor. In the maze of dim corridors, she walked herself around in circles twice before finally locating the familiar cul-de-sac.

Picking her way down the dark hall, she collided with a janitor's abandoned mop bucket near the door of STOESSEL & CO., IMPORTERS. The clattering pail spilled a foul-smelling puddle across the dull linoleum.

Temple backed against the wall, and listened for a moment. Not a sound

Cautiously, she crept to the next green glass door. The office inside was pitch dark. Slipping the gold American Express card from her wallet, she jiggled it in the doorjamb until the lock sprung with a clean little *pop*.

Inside, she waited for her eyes to adjust to the darkness, then scanned Timm's shabby, claustrophobic room. She crossed to the desk, draped her scarf over the lamp there, and snapped it on. The shaded light gave off a muted yellow glow.

Timm's desk was stacked with files, folders, and old newspapers. First on the pile was a fat folder marked "Preservation Plan," and inside was a yellowing, coffee-ringed letter topped by the seal of the City of New York.

Dear Ogden,

I'm taking time out to drop you this personal note regarding your recent proposal to the Mayor. Though he appreciates the good intentions of your offer to assume management of the city's architectural resources, such a plan, no matter how justified and well conceived, would be inappropriate given the city's current fiscal condition.

Personally, I'd like to say I find your idea intriguing. I, too, am a lover of old buildings and old things. And I am equally concerned that private owners do not share that love. But the city cannot put itself in the position of condemning structures without free-market compensation, merely to pass them into the hands of private groups such as yours.

However, if you are able to attract sufficient capital investment to acquire structures independently, the city will of course do all it can to aid your efforts at preservation.

Hope to see you at our next reunion.

> *Paul Congreve*
> *Office of the Mayor*

Temple rummaged through the rest of the file. Each page described a Manhattan property of some architectural distinction. Beneath each physical description were the name and address of the current owner, along with pencil notes detailing possible purchase prices, code violations, the owner's financial situation, and, in several cases, some rather intimate personal foibles.

Closing the folder, Temple dug deeper into the stack of papers on the desk top. Most were newspaper clippings on the Times Square area. Underneath them, though, she found a brown stenographer's notebook filled with O. M. Timm's meticulous scrawl.

Quickly, she flipped through the spiral bound book. The first page read:

> *TRIQUARTERLY STORY———*
>   *(Cover?)*
> *Deadline: Wednesday*
>
> *Length: 2,000 wds + Lopez sidebar*

The next several pages were covered with notes from interviews with the mayor, the head of the Urban Development Corporation and the lawyer for the landmarks commission.

Then came notes on Timm's chat with Temple and Frank. A page headed "*Cornerstone*" was blank.

The last scribbled page was titled:

QUESTIONS

—*How much does Coughlin really know?*
—*What could he possibly not know?*
—*Rumor of Grant's gold true or false?*
—*If gold is in building, where?*
—*In what form—bricks? jewels? coins?*
—*If gold there, how obtain?*
—*Figure motives for everyone!*

Temple replaced the notebook and checked that she'd examined everything on the desk. Then she swiveled the chair around to look behind her. There, on top of an old Underwood upright, were several sheets of yellow copy paper. The top page was slugged:

DRAFT/TRIBECA COVER: EMERALD/COUGHLIN'S

Temple skimmed through the raggedly typed pages and discovered nothing new—except Timm's editorial slant. He portrayed the block struggle as a sprawling morality play, with McQueeney the redeemed conniver who "shakes his fist from the confines of his wheelchair and says this time he will not play along with the boys in the smoke-filled rooms."

Frank, however, was cast in a different light: "Wavering, the man stands to lose all by seeming to serve no one's interests but his own. If he must be so indecisive—and so selfish— does this opportunist deserve to judge the people of New York?"

Suddenly, Temple was aware of an even-cadenced *tap . . . tap . . . tap . . .* growing louder in the hall. The sound of a man with a walking stick approaching.

She dumped the unfinished article back on the typewriter, clicked off the lamp, and retrieved her scarf. Then she darted to the door of Stoessel's adjoining office and began fumbling at the lock with her credit card. . . . She wasn't getting it in time.

An oath of surprise in the hallway. Frantic splashing, and then a splattering final thud. "Blast!" cried the voice of O. M. Timm.

Temple concentrated harder.

Stoessel's latch clicked obediently. She ducked through the connecting green glass door just as Timm's key was rattling the other one. The last thing she saw as she eased Stoessel's door shut was O. M. Timm backing into his office, wiping his wet behind: ". . . have that peon drawn and quartered," he muttered under his breath. She heard the cane clatter into the umbrella stand.

When Timm snapped on his light, Temple instinctively cowered against the separating wall in the strange, greenish half-light. She ran her finger along her credit card's mangled edge, realizing she'd have to call for a replacement.

Then she heard a series of light clicks, and Timm started speaking. He was making a telephone call. "Good evening, this is O. M. Timm . . .

"Yes, no doubt you're surprised to hear from me. I'm sorry to disturb you at this hour, but I've come across some information that may alter our relationship somewhat . . .

"Let's just say I now understand the special appeal of the Coughlin property—and why you might be prepared to kill to obtain . . ."

Timm paused only a moment.

"Please, please . . . Your methods don't concern me. I simply state that I'm persuaded you're well aware the death of Casey Coughlin was no accident. No doubt, I should share my observations with the surviving Coughlin brother, but I thought we might discuss another arrangement . . .

"That's right. You'll make it worth my while to keep him in the dark, will you not?"

After a moment, Timm chuckled.

"Yes, as good causes go, I am certainly at the top of my list. What time would a meeting be convenient?"

He listened some more.

"I'm afraid I'm tied up with my rehearsals most of the day. Suppose I find you later on? . . . Certainly. Until then."

Timm hung up and clapped his hands together. Then Temple

heard the sound of paper tearing, and something being tossed into the wastebasket.

She bent to check the keyhole—and knocked over an ice bucket next to her in the darkness. The other office was suddenly silent. Soon she heard Timm's quiet tread, and his shadow loomed larger and larger on the frosted glass. The knob on the connecting door turned slowly to the left, then slowly to the right.

Temple let out a long, soft moan. Then she mewed in a little-girl voice: "Ohh, Stessy . . . Ohhhhhh, *Stessy* . . ."

After a moment's hesitation, Timm's bulky shadow retreated from the door. Temple took a deep breath and sighed audibly.

A series of light *clicks* and Timm was on the phone again:
"And how is my merry widow this evening? . . .

"Splendid. You might even break out that special sherry of your husband's, hmm? I'm in a mood to celebrate . . ."

He chuckled uncomfortably.

"Of course, I'm in the mood for that too . . .

"Please, Millicent, not over the phone . . . Er, you'll have that contribution for the landmarks fund? . . .

"Excellent. I'll be along shortly . . . dear."

He cradled the phone and began moving around the office. A file drawer slid open through the wall by Temple's shoulder and then slammed shut. As he moved toward the hall door, she heard the heavy cloak swirl around his sloping shoulders. Then a moment of silence.

Temple filled it with a long, ecstatic sigh that looped through the air like a roller coaster.

Timm grunted and clicked off his light. Locking his door, he strolled past his neighbor's office muttering, "Animals."

His walking stick tapped away down the hall, paused while he skirted the puddle, and tapped onward.

Temple remained motionless until the corridor was silent again. Then she let herself back into Timm's office, shaded the desk lamp before snapping it back on, and headed straight for the wastebasket. Lying on top of the other rubbish were several sheets of yellow copy paper, torn in half. O. M. Timm had thrown away his own precious cover story.

Moving quickly now, she turned to the filing cabinet she'd heard slamming shut. The drawer marked "A-B-C" was just shoulder height. Pulling it open, she flipped backward through the files until she came upon one marked "Coughlin's Saloon."

The top sheet of paper was yellowing with age. Its letterhead read:

Sisters of Saint Joseph, Saratoga, New York
January 9, 1932

Dear Inspector Coughlin,

I contact you reluctantly regarding a sensitive matter.

Twenty years ago, Mrs. Helen Josephine Mansfield Reade came to us seeking the shelter of our Lord. Though her past had been filled with trouble, her desire for sanctuary and repentence was real. Recalling the words of our Lord—"I came for sinners, not for saints"—we took her in. She lived among our order, devoting herself to charity, until 1929. Then, hearing the Lord's call, she traveled to Paris and died there this past October 26.

Mrs. Reade's good works paved the way for her passage into the Kingdom of Heaven. That we may continue bringing light into the lives of those we teach, she willed all her wordly goods to our order.

In her last communication to us, a letter just recently received, she wrote of a considerable quantity of money— in gold—which she asserts was rightfully hers. She claims it was left to her by a Mr. James Fisk, but was denied her by his heirs. It appears that the house he built for her—with the gold inside it—is now in your possession. Her past legal actions have proved useless, but it was Mrs. Reade's last request that we assume responsibility for recovering her legacy and putting it to the Lord's work.

My first thought was to contact my dear friend, the Governor. But before I trouble his valuable time, I am appealing to your good will and sense of Christian duty.

As our Lord tells us—and Mrs. Reade discovered— if a sinner repents, he will be admitted to the Kingdom of Heaven. But if a devout man has sinned at the end of his life, he shall suffer another fate.

I trust I can count on you to do the right thing now,

Inspector Coughlin. We await your thoughts on this matter.

John Coughlin's reply had been mailed without delay:

January 15, 1932

Dear Mother Superior,

Some houses come with ghosts. Mine came with a legend attached to it. But there have been many men, both good and bad, through here in the half century since the days of Josie Mansfield and Jim Fisk. By the time I retired from the force and acquired this property, the only gold mine left in it was the speakeasy which I promptly closed down—being, as you hoped, a man of Christian conscience.

I am sorry, but if Mrs. Reade's gold was ever here, it is not any longer. My lawyer tells me that this was pointed out to her in the aftermath of her unsuccessful lawsuit against Fisk's widow. Gold-diggers never stop digging, I suppose.

However, as a God-fearing man, I have sympathy for your plight. The current depression has left me better off than many of my fellows. After 32 years on the force, I receive a healthy pension, and it is only fitting that my good fortune be shared. Thus I am enclosing a donation to your order in the name of Josie Mansfield Reade. I will arrange a similar tithe annually, and will do my best to see that this commitment is kept by my heirs even after I myself have knocked on the Gates of Heaven.

I hope this arrangement suits your needs—and the Lord's.

Faithfully yours,

Inspector John F. X. Coughlin (ret.)

Apparently, the arrangement was satisfactory, for the correspondence ended there. The rest of the file marked "Coughlin's" was filled with the historical data on Josie, Fisk, and McManus that Timm had revealed two days ago.

Temple replaced the folder, took a deep breath, and moved on to the drawer labeled "D-E-F." The first items in the file marked Emerald were copies of Timm's press releases on the theater and the benefit show. But underneath them was a Xerox of the deed to the theater, dated 1926.

Temple's eyes started running down the page—then flew back up to the top as a familiar name echoed in her mind. The Emerald Theater had been deeded by its builder to a limited partnership composed of Michael McQueeney . . . and Arnold Rothstein.

Rothstein. The J. P. Morgan of the underworld. The man who put the "organized" into organized crime. The man who Uncle Mickey had not wanted to borrow from, who was shot by Mickey's boss, McManus, who himself owned the Saloon before Inspector John, who was Mickey's cousin and who covered up Rothstein's murder and . . .

History was a tight little world—swirling in upon itself.

Temple snatched up the last page in the file. This was another deed, dated 1929, and it named Dora Driscoll as trustee of the Emerald for the sole owner, Michael McQueeney.

Footsteps echoed down the hall again—more than one person, no walking stick—making Temple shut the filing cabinet quickly and snap off the light.

"Whoopsie!" A woman giggled. "Look out for the water."

There was a faint jangle of keys.

A flood of greenish light shot out of Temple's old hiding place.

"Come out, come out, wherever you are." The other woman giggled again. "See? Nobody here. That man downstairs was just kidding us."

Stoessel's door banged shut.

"Let's see those toes now," a man's voice barked. "C'mon, show me your toes!"

Temple began straightening Timm's office quietly as the furtive movement of the pair next door cast giant silhouettes on the green glass door. She messed things up a little more for effect, then stealthily let herself out into the dim hallway.

"Oh, baby . . . That's it, baby!" the floozie called encouragingly.

Temple grinned as she ducked into the elevator. "Attaboy, Stessy."

Twenty-eight

Temple whirled into Coughlin's Saloon and found Frank nursing a drink next to Dora at the bar. She pulled up a stool.

"Boy, have I got news for you!"

He glanced at her noncommittally. "Where have you been?"

"Saratoga." She sneezed.

Coughlin nodded. "Lovely up there this time of year." He looked away.

Temple watched Pat lay an Armagnac down in front of her. "What have you two been feeding this guy—wormwood?"

The bartender shook his head. "Himself has been to see the mayor today."

"And?"

Coughlin chuckled humorlessly. "It was like an audience with the Wizard of Oz. Every time I asked him what the city was planning, he smiled and asked me about *my* intentions. Then he promised to keep an eye on the situation, gave me a few pats on the back—he treated me like . . . like a voter."

He knocked back a hit of scotch. "What's your news?"

"All bad, I'm afraid. Did you know Timm was writing an article about you?"

"Very flattering," he mumbled absently.

"Oh, no, it's not. He's ready to accuse you of being unfit for public office."

"Is he now?"

"He's going to say your uncle did business with Arnold Rothstein."

Dora raised her eyebrows. "He'd have to prove it first."

"I've seen a pretty convincing piece of paper—the partnership deed on the Emerald."

"How do you know all this?"

"I've been poking around in Timm's office." Temple tangled herself in her cape coat as she tried to pull it off. "That glory hound is out to ruin you, Frank."

130

Coughlin scowled. "Since when is snooping on him your job?"

"He's double-dealing you, dumbskull!"

"He'll have to stand in line." Coughlin turned back to the bar and tapped his glass for Pat to refill it.

"Would you look at me, please? You're a million miles away these days."

"Me?" He spun on his stool. "I tried to get you all last night. What were you doing in Saratoga?"

"Following Timm." She drummed her fingers impatiently on the bar. "I tried to call you too. Where were *you?*"

"Me? Out, I guess."

"Out?"

"Yeah. You know the place? I'd tell you about it, but I know you want us to be independent, right?"

"Yeah . . . No . . . Oh, fuck you, Coughlin. You're in a weird mood, you know that?"

"I had noticed that, yes, ma'am."

Pat and Dora exchanged glances and moved off discreetly down the bar.

"Frank, don't you care at all what Timm's up to? If he publishes just half—"

The color TV over the bar crackled to life. Filling the screen was the craggy face of Ron Stone, anchorman of WSAV-TV News. His impossibly red hair bounced with a life of its own.

". . . reporting from our studio, and the streets of New York, 'Savvy News' roving reporter, Jimmy Shelby."

Dressed to the nines in a suede trench coat with its collar up, Shelby grinned from the steps of the Emerald Theater.

"Once upon a time," he drawled, "the theater behind me was the home of a leggy line of chorines and a nightly vaudeville extravaganza that starred the likes of the Marx Brothers, George Gershwin, and the young Eubie Blake."

A montage of photos flashed by on the screen.

"But today's Emerald isn't the gem it used to be . . ."

The picture was now a closeup of the deteriorating wall that had once held the faces of Glee and Glum.

"This week, this block is the front line of the battle to save New York landmarks from the wreckin' ball. In the last few days, I spoke to people for and against the rumored development . . ."

The picture fractured and re-formed into the image of New

York's balding chief executive. Shelby's off-camera voice posed a question: "Mr. Mayor, is it true your administration is ready to sacrifice this historic block of buildings?"

"No, not at all. I don't know why people always insist on impugning my motives. I am not Nero. I am not in favor of random destruction. But I am in favor of construction that creates jobs, that builds the city's tax base, and attracts more people to our entertainment zone."

"But if..."

The mayor waved Shelby's question off. "Now, in the case you are speaking of, we are not aware of any development plans. There is no story here beyond the myths being advanced by a self-promoting band of loudmouths."

The screen blinked again. In the cluttered office at the bottom of Broadway, Shelby was pointing his microphone at Ogden Maldwyn Timm.

"As head of the preservation effort, how do you respond?"

Timm pursed his lips. "The mayor suffers from premature articulation. What good will it do the city to line its pockets at the expense of its soul? I will lie down before the bulldozers rather than allow them to harm a single brick of this block."

"But sir, you don't mean every single structure on that block is worth saving?"

The camera cut away to a pan of the tinned-up warehouse and decaying tenements. The troupe of mimes in whiteface marched by on the sidewalk in mock military formation, giving the camera crisply mimed salutes.

Timm's disembodied voice chuckled. "There are always compromises to be found."

The image crackled and returned to Shelby live in the studio. "But what about the folks who live on the block? We spoke to a couple of 'em..."

Several block property owners flashed across the screen, each expressing fervent support for the move to develop the block.

When the TV screen suddenly featured a brawny barman identified as "Coughlin's Saloon's manager," Pat stared down the catcalls of several barflies before returning his attention to the set.

"...I think they're runnin' scared is all. They smell the big money and want a bite of it. And they seen when someone turns his nose up at it, he ends up dead."

Shelby raised an eyebrow. "That's quite a . . . conclusion. You're referrin' to the death of Casey Coughlin, owner of this saloon?" The camera pulled back to pan the premises.

"Indeed I am."

"And you're sayin' his death last week was the result of his refusin' an offer to purchase this property?"

"I'm sayin' no such thing, young fella. All I'm sayin' is, the police callin' it an accident don't necessarily make it one."

A voice-over from the studio: "To answer the Saloon manager's charges, we sought out Police Commissioner Powers."

The image shifted to an office at One Police Plaza. The commissioner sat at his desk, speaking directly into the camera.

"We had determined Mr. Coughlin's death to have been an accident. However, as a result of unsubstantiated charges leveled by certain parties, his insurance company asked us to continue our investigation."

Shelby furrowed his brow. "What's their interest, sir?"

"Well, if the death is indeed an accident, the insurers will have to pay a substantial amount. But if the deceased's beneficiaries played any part in this 'accident,' they could deny the claim. Understand?"

"Not sure I do."

Powers glanced at the camera slyly. "Let's just say, when somebody points a finger, we always wonder if he might be trying to divert our attention *away* from something."

The scene shifted back to Shelby behind the desk in the studio. "So the police file remains open, and the battle rages on. In the next coupla days, the preservationist forces begin a public campaign that'll climax next Monday, in a benefit performance at the Emerald. 'Savvy News' will be there, and I recommend you mosey along too. Ya never know—it might be your last chance."

The face of Ron Stone filled the screen again, his hair jiggling up and down. "Jimmy? Who was the commissioner referring to?"

A momentary look of worry shadowed Shelby's face. "I don't think the will's been probated yet."

"But isn't his only relative Civil Court Judge Frank Coughlin? Is the commissioner implying the judge had a motive for murdering his own brother?"

Shelby fidgeted nervously. "I 'spect any confusion will be cleared up in the next coupla days, Ron."

"Thank you, James . . . And now, for a new way to keep your pet cat from annoying your overnight guests, here's—"

Pat reached up and snapped off the set. "Now, there's a fella could use a baseball bat on the noggin to clear up his thinkin'."

"Don't tempt me," Coughlin muttered, still glaring at the darkened screen.

"Frank, don't you—"

His head snapped around. "Hey, it's great publicity for the show, Temple. Really. You're doing a helluva job."

"But I didn't—"

"Look, haven't you been letting your career slide lately? Why don't you go slap some goo on your face and get a good night's sleep?"

Temple fought to calm her breathing. "Why are you doing this?"

"I'm tired of you pestering me." He turned his back on her. "Leave me alone."

"What do you mean 'leave you alone'?"

"Like, without company. Solo. Buzz off." He took a slug of scotch. "Get the idea?"

Temple blinked and looked across the bar at Pat, who was polishing a beer glass intently. He dropped his eyes and ambled away.

"Let me get this straight. . . . Are you breaking up with me?"

"Why not?" he said into his glass. "We aren't going anywhere."

Temple stared at the back of his head, too stunned to speak.

"Oh, and here . . ." He reached into his pocket and dangled the keys to Paradise over his shoulder without looking. "Some other jerk is bound to want a modern woman like you."

She poked her chin out bravely. "Great . . . I'll need another set if Remy comes to visit . . . I guess."

Down by the beer taps, the helpless bartender watched her reach reluctantly for her keys.

In the mirror, Coughlin was looking at her as though trying to figure out what he was leaving behind him.

Temple's heart was dissolving, leaving her body like an emptying hourglass. She'd run out of time with him, just like that.

Twenty-nine

Temple barely had enough strength to heave open the heavy metal door on Great Jones Street. She trudged wearily up the crooked staircase, fished out her keys, and let herself into Paradise.

A small white business card fluttered to her feet. She knelt, staring at the engraved name and address:

> Hon. Francis Coughlin
>
> Civil Court of the City of New York
>
> 111 Centre Street
> New York City 10013

Flipping it over she read the message in his masculine scrawl: *"Sorry I deserted you on the sidewalk this morning. Let's talk— okay? I'll be at home. —F."*

This morning? Yesterday morning. He'd come by while she was in Saratoga—but he hadn't let himself in.

"Great timing," Temple muttered as she bolted the big door behind her.

Shucking off her mismatched gloves, scarf, and boots, she found the loft freezing-cold and drafty. Even the gas heater was letting her down tonight.

Shivering, she rewound her message tape before walking into the kitchen. She put a pot of water on to boil, and began mixing Droste's hot chocolate with a dash of Cointreau in a thick mug while her messages played:

This is Temple talking. Home is where the heart is, but mine is out to lunch. If you've got some heart to spare, leave it here, along with your message, after the tone.

BEEP. "Is this the world's prettiest girl? Lewis Tedesco here. You know . . . double-O-seven? Love the publicity you're getting for that *Comedy of Errors*. Now, about the Bond film . . . I don't want to pressure you, but we'll be shooting the dolphin-riding sequences in the Bahamas in a few weeks, and I'm going to have to make some decisions. . . . So call, huh? Love ya . . . Mean it."

BEEP. "O. M. Timm, young lady. I'm afraid I've been called out of town, and won't be able to escort you to the ballet tonight. Mrs. Onassis will have to wait. If you want them, the tickets are in my name at the box office."

BEEP. "It's Frank. Give me a call when you get in."

BEEP. "Jimmy Shelby, CBS News, New York. . . . Not really, but it has a nice ring to it, right, darlin'? It's Thursday and I been all over that block with a minicam crew. Where were ya? Anyway, my grand debut is at six tonight and I need ya to Betamax it for me."

BEEP. "It's Van, Temple. Listen, I've run a D and B on our friend McQueeney, and I think you can stop worrying about him. The man's certainly well-fixed—he may have a few million to buy property—but nowhere near enough to finance a skyscraper. He's comparatively small potatoes . . . Feel better?"

BEEP. "Hi . . . I stopped by last night, but, uh, you must have been out. Didn't you get my message yesterday? Look, I want to explain why I can't have you going off like a loose cannon anymore, all right? I'll be out a couple hours—got an appointment with the mayor. See you later?"

Temple made a face at the machine and snapped it off.

Picking up her scalding cocoa, she headed for the stairs, where a blast of winter air chilled her even more. On the landing was a terrace door leading to a tiny patio on the airshaft. Temple used it during the summer—it caught two hours of morning sun—but in winter she stapled plastic sheets over the door to seal it. Now the plastic was pulled away and the door was awry.

Locking it shut, she crept down to her twilight blue bedroom and peeked nervously into the closets, bathroom, and under her white brass bed. . . . No intruders . . . Nothing stolen.

The telephone rang. Only Coughlin was allowed to call this late.

Let it ring, she decided with satisfaction. Warming her hands over her steaming mug, she waited for him to go away. Eight times, and then it stopped.

Temple padded over to her closet and pulled out the skimpy dress she'd worn the night she met Frank. A silvery snippet of gossamer, too thin to warm her in the chill of winter. Gently, she put it back, and began changing into her most chaste long flannel nightgown.

She went to the bathroom, washed listlessly, and brushed her teeth.

The telephone rang again.

Returning to the bedroom, Temple counted rings...four...five...

Wanting him wondering where she was...seven...eight...

Letting him taste his own bitter medicine...eleven...twelve...

She pulled out the phone's modular plug, but it kept on ringing upstairs....thirteen...fourteen...

Temple began turning down the lacy white bedspread ...fif—

All at once she noticed the bedside drawer was open. The Avedon photo she'd meant to blow up for Frank was discarded on the broad-beamed floor. One piece was cut from it with pinking shears, leaving her winking face contorted closed.

The missing piece was impaled on Temple's snow-white pillow—one of her own knives thrust right through it, its glinting blade stabbing deep into her lovely open eye.

Still ringing.

Frantically, Temple pulled at the twisted phone cord. Clumsy fingers played with the tiny phone plug.

Finally.

"Frank!"

The only reply was the steady, hollow drilling of a dial tone.

FRIDAY

Thirty

The *Comedy of Errors* rehearsal was off to a lazy start. By the time Temple slunk down the aisle in jeans, a Danskin, and Capezio sneakers, bored Molineux models were fidgeting impatiently, their shapely limbs draped across the front rows of the Emerald Theater. She collapsed into the seat next to Chloris Ames. "What round is this?"

"Hasn't started yet, hon, but you look like you already lost the fight." Chloris reached into her bag and offered a container of Covermark and a mirror to her disheveled friend.

Temple shook them off. "Not feeling pretty today."

She knew she looked dreadful—and didn't care. Her eyes were dim after a night of staring into the dark, wondering if she could call Frank. Her whole face sagged like soft putty and her mouth didn't have a smile for anyone.

"Why so glum, hon? You're wearing a face like Emmett Kelly."

"God," Temple muttered. "Another damn Irishman."

If her day rate were two cents today, she'd be overcharging.

Directly in front of them, Nina Vartell spun around in her seat. "Ooooh, Ms. Temple, you look so pretty today. Do you hear the Hollywood agent comes to cast for James Bond? Is so exciting, yes?"

Temple shrugged noncommittally at the ice-blonde French girl.

"So, how is your cute *ami*, eh?"

"You want him? He's yours."

Chloris's hawk-wing eyebrows shot up to her bangs.

"He seem very nice," Nina purred, "but he never carry the drugs, *c'est vrai*? I think he is...mmm, too mature." She mimicked an exaggerated yawn.

Before Temple could reply, the ice-blonde mademoiselle turned and whispered to the girl next to her. While they giggled

138

secretively, Chloris leaned into Temple's ear. "Don't let her put the psych on you now. She's got the hungries for your role."

"Does she?"

"Honey, that girl files her teeth. What's with you today? I've never seen you so frayed around the edges."

Temple sighed. "I can't get into this today, Chlo."

"Wanna sneak out back and smoke a joint? I got some angel's breath from my local Rasta."

"Wouldn't help."

Finally, the skinny, hyper director/choreographer came skipping down the aisle. Today his sweater was decorated with owls. The red booties he wore outside his pants were circled with tinkling little bells.

"Sorry I'm late, everybody! My name is Logan, and you'll do as I say. Let's try to make up time. Can we have all the Molineux models onstage, please?"

"Boys or girls?" someone called.

Logan looked confused. "Boys, girls, what's the difference? It's all flesh to me. Where is our headliner, Ms. Kent?"

"Present." She gave a limp wave. "And it's Miss."

"Okay—you stand in the center, everyone else on both sides. Tallest people at the ends."

After a few moments of beautiful pushing and shoving, fifty Molineux mannequins were lined up across the stage. Logan unlatched speakers from a portable minicomponent stereo and cued up some bionic boogie. "Let's shake it!" he commanded. "Show me what you can do."

They all began rotating in place, each according to his or her own conception of cool. The dozen or so boys all danced the same, with a studied casualness they mistook for nonchalance. The younger girls were as boisterous and unbridled as their enthusiasm for their careers. Many of the older women's dancing was marked by distraction or blank dispassion—barely acknowledging the music at all.

Logan began hollering from his aisle seat ten rows back. His face was almost as red as his boots. Flipping off the music, he launched himself out of his seat and fairly flew toward the stage.

"Ms. Kent!" he snapped. "This is a follies, not a funeral. Turn it on for me, all right?"

"I—I'm sorry, I left it at home today. I swear I'll bring it tomorrow."

"Cute, peaches—but let me warn you. I am known for my killer instinct. Don't give me cause for homicide."

Temple lifted her hands in surrender. "Last thing in the world I'd want. I'm just not used to dancing without a little eye contact, know what I mean?"

"It shows. Wait until Monday night—you'll have all the eye contact you can handle."

Nina tittered behind her knuckles.

The director leapt deftly to the stage. "How many of you have *any* professional dance experience?"

Two of the models raised their hands.

"Theater experience?"

A few more hands went up.

Chloris Ames cracked, "What about ballet school?"

"All right. How many?"

This time over half the models shot their hands into the air.

"I really am enthralled. This will be *such* a disaster. Now listen. The general theme of the evening is famous people parodying their own images. You are the accompanying razzle-dazzle. There are going to be enough people making fools of themselves up here Monday night—most of our celebrities will be doing this with no rehearsal—so at the very least I want our chorus line to look sharp."

The models nodded obediently.

"You'll be onstage as a group four times—at the open and close of each act. The first time out, you're going to dance—or, rather, attempt to dance—mmm, sort of like you just did. You'll be total klutzes.

"Your second time out will be a fashion show, only we're going to get a few things wrong. Actually, it should be a kick. The third time out, you'll dance again—better, but not by much. And for the *pièce de résistance*"—Logan touched his forefingers to his thumbs and closed his eyes as though savoring a gourmet meal—"you're going to dance the spangles off the Rockettes. The shock will bring the house down, I promise you.

"Now I'm going to teach you a couple of easy sequences—fast. Which means you learn fast, and no bitching. I'll be getting enough of that from our so-called stars, you dig? Okay—let's bop!"

* * *

Temple's thoughts were on autopilot from the hurry-up-and-wait pace of the rehearsal when a glint of light drew her eyes to the trap door of Michael McQueeney's private hideaway. The shining chrome wheels of the old man's chair rolled away from the opening, followed by two trousered legs and a gnarled black walking stick. Then the trap swung shut.

"...don't you think, Temple?"

"Uh, beg pardon?"

"Your lines..."

"Lines?"

"The squiggly black things in that book we gave you Wednesday. Are they at all familiar?"

"I'm sorry. I'm a little distracted today."

"A little?" The hyperkinetic man behind the footlights sighed audibly. "Take it from the top, please."

She turned her back, took a deep breath, and faced the empty house again: "Umm... Good evening, ladies and gentlemen, and welcome to *A Comedy of Er*—"

"Ms. Kent!" Logan's voice slid up several octaves into another register. "Is my exasperation showing?"

"I'm afraid it is."

"Good. The rest of us are rehearsing act *two* now. I think we'll continue without you."

Behind her, Nina Vartell snickered. Temple scratched her back with her middle finger.

The owls on the director's shirt regarded her coldly as he approached the stage. "I'll expect you to know your lines tomorrow at two P.M. sharp. If you don't, don't come. Am I making myself clear?"

"Crystal. What about the dancing? I could use the practice."

"Self-knowledge is a wonderful thing, isn't it?"

"*Au revoir,*" Nina tittered, "Ms. Headliner."

Temple's friends looked away awkwardly.

Backstage, the entire theater community was pitching in to help the Emerald mount its seven-day wonder. Carpenters were hammering sets together. Stagehands from all the Broadway houses carried props and flats through the wings to painters already finishing a backdrop. Electricians toyed with the lighting overhead.

Sitting on a crate near the hall to the dressing rooms was Jimmy Shelby. He eyed her warily. "Hey, Ms. Kent."

She scowled as she swept by to the changing rooms. "What's all this 'Ms.' garbage today?"

Jimmy trotted after her. "You ain't seen the *TriWeekly* yet?"

"I forgot about it. Why?"

"Uh . . . never mind." He nodded back at the stage. "Only job I ever saw where foulin' up gets ya the day off."

Temple frowned. "What are you doing here?"

"I got news for ya."

"Last night's was quite enough."

Shelby looked wounded. "I'm comin' to make amends, T-Kay. I turned up another Cornerstone fella."

"Just what Frank needs—another spineless sell-out." She pulled on her coat and began buttoning up.

"No, no, darlin'—a Cornerstone *employee*."

Temple looked up quickly. "How did you do that?"

"Darlin', these ears could hear a raccoon lick his lips at five hundred feet. These eyes could—"

"Shelby . . ."

"I was pokin' around that warehouse with the chained-up door, when I saw this guy in civvies let himself in with a key."

"Civvies? As opposed to what?"

"As opposed to his regular uniform. Turns out Officer Falcone is moonlightin' as Cornerstone's night watchman. Got an office an' everythin'."

"Have you, uh . . . told Frank yet?"

"I was kinda hopin' you'd tell the big guy for me. Seein' as he might not be too fond of me today. 'Sides, I gotta hustle over to the U.N."

"Hard news?"

"You betcha. There's a guy in a penguin suit says he's the ambassador from the South Pole."

Temple eyed him drearily. "They'll probably give him a seat in the General Assembly." She headed for the door.

"Hey, T-Kay? Will you fill in the big guy if you see him before I do?"

Temple smiled wanly. "Not if he sees me first, I'm afraid."

Thirty-one

Temple was stepping out of the theater when she heard a familiar burbling roar coming nearer. She ducked back inside the Emerald's lobby just as Frank Coughlin coasted by on his motorcycle.

On the opposite sidewalk, Patrolman Falcone stopped showing off his stick-twirling to a gang of kids long enough to watch the young judge vanish into Coughlin's Saloon.

Temple headed up the street in the other direction, hoping the cop would think she'd missed Frank by mistake. At the green shanty newsstand on the Broadway corner, a pile of *TriBeCa TriWeeklies* was stacked by the sliding plastic window. The cover story was something about the politics of nightclubbing.

She bought a copy and began flipping through it. No Timm exposé anywhere. But on page 47, right across from an ad for an erotic lingerie shop, was Sasheen Lopez's column, framed by a montage of Temple's magazine covers and Jimmy Shelby's photos.

TEMPLE KENT GIVES GOOD HEADLINES
by Sasheen Lopez

Million-dollar supermodel Temple Kent is the star of A Comedy of Errors, this Monday's landmarks benefit at the run-down Emerald Theater off Times Square.

Recently, Ms. Kent heard there was graffiti about her on the men's room wall of Le Gillon, a swank eatery with the Euro-Trash coke and champagne set. She barged in to check it out, but couldn't recognize the hand behind the free PR. Thus she had to settle for revising the scrivener's message.

I met Temple Tuesday and I can confidently report that the words currently adorning Le Gillon's walls are true: Temple does, indeed, give good headlines.

Now for the bad news.

Ms. Kent is a pampered elitist from a Social Register family, with no idea of the bread and butter issues involved in the battle to rebuild Times Square. Immigrant families one step off the steerage deck can't understand why anyone would want to keep them from raising the quality of life in a deteriorating neighborhood.

Temple Kent's family came to America under slightly better circumstances—and they've yet to notice that anything has changed. The Mayflower brought their servants, Temple claims. Her relatives "came on their own boat after the crops were planted." Obviously, the Kents don't like getting their hands dirty.

Unfortunately, Ms. Kent seems to have inherited her family's tenuous connection to reality. A Wellesley dropout, she fell into modeling, for lack of anything better to do, sidetracking for a stint as a transatlantic plaything. ($50 to the snitch who fills me in.)

She's fallen into her latest role with about the same commitment. The benefit in which she's set to star is supposed to save landmarks. I asked her what she knows about landmarks. "No more than the next person," she explained. "I just like knowing they're there." . . . Heavy. So I asked why she's doing this benefit.

"My boss asked me to. I've been concentrating on my career so much the past few years, I thought it would be nice to show a little civic spirit."

Let me admit a prejudice. I don't like people who say they're doing the public a favor—as Temple did over and over—and then try to use the press for their own aggrandizement.

"I'm not famous," insisted the cover girl.

"I've never understood the compulsion to be in the spotlight," she declaimed from hers.

"I really don't want to be discovered," protested the girl who protests too much.

But when she heard this column might be subordinated to another, longer landmarks article, her nascent competitiveness was quickly aroused. She wanted to hear all about "what's knocking me into a sidebar."

I'll let you in on a secret: This year's model is precisely what we all think she is in our secret heart of hearts—a dropout earning an executive salary posing for pretty pictures, a model cheekily fobbing herself off as committed, a sphinx without a secret who quotes the wisdom of Robert Redford.

Who wants to pay good money to see a performance by someone who warns you right off: "I tend to freeze in front of large groups of expectant Homo sapiens"?

"I'm supposed to act totally inept," Ms. Kent confided.

Must be typecasting.

Temple gazed sightlessly across the confusing muddle of Times Square. Then she read the article more slowly, surprised that a stranger could cut her so deeply.

Folding the paper under her arm, she looked around for direction. Anywhere but home, she decided, where the telephone would ring all evening. Anywhere but where people would recognize her face. She pulled her scarf up over her nose and started wandering north.

When she reached Columbus Circle, she found a pay phone, checked the number in the paper and dialed the offices of the *TriBeCa TriWeekly*.

"Hullo? *Tri-Tri*."

"Hello," said Temple. "This is the Grand Union Motel in Saratoga Springs calling. Would you connect me with your editorial department?"

"Uh . . . I don't think they're in right now. It's Friday."

"I see. Well, could you help me? We had a guest here the other night who said he worked for your paper—a Mr. O. M. Timm? We gave him special accommodations because he promised to mention us in the article he was writing. And now the new *TriWeekly* has come in, and his byline's not in there anywhere. Was his article . . . postponed?"

"Hold on. . . . Ma'am? I'm afraid that assignment has been canceled."

"Oh dear—you mean permanently? Was there something wrong with it?"

"You got me, lady. They said in back that Om called in and canned it himself."

"Oh, gosh, you can't trust anyone these days. He was so convincing."

"He always is," the other voice sighed.

Temple hung up. She unfolded the paper, glared at it one more time, and tossed it into a trash barrel.

Watching the yellow taxis swarm into Friday afternoon's rush hour, Temple knew she had nowhere to go. Loneliness wasn't an empty feeling, she realized. She felt bloated with it. Perhaps she could walk it off . . .

Disconsolately, she wandered north in the blue winter light, drifting past the heroic white Spanish-American War Memorial, into the barren glades of Central Park, where the snow on the ground was still clean.

There were so many ways to be lonely. For the love you

were losing. For the one stillborn before it ever had a chance. For the one you dreamed of, but couldn't hope for anymore. For the one you always meant to go back to someday, until even "someday" was gone.

Rounding a frozen pond, Temple came across a group of children sledding down a small hill. While their mothers fretted and called them home, they hurtled their toboggans and saucers into one more reckless ride. Temple could practically smell the wet woolen mittens.

So she was lonely for being small, too, when everything came easily. For the father who'd always loved her just enough.

A hansom cab trotted by on the drive, the old horse's hooves clopping bravely on the pavement. Temple followed it out of the Park at Seventy-second Street and Fifth Avenue. Trudging south toward home, she spied a familiar distinguished mansion through the deepening dusk.

Of course. It was the Frick Museum.

She turned up Seventieth Street, walked through the lobby and into the Fragonard Room. Temple's eyes were drawn to Clodion's terra cotta statue of two nudes embracing, with Cupid pushing them together. Just then, a couple of kids in the first blush of love cruised by, whispering and giggling as though they'd just discovered sex. Ignoring the paintings, the boy patted his girl's bottom so affectionately, she almost sat into his hand.

Temple looked away—toward the opposite wall and the Fragonard panel entitled *Rêverie*. In it, a woman lay limp at the foot of a column, her eyes devastated by love: She missed someone too. Atop the column was another Cupid, this one pointing toward the door. Telling Temple she didn't belong here anymore.

Thirty-two

Ummm... Leave a message and... uhh... I'll, uh... call you back when I can.

BEEP. "Temple, it's Van. I'm trying to track down Frank to thank him for okaying the cast party after the show at his Saloon. Give him my best, will you? By the way, I hope you realize intelligent people don't believe everything they read... See you Monday."

BEEP. "Oh, Satin. I know that voice. It means my little girl is feeling blue today, eh? Well, I have got good news. A deal that gets me a plane ticket! You find a piano tuner, little doll, and I will call Sunday. I can't wait to see you...."

BEEP. "Oooh, Ms. Temple, this writer is very wicked, yes? Is not fair they end your career so soon. Ah well, *c'est la vie*...."

BEEP. "It's Tina. Now don't you worry about a thing, dear—everybody knows that paper is run by morons for idiots. I've already got the article lining my parrot cage. Just keep your chin up and remember: Your friends still love you. Call me at home tonight if you feel like talking to a smart old broad."

BEEP. "Hey, got any tickets? It's Radie. Jimmy said I should call you and get on the comp list, so, uhh... is that okay?"

BEEP. "Do I talk now? It's your mother. Nothing important. Mr. Eaton says hello. Do you want me to come down for this show of yours? I know you haven't been onstage since you played Peter Pan in summer camp... Let me know."

Temple reset her machine to "Answer Phone" so she could screen her incoming calls. Then she plunked down in front of the TV for fifteen minutes before she realized she was ignoring the network news.

She headed for the kitchen to gratify the familiar gnawing

in her stomach as simply as possible. Opening a tin of smoked oysters, she choked on their pungent odor—like something old found on the shore of a salt pond.

Snapping on the radio for company, Temple recoiled from her usual rock station and turned to easier listening. Maybe she was getting older after all. Wandering into the bathroom, she scrubbed the floor for half an hour for the illusion of usefulness. Then she caught sight of herself in the mirror. No wonder she'd been asked to leave the rehearsal. A little self-help was definitely in order.

Hopping into the shower, she washed her hair until her scalp tingled. After toweling off, she painted her face with a private salon mask that smeared on electric blue and peeled away a sheet of dead gray skin. Then she stung her face with astringent before soothing it with moisturizers.

Stripping her fingers and toenails of polish, she rubbed in an emulsion originally developed to strengthen horses' hooves called Ecrinal cream, pushed back her cuticles, and rubbed on more cream. She completed her pampering by sliding her extremities into white cotton gloves and booties.

Then Temple tried lightening her mood with a roach she found in the ashtray, and finished the last three Famous Amos pecan chocolate chips from her cookie jar.

After all that, she still didn't feel one bit better.

The telephone rang. When Temple's machine kicked in, intercepting the call with her prerecorded voice, she waited to eavesdrop on the incoming message:

BEEP . . .

But no one spoke. The other end was silent, except for the faint sound of church bells chiming—a familiar sound that meant Sunday mornings with croissants and newspapers.

Sunday mornings. They were the chimes of Saint Luke In The Fields, in the far West Village.

Temple picked up the receiver. "Hello?"

The other phone disconnected.

She started to call Frank back—and then hesitated. She dialed long-distance to Massachusetts instead.

"Mom?"

"What's wrong, Sunshine?"

"Wrong? I got your message, that's all."

"Oh. Well, I wanted to hear all about Betsy's wedding."

"She wore white. Pamela thinks she was bluffing."

"You don't sound very cheerful, Temmy."

"Uh . . . things are not specifically too great."

"Frank things?"

"How do you always know?"

"When your romances are all right, the rest doesn't bother you."

"Oh, Mom. Frank's brother died Saturday night. The police say it was an accident, but Frank thinks he was killed. And so do I."

"Killed? In heaven's name, why?"

"It's a long story."

"I'm sitting down."

The radio in the background was playing a medley of Duke Ellington hits.

". . . And now, fifty years later, the same people who used his grandfather to cover things up are trying to tell him his brother died accidentally."

"How's Frank taking all this?"

"Right on the chin. He keeps trying so hard, but he doesn't get anywhere. I've never seen him so discouraged . . . so alone."

"Not *all* alone."

"Casey was the only family he had, Mom."

"He still has you."

"Yeah, well . . . He doesn't want me anymore."

"What! . . . Temple, you're crying."

"Very perceptive, Mom. He . . . I think we broke up last night."

"What haven't you told me?"

"Before all this happened, he asked me again about moving in with him."

"That's a funny way to break up."

"I ducked the question."

"I knew I didn't want to hear this."

"Mother! You're the one who told me, 'No man buys a cow when they're giving milk away for free.'"

"That was your father, not me. And Frank wants more than milk, Temple. I just don't understand you. You put so much into modeling—something you don't give two hoots about—

but ever since your father died you've been scared to death to commit yourself to anyone or anything really important."

"That's not fair."

"I'm sorry. You're right. You bought this house back for me, and I love you for it. But you run away from men every time they start to get serious. First the blond Crandall boy. Then that nice Todd Sears. Then that awful Remy from Europe—who was the only one you were right to run away from—"

"Enough!"

"Right! That's what *I* think. But here you are, shying away from the best of the lot. Can you blame him for thinking he's wasting his time?"

"But . . . I gave him my keys."

"Well, aren't we liberated. Does that mean he knows your house is his home?"

Temple didn't answer.

"It's awful to lose an admirer, isn't it? Listen, Sunshine, every mother finds fault with her child one way or another. The ones who discuss it with them are generally making a mistake. But I think it's time to risk it."

"Oh, goody."

"Temple . . ."

"Okay. Blindfold's on. Fire away."

"Let me start with a question: If Frank isn't the man for you, fine—but what *do* you want?"

"I don't know . . . Independence?"

"Oh, nonsense! Independence is wonderful as long as it provides you with an opportunity to discover what you want. But it's not an end in itself. Part of growing up is knowing when you believe in something enough to take a stand."

"I know . . ."

"I'm just worried you've been looking so long, you've forgotten what you're looking for. Or won't know how to keep it when you find it. There's a centrifugal force to these things. If you *are* already with the right man, what's the point of running backwards to independence? Don't be so . . . contrary."

Temple listened as Ellington slid into "Mood Indigo."

"Well, what should I do?"

"Have you thought about what life will be like without him?"

"Oh, you know. Another two or three years in the wasteland."

"And what are the odds you'll run across a better man than Frank?"

Temple gazed around at the empty loft which was suddenly such poor company. "I don't want to lose him, Mom."

"Hallelujah, my daughter is growing up."

"But I don't know if he wants *me* anymore."

"A man doesn't fall out of love in one night, you know. It sounds to me he's got so many other problems at the moment, he can't afford a girl he can't count on. Of course, you'll have to convince him you're serious."

"But how?"

"When there was something standing between your father and me, I wouldn't give up until we'd get it right. But I mean together, Temple. If you aren't both willing to support each other as allies, there's certainly no future in getting married."

"I . . . Married?"

"Oh, my, did I say a dirty word? Well, it happens to the best of us—but if you're not sure, why not just try living with him for a while?"

Temple giggled. "What would your friends at the Garden Club say?"

"Like mother, like daughter, I suppose."

"Mother! What do you mean?"

"To tell the truth, Thad Eaton asked me to marry him last month—and I had to tell him no. I'd end up comparing him to your father, and it wouldn't be fair. But I do care for Thad—very much—so I came up with an alternative."

"I'm not sure I want to hear this, Mother."

"Well, at least you're laughing again. All right, I'll spare you the sexy details."

Temple's buzzer sounded: a long, a short, another long.

"Mom! Frank's at my doorbell!"

"Well, let him in . . ."

Temple skipped to her buzzer and pressed it a few seconds. The Duke on the radio started playing "Satin Doll" as she picked up the phone again, and yanked off her white cotton gloves.

"I'm glad you called me, Temple. I'm . . . proud."

"You called first."

"I know when my child needs me."

"Thanks, Mom."

Temple cradled the receiver, raced to the mirror, and began

primping with a smile on her face. Then she waited for Coughlin to knock, humming along with the familiar piano music she had loved so much.

But there was no knock.

After a long moment, she cautiously turned the locks and poked her head out into the hall. There was no one on the landing, and no one on the rickety stairs.

Temple reluctantly locked herself back in. Returning to the futon, she shut off the radio and dialed the West Village. Coughlin's phone rang on and on—but no one was home.

Out on Great Jones Street, a couple of rock 'n' roll kids shied away from the scowling man with the purple lilacs in his hand. Furiously, he dumped them in the gutter before leaping onto his motorcycle. He kicked the machine into gear.

Recklessly rolling his wheels over the undelivered flowers, he popped his clutch, pulping the tender blossoms on the pavement as he skidded around the corner with the jaunty strains of Remy's favorite melody still tinkling in his ears.

SATURDAY

Thirty-three

Temple knocked the phone to the floor. She leaned out of bed and groped for the receiver among stripes of sunlight.

". . . Hullo?"

"Well, top o'the mornin' to ye!"

"You wanna bet? . . . Who is this?"

"Why Patrick Xavier Duggan, a'course! At yer service."

". . . Pat?"

"Now ye've got it. I thought I might be lettin' you do me a favor this fine mornin'."

Temple looked for her bedside clock: 8 A.M.

". . . Like what?"

"Well, it seems a friend o'mine took the most terrible tumble last night. Fell off his motorcycle, he did, right in the middle o'—"

"Oh, God." Temple sat bolt upright in bed, "Is he all right?"

"Well, his ankle is broke, but aside from that he's fit as a fiddle. 'Course his pride is bruised somethin' fearful."

"What happened?"

"Ah, I'm afraid that may be the fault o'yours truly. The boy come in late last night in the blackest mood y'ever did see. Drinkin' like he was tryin' to drain the Irish Sea, he was. I tried to jolly him out of it, but there was no stoppin' the lad. Well, it's his liquor, ain't it? He went bangin' out o'here at closin' time and roared off like a banshee. Next thing I heard was the most terrible crash. And now he's at the Roosevelt Hospital needin' someone to help him home, bein' on crutches like he is. I thought maybe you . . . ?"

Temple sighed and sank back into her pillows. "Oh, Pat. I don't think he wants to see me."

"Now, there's where yer wrong, me girl. He's in love, ain't he?"

Temple pulled the quilt up under her chin. "I don't know."

"Oh, but ye *are* ignorant. Don't ye see it, Red? He's fearful worried for ye. Why else would he send ye away?"

Temple wiggled her toes hopefully. "Wouldn't it be better if you took care of him?"

"Can't do it, me girl. Got to finish me chores or the wife won't let me watch the Notre Dame game. And the beautiful Mrs. Duggan has enough trouble already, takin' care o'one man."

"What if he starts barking at me again?"

"Why, then ye bark right back! I'm afraid yer goin' to have to tell the boy no one else'll have him. Now I've done me duty, and that's the end of it. He's in yer hands now, girl—like it or not."

Pat hung up before she had a chance to reply.

Thirty-four

Temple was halfway down the hospital corridor to Frank's room when she noticed a poised, familiar looking redhead walking toward her. The woman she'd seen through the window at Frank's house. The redhead smiled noncommittally and vanished into the elevator.

Temple glanced down at the teddy bear she'd brought him and wished she hadn't made the effort. She paused outside Coughlin's room, took a deep breath, and looked in.

His right ankle was sheathed in a plaster cast, propped up on pillows. Leaning over him was a cute blonde teenager wearing the pink and white frock of a candystriper. She was doing her best to fluff up his pillows, nearly smothering him with a faceful of breasts in the process.

Temple leaned in the doorway and crossed her arms. "Suffering much?" she asked. "I hope."

Coughlin peered around the girl; he looked stunned. Then his eyes lit up, and his crooked smile began to rise. "Aww, Teddy, you brought me a girl."

Temple strolled up to the bed and sat on it across from the candystriper, peering at the volunteer's black plastic name tag.

"Jeannie?"

"Yes, ma'am."

"Would you go practice somewhere else, please?"

"Uh . . ." The girl began to blush. "Practice?"

"Makes perfect. But this case is out of your league."

The teenager flounced to the door, snuck Frank a cute little wave, and scooted away.

Temple sat the teddy down squarely on his chest. "Anything else I can get you, Humbert? . . . More milk?"

He grinned sheepishly until the smile slowly dissolved. "I stopped by last night. Before this happened."

"Did you?"

"Yeah. You were, uh, busy, I guess?"

Temple shrugged. "I'd tell you all about it, but we've already broken up, right?"

Coughlin gave her a withering look and glanced away.

"What happened to the ankle?"

"I fell off my motorcycle." He looked embarrassed.

"Clumsy of you . . . I saw your girlfriend on the way out."

". . . Girlfriend?"

"The redhead."

"Oh, her." A half smile flitted over his face. "She's just a friend."

"Uh-huh. She looked friendly. Can she take you home okay?"

"I don't think her husband would appreciate that."

"Aha . . . too bad. Well, maybe the candystriper would have you. She seems an eager little girl."

"Yeah, but I think she's jailbait. Besides, her breath smells like Juicy Fruit."

Temple smiled. "Looks like you're stuck here for the rest of your life, then."

A sharp rapping interrupted them. Standing tall in the doorway, Officer Falcone was beating a tattoo against the wall with his nightstick. "Yo! Frankie!"

Coughlin groaned quietly.

The handsome cop swaggered into the room and sat on the bed close to Temple. "Too bad about the ankle, fella. You gonna be okay, or, uh, you gonna be a gimp from now on?"

Temple glared at the Cornerstone cop, poking an elbow into his side. "Do you mind?"

"Huh?"

"Four's a crowd. Guns make the bear nervous."

"Oh, sure, sure." The patrolman eyed her uncertainly and flopped into a visitor's chair. "So, Frankie, what went down? You fell off your bike, huh?"

"Some clown knocked me off."

Temple raised her eyebrows at him swiftly, but didn't say a word.

"No kiddin'? Fuckin'-A." Falcone pulled a notebook and pen from his uniform. "Time?"

"Two A.M."

"You get a good look at the bastard?"

Frank smiled wryly. "Just what I said—some guy with curious circus makeup all over his face."

"Think you can make him?"

"No, it could have been anyone. I was slowing down to take the corner at Broadway, leaning into the turn, and he jumped off the curb and threw a stick under my wheels." Coughlin held his hand in front of his face and flipped it over.

"So you think maybe it wasn't an accident?"

Frank stared at the cop incredulously. "I think definitely it wasn't an accident."

"Second the motion," Temple murmured.

"Hey, babe?" the cop snapped. "Keep your pretty little nose out of this—check?"

Frank glanced up at her and winked.

"I'm out," she promised softly. "I'm out. I'm out..."

"So, Frankie, no description of the perpetrator, then. What about his offending stick? Can ya give me anything?"

"It wasn't very long. Just about...maybe the size of that nightstick there."

Temple glanced at the shiny black staff hanging from Falcone's belt. "Is that a new one, Officer?"

"Huh? Uh, no, I just like to keep it polished, is all." The cop gave her a peculiar look and shifted uncomfortably in his chair. "Say, listen, fella. I'm gonna check into this and nail the bastard—you got my word. But meanwhile, the commissioner wants me to ask you a couple of questions. Routine, y'know?"

"Fire away."

"Well, like any chance you coulda been drivin' while intoxicated, Frankie?"

Coughlin shrugged. "He wants to revoke my license? Take it. It's in my wallet. . . ."

"Hey, gimme a break here—I just work for the man. He was wonderin' if maybe you was bein' reckless . . ."

"The guy who shoved the pole under my wheels was reckless—not me."

"Sure, sure. Well, I believe ya. It's just, the commissioner was thinkin' . . ."

The judge eyed the cop. "That's what he's good at. Thinking what?"

"Well, like maybe you coulda hurt yourself . . . on purpose."

Coughlin furrowed his brow. "Why? Because I like hospitals?"

"Candystripers," Temple corrected him softly.

"I dunno, Frankie. He's got some cockamamie notion about ol' Casey's death. I mean, you weren't in the room when it happened, and you will inherit the Saloon, right?"

Coughlin stared at him without answering.

"Look at it his way. This bum leg coulda been a setup to make you look innocent—know what I mean?"

"Christ," Coughlin muttered, shaking his head. "Good thing I didn't get killed, too, or I'd *really* look guilty. Know what I mean?"

"Damned straight," the cop nodded. "So, uh, how about it? You got anything you want me to pass on to the commissioner?"

"Yeah," Frank nodded grimly. "You tell the commissioner he sucks dead rats. Write it down in your little black book there: S-U-C—"

"Time to go, Officer." Temple got to her feet.

"I decide when I'm done with the questions, babe."

"Suit yourself." Temple reached under Frank's side table for a gleaming stainless steel bedpan. She removed the sanitary band around it before handing it to the bedridden man. "But Frankie here has the greatest throwing arm you ever saw . . ."

Falcone stared at them a moment through his pretty eyelashes, then hoisted himself reluctantly to his feet. "Just doin' my job, y'know. No hard feelin's, right, Frankie?"

Coughlin scowled. "Don't bet on it."

The cop ambled across to the foot of the bed, sliding his nightstick lightly along the top of Frank's upraised plaster cast. "I'm supposed to tell ya not to leave town, but you won't be goin' too far on this—check?" He swaggered out without looking back.

Coughlin exhaled slowly and glared at Temple. "Will you kindly get me out of this place?"

"Later." She slid the bedpan under the nightstand. "They want to look at you again this afternoon and fit you for crutches. I'll pick you up after my rehearsal."

He groaned. "I feel like I've been stuffed and mounted."

"That gives you and Teddy something in common." She smoothed his covers and sat by his elbow again. "Do you realize this is the first time we've been alone in days?"

He looked her over with feigned indifference. "You wanna play Go-Fish?"

"No, I'm going to tell you a bedtime story."

"At eleven-thirty in the morning?"

"It's all about my trip to Saratoga . . . and our former ally Mr. O. M. Timm . . . and oodles of gold . . ."

Coughlin peered at her skeptically.

"Now just listen. Once upon a time, there was a funny little man who spent his whole life envying the treasures of others. Until one day, he stumbled across a secret that would make him very, very rich too . . ."

Frank forced his hand under the top of his white plaster cast and scratched himself irritably. "But Timm's producing the show to help us, Temple. Your theory sounds pretty farfetched to me."

"I know. I had to go pretty far to fetch it."

"Why wasn't it all in yesterday's *TriWeekly*?"

"Obviously, the gold is more important to him than the publicity and—"

Frank's hand darted across her lips. He was peering over her shoulder.

Temple craned her neck to see a furtive movement in the crack of the door.

"Care to join us?" Coughlin called.

Slowly, the door swung open. There, framed in the doorway, was O. M. Timm himself, his slouch hat pulled down over one eye, his cape draped over his rounded shoulders. He looked as though he'd spent hours practicing the pose.

"Oh, dear," the landmarks expert sighed as his eyes fell on the cast. "It's just as they told me. Does it hurt very much?"

"If only you knew," Frank muttered. "What's new on the landmarks angle, Ogden? How's that report for the commission coming along?"

"Oh, that." Timm crossed the room and sat on a window ledge. "You know, I had a chat with Mr. McQueeney yesterday about your grandfather's role in the Rothstein case. It's a bit . . . awkward, don't you think? Considering you're a judge?"

"I didn't plan my grandfather's career—and he didn't plan mine. That was fifty years ago."

"Just so. Still, if I were you, I'd hardly want to draw attention to your family's sordid past by applying for landmark status." Timm glanced squeamishly at the cast again. "And in light of recent developments, I can't in all good conscience recommend that you proceed until someone breaks your other leg."

"Don't worry about me. I'm not afraid."

Timm raised his eyebrows. "Well, bully for you—*I* am. It's all very well for you to defend your birthplace to the death, but I have no intention of participating in all this violence. First, your brother—and now this. I've received a telephone threat, too, you know. My goodness, I'm just a simple lover of architecture."

Temple stood up. "You mean you're backing out on us?"

"Young lady, it's fourth down and a football field to go. Time to punt. One day you'll realize that I'm doing us all a favor. Until that time, well . . . don't forget to eat your vegetables."

With a clipped nod of his head, O. M. Timm trotted across the room and was gone.

Temple glanced down at the man in the hospital bed, then spoke softly to the bear on his chest. "He has to believe me now."

Coughlin's eyes were still on the empty doorway. Without looking, he reached across the covers and gently squeezed her hand.

Thirty-five

"Thanks for meeting me, Shelby."

"No sweat. I was comin' in anyway. Saturday's the best chance for us rookies to get air-time."

The lanky cub reporter guided her through the lobby of WSAV-TV's news building and into an elevator.

"Y'had me worried backstage the other day, T-Kay. I was ready to have my sideburns scorched off after that news report, but that frost treatment ain't like you."

". . . It wasn't your fault."

"Anchormen have wild ways of gettin' their kicks. It's a game: Put the reporter on the spot. Least I warned ya 'bout that sloth, Sasheen."

"You wouldn't believe how she bent my quotes. You know that vicious last line about typecasting? Well, *I* said that; I was being self-deprecating. That creep stole all my best lines and used them against me."

"Forget it, darlin'. They're wrappin' fish in it already."

The elevator doors opened onto a brightly lit corridor.

"How come you're so interested in my footage of these mimes all of a sudden?"

"Just looking for acts to add to the *Comedy of Errors* show. You're sure you've got more film on them?"

"Tape—not film. Yeah, I do. Make a left." Shelby turned into a room marked LIBRARY, filled in a form, and handed it to the clerk.

When the man had turned away toward the racks, Jimmy muttered, "Remember, T-Kay, I don't want anyone up here recognizin' you. I got trouble enough around here as it is."

"Trouble is my business," Temple muttered. "Like what?"

He rolled his eyes. "Turns out I don't exactly have this job yet. I'm competin' in a week-long audition. Durin' which—this bein' your basic low-budget operation—I even have to pay my own cab fares."

160

"That sucks."

"You betcha. And so does the opposition. She's an oral specialist of the bottle-blonde variety and the boss loves it."

"Uh-oh . . . You've got trouble. How good a reporter is she?"

"You tell me. While I been coverin' this landmarks story, she's been slinkin' around the cat show at the Coliseum."

Temple frowned. "Mass market on white toast."

As the clerk returned with a pair of video cartridges, Shelby nodded glumly. He led her out the door, around the corner to an editing room.

Opening one of the boxes, he slid a black plastic cartridge into the three-quarter-inch machine and clicked on a monitor. As he fast-forwarded the tape to the section he'd aired Thursday night, miniature figures flashed across the screen. Then Temple was looking at what seemed to be a line of tin soldiers. Shelby slowed the tape to normal speed, and the mimes marched past in close military formation, snapping little salutes to the camera.

Their makeup features were indistinguishable, but obviously there were three males and two females. All five were young and agile; any one of them certainly capable of catching Coughlin off balance at a street corner.

"When did you shoot this?"

"Wednesday. Those kids are out there every day, advertisin' *The Mime Show* with an act of their own. They make pretty good money too. They're heaps of fun."

Oblivious to the cold, the mimes took over a corner of Broadway. Quickly, a huge crowd formed around them. The girl with red pigtails and the boy with star-studded suspenders sat with their spread legs toe-to-toe, forming a diamond, absorbed in a game of jacks — without jacks.

Another boy, wearing knickers and clumsy boots, tried to balance a cane on his nose.

The girl dressed as a lion tamer cracked an invisible whip over the head of a muscular but cowardly boy lion.

"How did you get these shots?"

"The station's got an old hippy van rigged up with one-way mirrors and hidden cameras."

The tape ended abruptly.

"That's it?"

"Just about. There's one more bit at the top of this tape."

Shelby loaded the other cassette into the machine. "This is last night when the theaters let out."

The scene was mid-block now, with Jimmy in the spotlight preparing his news wrap-up. As the fledgling newscaster tested his voice level, all five mimes marched past the camera in brisk lockstep, smiled clown-white smiles, and tossed him another snappy salute.

"So there ya see it, the backstage area continuin' to look like a scene from an ol' Andy Hardy movie, as friends of the theater work round the clock..."

Behind the beaming Shelby, the mimes faded out of the lights—then suddenly swung in formation into the parish house doorway. They huddled around another dark shape waiting there, deep in the shadows.

"... gettin' the old Emerald polished up for Monday night's show. This is Jimmy Shelby for Savvy News.... Back to you, Ronald."

Dimly, in the background, the mimes were scattering in different directions, all of them stuffing something into their pockets.

"That's it." Shelby began rewinding the tape.

"Wait a sec'!" Temple's hand flew to the STOP button. "Run it. Run it all the way through."

"Anythin' to oblige a lady." He punched PLAY and the figures moved again.

"... up for Monday night's show. This is Jimmy Shelby for Savvy News.... Back to you, Ronald."

As the mimes pocketed their hands again, the reporter in the foreground held his smile a few beats, then made a face at the camera. *"Cut!"* He walked out of the frame.

The spotlight swung away—and shone full on a uniformed man in the parish doorway, slipping his wallet back into his coat. Pinned in the spotlight, a startled Officer Falcone looked up with annoyance, then scurried off into the night.

"Now what in hell..." Shelby rewound the last minute and watched it again. "I didn't even notice."

"You weren't looking."

"T-Kay..." He eyed her curiously. "What's goin' on there?"

She punched REWIND and watched the tiny figures on the screen run backward all the way to the beginning.

"Listen, Shelby," she said at last. "It's been exactly a week since Casey's, uh, death. Maybe you ought to take that spy van out tonight and see what the block is like."

"What for?"

"Just to trace the normal routine. See who's out and about and making trouble."

"Sounds like a long shot, darlin'."

"True. But if anything turns up, you'll have the jump on the Cat Lady, won't you?"

Shelby snapped off the machine and stared at the blank gray screen. "That's a great idea, T-Kay. If I solved a murder, they'd *have* to hire me. You want to come along?"

"Can't. I'm baby-sitting tonight. For a very *big* baby. Just keep your eyes open, all right? I don't want you getting killed yourself."

Shelby packed the cassettes away and rose to his feet. "Darlin', when you're up against a Cat Lady, gettin' killed is just a minor annoyance."

Thirty-six

Coughlin hopped on one foot for balance as he peeled off his coat in the living room of Paradise.

"You don't have to do this, you know. I could lay up at Casey's and have Dora checking on me."

"As if one invalid weren't enough for her already." Temple locked the door behind him. "Besides, it's just for a few days until you're ready to move around on your own."

"Well . . . thanks, then. But you don't have to entertain me or anything. Just pretend I'm not here."

"Sure. It'll be just like the weekend you watched the Super-bowl."

Frank teetered awkwardly on his crutches, glancing around like a wounded giraffe, looking for a place to collapse. "Where should I . . . ?"

"Downstairs."

He eyed her uncertainly. "Are you sure?"

"March. But carefully, please."

It took him about three minutes to negotiate the back steps down to Temple's bedroom.

"Oh, I remember this place."

"Well, it's only been a week."

"Eight days," he muttered.

She pulled a silky blue robe monogrammed FC out of her wastebasket. "This ought to fit you. It was my ex-boyfriend's Christmas present."

"Funny, I got one just like it."

Sitting on the bed, he leaned his crutches against the wall, then stripped off his sweater and shirt.

"Need any help?"

"I can handle it." After pulling on the robe, he unfastened his pants and slid them down his legs. No matter how far he stretched, he couldn't work them over the end of his rigid plaster cast. Glancing up irritably, he caught her smirking at him. "Something amusing you, Kent?"

"There's a knife on the night table if you want to cut them off."

Scowling, he grabbed one of his crutches and used its rubber tip to shove off the trousers. It took him six tosses to hook a pair of pajama bottoms over his foot, but finally he succeeded in dragging them up around his waist.

When he lay back, exhausted, Temple plucked his clothes from the floor and fished out a bottle of pills. "You'd better take your painkillers before you get too comfortable."

With a sigh, he pulled himself up on his crutches and tottered down the hall. After a few moments, he called from the bathroom. "Temple! Where's my toothbrush?"

"Oh! I put it away. Try under the sink.... Sorry."

A few minutes later, he hobbled in, eyeing her curiously.

"Find it?" she asked.

"Mm. You bury your dead quickly, don't you?"

When he sat with his back against the white brass headboard, Temple grabbed an extra pillow, lifted his cast, and slid it underneath.

"Oww!" He flinched. "Will you stop helping me?"

"My mistake. Force of habit."

Coughlin plucked at the covers gloomily. "Look, it's not

that I don't appreciate your help. You just have this . . . tendency to jump into things you don't understand."

"I understand more than you think. For one thing, I have an idea who knocked you off your bike."

He leaned up on one elbow and peered at her. "You do?"

"I think so. Remember I told you in the hospital that Falcone was moonlighting as a nightwatchman in the Cornerstone warehouse? Well Shelby's got him on videotape—passing money to a bunch of street performers in clown makeup."

Coughlin's fingers reached under the top of his cast, straining to scratch an itch. "You don't say."

"Frank! Suddenly you're acting like you don't give a damn about anything. What happened to you while I was out of town?"

He shook his head unhappily. "You know, when I was a kid, whenever there was a problem in the neighborhood, the precinct captain would pay a call at the Saloon and talk to my dad. 'We're working on it,' he'd say. And then he'd come back in a week, and say, 'Case cleared. All taken care of.'" Coughlin scratched harder. "I thought I could count on those family connections forev—Oww!"

Temple eased his hand out of the cast, then sprinkled some baby powder down where it itched.

"Maybe you need a woman's touch."

"What do you want to help me for? I've been acting like a jerk."

"You are a jerk. I'll do it for your brother."

A brief smile flitted over his face. "What do you have in mind?"

"I could find those mimes. They're around the neighborhood all the time."

"And what are you going to do when the one who decked me pulls out another stick and comes after you with it?"

"You're the one who got his ankle broken. You want me to sit on the sidelines? Fine—that leaves you with an eighty-year-old man in a wheelchair and an arthritic old lady to do your legwork for you. What a team of cripples."

"Let's talk about it in the morning." He rolled to turn his back to her, but his leg twisted in the rigid cast. He let out another painful yelp.

"You know, Marlon, maybe it's time you gave up that bike."

He toyed with the knife on her night table. "Tell you what," he grumbled. "I'll give up the cycle if you quit playing with knives."

"I need my knives," she pouted.

"Why? Every time you pull one out you get into trouble."

Temple's eyes dropped to his broken ankle. "All right, deal. But get rid of it now, while you can't ride it."

"Already taken care of." He started to grin.

"Coughlin . . . Tell."

He chuckled quietly. "After I landed in the gutter, a couple of street kids rushed right over. I thought they were going to help me—but they were after the bike. Just laughed and waved at me as they rolled it away . . ."

He pocketed the knife from her table. "Want to surrender your weapons now?"

Temple shot him a sour look. "Let's just watch TV . . ."

She snapped on the set and curled up at the foot of the bed with her back to him. For two hours, they ignored the TV the same way they had through the autumn and early winter. Frank leafed loudly through the paper, while Temple played solitaire. Sometimes they glanced at each other curiously, unwilling or unable to raise the obvious questions.

Temple was watching a *Thin Man* rerun when she felt him sweep up her hair and plant a soft kiss on the back of her neck.

She stared over her shoulder, eyes wide with surprise. "What was that for?"

Coughlin looked baffled himself. "I don't know . . . Force of habit?"

"Must be the painkillers." She rolled off the bed and pulled her nightgown from under a pillow. "Hold the fort," she mumbled, heading off to the bathroom.

She was just stepping out of the shower when the telephone rang in the distance. "Will you get that, Frank?"

"If I can reach it," he called. Then, more faintly, "Hello?"

Temple listened as she toweled off.

". . . Frank . . . I thought so. How are you? . . . Fine . . . She's in the shower . . . No, no, just watching TV . . . Yeah, she certainly is . . . Well, I'm a patient guy . . . Right . . . Do you want her to call you back? . . . Okay . . . Okay, I'll tell her . . . Bye."

Temple cinched her burgundy velvet robe and walked in barefoot, just as he was hanging up. "Who was that?"

"The woman who gave you birth."

"Mom? No wonder you sounded so polite." She sat on the

side of the bed with her back to him. Looking into the mirrored wall behind the ballet bar, she began brushing her titian hair with long, steady strokes. "How was she?"

"Obviously not expecting *me* to answer."

"Does she want me to call her?"

"Tomorrow. She didn't want to . . . interrupt, she said."

In the mirror, Temple could see him gazing tenderly at the back of her head. "Something wrong?" she asked softly.

He shook his head just a fraction of an inch. "I like watching you do that."

She kept on brushing, humming to herself contentedly.

"Temple? I won't, uh . . . bother you, you know."

"I won't be home much anyway," she said, putting down the hair brush. "I've got rehearsals all afternoon tomorrow and—"

"No, I mean . . . now." Coughlin pushed himself over to "his" side of the bed to make plenty of room for her.

Temple smiled. "No problem." She pulled an extra quilt from the bottom dresser drawer and slung it over her shoulder. Then she reached to snap off the light. "Sweet dreams, mister."

She walked out of the room, heading up the stairs with the spare quilt dragging on the floor behind her.

In the darkened bedroom, Frank Coughlin murmured to himself, "This is very strange."

SUNDAY

Thirty-seven

"Breakfast!"

"Mmmm, whaa . . . ?"

"It's me—your ex." She was standing over him, holding a breakfast tray with three fried eggs—two easy-overs and one sunnyside-up.

"My . . . Owww!" Coughlin winced as he tried to sit up before remembering his ankle. Balefully, he watched her set the tray across his lap, then cross to the windows where she threw up the shades. Sunlight flooded the room.

"You're dressed already," he said, eyeing her blue flannel sailor's pants and cable-knit sweater.

"It's customary when going out in public. I'm late for rehearsals."

"Oh . . . You, uh, sleep okay?"

"Great," Temple lied, sitting on the bed facing him.

". . . Me too." He watched her burst her sunnyside-up yolk with a corner of toast and dip it before munching the runny crust daintily. "I think my next book is going to be about all the different ways girls eat their eggs."

"Mmm. Should be fun to research." Temple poked her toast into the running yolk and spoke with her mouth full. "I got you the newspaper, the TV control is right there, there's grass in the drawer, but we've run out of papers . . . the phone machine is off . . . Do you want anything as archaic as a book?"

Coughlin scanned the floor on his side of the bed. "Where's that mystery I was reading last week?"

"I mailed it back to you."

He looked at her blankly.

Temple shrugged. "I thought you'd want to see how it came out."

When he understood, he dropped his eyes. "Oh. Thoughtful of you."

"What about Falcone and those mimes?" she asked.

Coughlin paused with a forkful of egg halfway to his mouth. "What about them?"

"I could find the kids and talk to them. Find out what little services they perform for our man in blue."

"You're a model, not a policeman."

"Look, Frank, you don't grow up looking like this without noticing the effect you have on people. My looks are my ticket into the places where the answers are."

Coughlin returned his food to his plate. "Last night I would have said absolutely no."

"And this morning?"

"This morning . . . a qualified no."

"How qualified?"

He toyed with a slice of toast. "Up till now, I've been playing by the rules. It's the only way I knew how to play. But after I saw the mayor the other day and realized they weren't going to help me . . . Well, all bets are off. I'm on my own now."

"You've still got me and the bear." She plunked the fuzzy creature onto his breakfast tray. "We're going to help . . . whether you like it or not."

"Well . . . okay, Temple. But you can help my way—or not at all. Find out who those clowns are, but just get their names. Don't talk to them. And stay away from Falcone, all right? You call me before you do anything else."

"Aye-aye, sir."

"I'm serious. Don't get carried away. You'll be a sitting duck out there. If you get into trouble, nobody will be there to get you out. . . ."

"I know." She stood up, licking her fingers. "I should be back in time for dinner."

"Okay . . . I do love your geisha arts, you know."

She made a face. "Well, don't get used to them. In fact, you can do the dishes later for exercise. Sayonara."

Thirty-eight

Temple was waiting in the lobby of the Longworth Theater when *The Mime Show* box office opened for the Sunday matinee.

"Could you help me locate the kids who advertise the show? You know—that troupe of mimes?"

"I'm sorry, ma'am. I just sell tickets. If you don't want any, would you step away from the window, please?"

Wandering back out into Duffy Square, Temple crossed Seventh Avenue to the half-price TKTS booth, where she asked the young staffers the same question.

One of the kids turned to another. "Isn't that Marla's group?"

"Yeah, yeah. She was workin' here last summer, right?"

"Great," Temple beamed. "You know where I can find her?"

"Try around the corner at the U.S.O. She waits tables there. She's a regular hustler."

The low, white art deco building right off Times Square really had been a U.S.O., too—the one any World War II G.I. would remember—but it was now a chi-chi restaurant. Waitresses whizzed around the polished floor on roller skates, busily serving Sunday suppers.

When Temple sat at the bar and asked for Marla, the bartender beckoned to a brown-haired pro who was getting a standing ovation from one of her tables.

The waitress skated right down the stairs and hoisted herself onto an empty barstool.

"Okay if I ask you a few questions?"

"I only answer questions from female strangers on alternate Sunday afternoons—good thing you got the right week. What's up?"

"I'm thinking of hiring your mime troupe for a party."

"Yeah? Most of the parties we get invited to are in hotel rooms with weird out-of-towners."

"This is for real. You work with the guy who balances the cane, right? I saw him working alone the other night—he was incredible."

"When?"

"Real late Friday. Midnight, maybe later."

"Gee, that wasn't Bobby. We were dancing down at the Dirt Club until about six A.M. Beep-beep, toot-toot, get the picture?"

"Just the two of you?"

"And Hank."

Temple smiled. "Maybe one of the others was moonlighting."

"I dunno . . . Carl and Judy were probably together."

"Where can I find them?"

"You sure there's a party?"

"Sure I'm sure. Monday night at Coughlin's Saloon after the Emerald benefit. Lots of show biz types will be there. But I want to check you all out before I hire you. Where do I find Carl and Judy?"

"Carl's on the island visiting his mom. Back tomorrow."

"And Judy?"

"She's working. And she doesn't like to be bothered there."

Temple shrugged. "I have to decide this today. Should I forget it?"

Marla eyed her warily. "You aren't from her parents in Iowa, are you?"

"I didn't even know she had any. Why?"

"Her day job's, uh . . . different. Actors' Equity's unemployment rate is eighty percent, y'know? You gotta take what you find."

Temple nodded. "So what did she find?"

"Well . . ." Marla spun one of her skate wheels a moment. "Okay. It's a massage parlor just up the street—There's the Rub."

"She's there on Sunday?"

"Every day. Their legs never close."

Thirty-nine

The guard was big, so black he was almost blue, and dressed in a three-piece purple velveteen suit. He squinted at Temple from behind rose-colored glasses.

"You sure you got the right place, sweet thing?"

"This the rub?"

"This There's the Rub. 'S for dudes."

"Why? Your sign says you're selling massages. Total satisfaction guaranteed."

"Once you see what they sellin', you won't want any. An' if your old man's inside, he don' want to see you." He stepped in front of the orange door and crossed his arms like a harem guard.

Temple frowned. "What's your name?"

"Me? Who wanna know?"

"I'm swearing out a formal complaint. Public Code 463.2C specifically states all business premises shall be operated without regard to sexual gender and constitutionally repudiated without undue adjudication of personal liability and *quid pro quo* sexual prejudice . . . Or else."

The man-mountain blinked. "That a fac'? His mouth creased into a smile until a gold tooth winked amiably. "Boss says I'm s'posed to search all customers. You wanna stick 'em up?"

Reluctantly, Temple raised her arms over her head, wondering how much of a feel he could cop through three inches of goosedown. "Don't overdo it, okay?"

The frisk was quick and professional. "Armed and *daªan*-gerous," he murmured appreciatively, before buzzing her into the waiting room.

The chamber was lined with purple fake fur, covering the walls, the floors, the ceiling—even the cashier's desk—like the inside of a pimp's van. Three men were fidgeting in separate corners of the gloomy parlor. As soon as they caught sight of

Temple, they sprang to their feet in unison, thrusting scarlet tickets into her face.

"Hey, doll. Haven't I seen you before?"

"Only in your dreams."

The receptionist behind the register looked up from her book, startled. "You can't be the new girl."

"I'm a civilian. Can you call 'em off, please?"

The girl glanced at the three men circling Temple like hungry animals. "She's got the clap, boys."

The blonde receptionist was wearing a green Lacoste shirt, jeans, and penny loafers. She should have been working in a college bookstore.

"What's your pleasure, miss?"

"I'm looking for Judy."

"Yeah? Why?"

"Marla sent me."

"Why?"

A plump brunette in baby-doll pajamas pushed through the swinging double doors, reading a paperback romance. With a last, disappointed look at Temple, one of the men broke off from the circling group and handed her his scarlet ticket. Without dropping her paperback, the brunette led him through the swinging doors that went someplace Temple didn't want to know.

As the other two began closing in on Temple again, the fair-haired girl at the register waved them off. "I said she's not working, fellas."

One man backed into his seat glumly.

The other one, a ratty-looking guy, faced off with the cashier, resentment staining his face a dangerous hue. "Her or none," he groused. "Don't get none like her in Cleveland."

The girl turned a page in her book without looking up. "You know where the door is."

"I want my money back!"

She yawned and pointed to a hand-lettered sign: NO REFUNDS.

"Lookit, lady, I—"

Suddenly the outer door swung open, and the man-mountain glared inside. The buyer from Cleveland glanced into his huge face and reclaimed his purple fake fur corner, muttering to himself darkly.

The guard winked at Temple. "*Daaaan*-gerous," he chuckled softly.

"Judy doesn't go for women," the cashier mumbled without looking up.

"I'm here to talk business."

"What business?"

"I'll explain it to Judy. I have a job for her."

After a moment, the girl marked her place and closed her book: *The Cherry Orchard*.

"Take the desk a minute, Ahmed. We're going back. And watch our friend over there. He's a whiner."

The blonde held open the double doors, enjoying Temple's discomfort as she peered down the hallway.

"Judy's waiting," she cooed.

Temple was in the woods at night—only the trees made noises like bedsprings, and the animal sounds were at once awful and comic. The dominant odors were mildew and disinfectant. Every ten feet along the dark hall, there was a thin door. When the one next to Temple opened abruptly, she darted ahead so quickly she bumped into the cashier, who had stopped before an unoccupied cubicle.

The girl raised an eyebrow. "Shall we step into the boudoir?"

Temple squeezed past her into the tiny, rancid room. On a carpeted platform was a plain single mattress with a clean sheet draped over it.

The blonde followed Temple in, closed the door behind them, and leaned on it with her arms crossed over her book.

"So?"

". . . You're Judy?"

She nodded warily.

"Marla sent me over here. I want to hire some mimes for a party I'm tossing Monday night."

"Yeah?" Judy's whole face lit up.

"You worked at the Simmons bash on Friday, right?"

"Uh . . . Simmons?"

Temple nodded. "Ruthie said some kids from *The Mime Show*. Wasn't that you?"

"Damn." Judy looked crestfallen. "No . . ."

"Oh, too bad. Well, maybe it was Carl."

Sally shook her head. "He was with me."

"Around midnight?"

Judy's eyes narrowed. "What are you, a cop?"

"Right. The name's Julie. I'm with the Mod Squad. C'mon, do I look like a cop?"

"You sure ask a lot of questions."

"I have to know what kind of people I'm hiring, don't I? How much do you make on the street?"

"Maybe thirty dollars a night—each."

"I'll pay you fifty each on Monday. If I start getting some answers."

"Oh . . . Well, we were at his place all night. He helps me forget about this place. Okay?"

Temple nodded. "Who do I talk to—Falcone?"

Judy flinched. "Falcone?"

"Yeah, I saw him giving you money the other night. He's your manager?"

"That's a laugh. We give *him* money. If we don't pay, he runs us off the block. Carl calls him Officer Scrotum—the bag man."

"You were paying him?"

"Yeah, he takes a one-third share."

Temple pulled out her leather address book, scribbled on a blank page, and tore it out for Judy. "Monday night at eleven sharp. Bring your friends—your mime friends, not these."

"Sure." Judy folded the address and slipped it into her book. "And thanks. I'm sorry I was so suspicious."

"Can I ask you something? Why do you work here?"

"I get paid for reading . . . just reading. And I can cut out for auditions whenever I want."

"You must get a funny view of humanity working in a place like this."

Judy smiled wryly. "There's the rub."

Forty

The massive, red brick warehouse down the street from Coughlin's Saloon had seen better days—but never much better. The fading black stencil on the garage door identified it as PROPERTY OF CORNERSTONE EQUITIES—NO TRESPASSING, and Cornerstone's chunky rock logo punctuated the message.

It was growing dark as Temple left her rehearsal and began wandering up and down in front of the building, looking for a way inside. The front door was gated, chained, and padlocked. Across each tinned-up window, a graffiti artist had written *Futura 2000* in electric red script.

Temple ducked down the alley beside the warehouse inspecting the tin-covered windows. One was loose in a lower corner. When she tugged, it bent away from the window easily, as though it had been pulled away many times before.

Glancing furtively up and down the alley, she yanked the tin farther, dug the toes of her cowboy boots into the crumbling brick wall, and hoisted herself over the sill.

Inside, it was pitch black, but whoever had been through the opening before had conveniently positioned an old crate below it. Temple stepped down safely. Reaching back, she replaced the tin, then stood near the wall until her eyes could adjust to the dim light.

It was a vast, empty concrete space. Far in the back, mismatched sofa cushions on the floor circled a makeshift table that was actually a huge wooden telephone cable reel. On it lay a charred spoon, the remains of a candle, empty glassine envelopes, and a pile of played matches. Heroin addicts were using the place as a shooting gallery. Falcone's informers?

A sudden scratching noise against the opposite wall made Temple start. A rat as big as a rabbit was regarding her curiously, scratching its snout with one brown-gray paw. The look on its face was just like the one on the buyer from Cleveland in *There's the Rub*.

When it began inching toward her, Temple grabbed a bottle and hurled it wildly in the little monster's direction. The creature scampered along the wall and disappeared into the innards of an old, doorless refrigerator.

Nervously surveying the rest of the room, Temple spotted a partitioned dispatcher's office by the loading dock behind the garage door. Sighting by the cracks of light, she picked her way toward it. The door hung open.

In the middle of the cubicle was a gray, slate-topped desk, tilted slightly because one leg was missing. Temple switched on the desk lamp and was almost surprised when it worked. She aimed it around the windowless room.

In one corner was a green metal locker. The drawers of the desk were all empty. A pair of battered black work shoes lay on the floor in the knee hole.

Opening the locker with a tiny rattle, Temple found a battered briefcase with a luggage tag reading *FALCONE—MID-TOWN NORTH*. It contained several sticks of makeup, a jar of cold cream, a towel—and a small metal tin with the label CLOWN-WHITE.

Grimly, she rubbed some of the thick white greasepaint between her fingers—it was fresh. She wiped her fingers on the dirty towel, carefully replacing the makeup, and turned to go.

Tacked to the back of the door was a tear-away day calendar showing the correct date. Obviously, Falcone had been here in the last twenty-four hours. In the space for tonight, he'd scrawled an appointment in red ink. *"Meet the Boss: 7:30—769 W. 51 St."*

Temple was noting the information in her own address book when a loud bang echoed through the cavernous warehouse. Her spine stiffened before she forced herself to click off the light. Please, God, let it be just the rat.

But rats don't shuffle, step by step.

Temple crept to the doorway, unwilling to step on anything noisy, but too afraid to wait for whatever was coming. A dark shape was moving through the shadows. A tall shape, sure of its path through the debris. It was a man. Moving closer, heading straight for her . . . and then a tumble into the mismatched sofa cushions, followed by a long, contented sigh.

A rustling in the darkness.

A match flared. Smaller shadows broke away and fought

on the ceiling above him. He fumbled on the table awhile, seemed to grab his arm—and then stiffened suddenly.

Finally, he lolled back, sinking into the foam rubber, and didn't move anymore.

Temple counted to a hundred. She counted to a hundred again, then once more to be sure. Finally, she snuck out of the dispatcher's office and moved across the floor as quickly as she dared until—

Damn! She kicked over a paint can that clattered across the cement floor.

Temple ran for the window now, scrambling through the opening, tossing one last frightened glance over her shoulder.

But the junkie on the cushions didn't notice. His eyes were as empty as the rest of the warehouse. He wasn't going anywhere at all. He'd already been delivered.

Forty-one

It was nearly 7 P.M. when Temple took the last bite of her salad and slugged down the tail of her second Armagnac. Pat ambled over to lean his thick white forearms on the bar.

"How's the cripple, Red?"

"Restless. How are things around here?"

"Tip-top. That engineer fella Francis hired come by yesterday, givin' the place the once-over."

"And?"

"It's sound as a rock, he says. Built with first-class materials back in the old days. But the repairs are like to be six times as dear on account of it."

Temple leaned her stool forward on two legs. "Did he find anything . . . unusual?"

"Depends on what ye think's unusual." Pat winked and began polishing a glass.

Temple eyed the white-haired man closely. "Tell . . . please."

He put down the glass, smoothing his clean white apron.

Then he leaned down and pulled open a trapdoor in the floor behind the bar, pointing downstairs with his thumb.

The model's eyes widened. "That's where you wouldn't let Mr. Timm look the other day."

"Ah, him, and his old wives' tale about gold. This is my turf and I get to say who crosses it."

Temple grinned at him, batting her eyelashes.

Pat dropped his bar rag and called toward the dining room. "Master Peter!"

"Yo?" the busboy yelled back.

"Mind the bar, would ye?... C'mon, Red. Let's go prospectin'."

Quickly, she skipped around the bar and followed Pat down the steep narrow steps to the basement. Long hoses from beer and soda kegs ran up through the bar floor to the taps that served the thirsty. Just past the stairs was a locked cage filled with supplies—cartons of booze, champagne and bottled beer; industrial-size containers of ketchup, mustard, and lard.

"This was the old kitchen," he said, leading her into another cold room. "They was always in the basements o'the fancy houses in them days."

Pat pulled the chain of the bare ceiling bulb, lighting up the spot where a giant storage cooler had been pulled from the east wall. The plaster there was freshly chipped away, revealing a hidden dumbwaiter.

"Does it work?" Temple opened the little wooden door.

"That it does. Mr. Engineer was a little fella, so he hopped right in and I pulled it up and down. He looked for your gold, Red, but there's nothin' up there but air. See for yourself, if ye like."

Temple took the flashlight he offered and shined it up the shaft. She saw only brick and broken spider's webs. "So, the master liked his breakfast in bed, huh?"

"Ye've got the wrong wall." Pat replaced the flashlight on a convenient shelf. "This here runs right up to old McQueeney's apartment in the theater."

"Oh . . . right. I saw the other end."

"Francis's grandpa sealed it up when he took over the place, and it's been that way until yesterday."

"One more useless back alley to the past," Temple muttered.

A few minutes later they were back in the bar.

"Frank called while you was down there," said the busboy,

relinquishing his post. "Says we should keep our fingers out of the till."

"Want to call him back, Red? Use the phone behind the bar."

"No, I've, uh, got an errand to run." Temple struggled into her coat. "I'll head back home later...I guess."

"Well, that ain't very loverlike. What's botherin' ye now?"

"Oh, Pat," she sighed. "I just can't face him empty-handed."

"Ah, don't be daft. Findin' El Dorado is impossible, ye know. Why do ye think they call it the *Lost* City of Gold?" He sat on a stool and peered at her keenly. "Important as solvin' yer mysteries is, don't fool yerself they're all that's standin' between you 'n' Francis."

Temple stopped playing with her buttons. "What do you mean?"

"Yer both carryin' around loads o'baggage that can only slow ye down, girl. Francis's family left him a vision of a fairer world that's about as real as those movies they show next door. Once he stops tryin' to canonize three generations o'dead Coughlins, he'll be makin' his own rules."

"You sound like a shrink."

"Well, ain't that what a barman's s'posed to be? What's a saloon but a poor man's apothecary?...There's an old suitcase ye'd do well to discard yourself, girl."

"Me?"

"I understand yer shyin' away from livin' with the man. Still holdin' back on life. Now, think how free ye'd be to enjoy what ye got, if ye weren't always waitin' around for more."

"But—"

"But nothin'. Yer so busy chasin' the future, and he's so busy chasin' the past, yer both losin' sight o'the now. The beautiful Mrs. Duggan and me near lost each other the same way, ye know, hidin' ourselves from the truth. It was Francis who showed us the light."

"How did he do that?"

"By pullin' us far enough apart to recognize what was slippin' away. I do believe the two of you had best be findin' the cities o'gold inside yerselves first, girl. Then maybe the price o'happiness won't seem so high."

Temple tucked her scarf around her neck. "What price?"

"Why, trustin' yerselves, Red. There ain't no other way."

Forty-two

Temple shuffled cautiously westward over the slippery sheet of ice that was Fifty-first Street. As she left the theater district behind, the cheerful neon marquees shrank and dwindled, finally disappearing altogether. Soon, even the streetlights were scarce, and the dark winter night closed in around her.

When she approached 11th Avenue, gusty winds off the Hudson whipped her ears painfully. A scrap of paper rattled in her hand: "769 W. 51."

God. There was another block to walk yet—at least. Temple had never come this far west before, past the line where civilization ended and the wilderness began. An urban wilderness of tinned-up tenements, decayed industry, and glazed, buckling sidewalks. She was nearing the waterfront.

Across the pitted street was a black limousine, waiting with its engine running. She inched past it, toward a narrow doorway where a single, naked bulb gleamed over No. 769.

Peeking inside, Temple was surprised—and relieved. A well-dressed crowd was chattering gaily there, sipping wine from little plastic cups. In the entryway was a large blue posterboard covered with a dozen black and white photos and the scrawled title "*Meet the Boss.*"

Temple slipped inside and scrutinized the Off-Broadway theatergoers carefully. Officer Falcone was nowhere in sight.

When the lights flickered off and on, off and on, she bought a four-dollar ticket from a girl behind a card table and mingled with the crowd. Even inside the tiny theater, where her eyes could pick through the assembled faces at leisure, there was no sign of the obnoxious cop.

And then the house went black, blinding everyone.

There was a burst of automatic weapons fire.

The lights came up on an Italian funeral, with half a dozen mourners in Mafiosi drag surrounding a bronze coffin.

The deceased lay resplendent in a silver sharkskin suit, his handsome face painted a deadly white.

Police Officer Falcone made a very credible corpse.

Far more credible than the playwright's *Godfather* parody, which hung on a premise as slight as it was whimsical: What if the dead *capo* in the coffin really *were* Marlon Brando?

After half an hour of "dese," "dem," and "doze," Temple gave up on the play. Closing her eyes, she silently ran over her *Comedy of Errors* lines, smoothing away the burrs and rough spots until she was satisfied.

The lights went up at last. Falcone hadn't breathed, let alone left the stage. Temple followed the actors' excited relatives backstage. All of the performers were being lionized by friends and family in a cramped little dressing room. All except the man by a locker in the far corner. Sitting by himself, Officer Falcone was wiping off his clown-white, sullenly watching his fellows collect their kudos.

When he saw Temple approaching, his face lit up as though he were greeting a long-lost friend. All eyes were suddenly on him and his pretty visitor.

"Uh . . . What are you doing here?"

"Just checking out the competition. Been rehearsing much?"

"Every night for the last three weeks. I even helped with the set. Hey, you know how rehearsals are, right, babe?"

"Temple. Try calling me Temple . . . What about the night you came to the Saloon to offer condolences?"

Falcone furrowed his brow. "Oh, yeah. The director was sick that night. Why?"

"I'm interested in how you spend your free time. It must be tough, walking a beat, rehearsing here every night and working for Cornerstone too. How do you manage?"

"You gotta be kiddin'. I don't work for Cornerstone."

"Sure you do, Falcone. You're the night guard in the warehouse."

"How the hell . . . ah, never mind. I moonlight for Security Services—it's a private guard service. Can't make ends meet on a cop's draw." He eyed her speculatively. "You got a lot of nerve for a broad, you know that? Givin' a cop the third degree."

"I'm a taxpaying broad. You work for me."

"Yeah? Well, right now I'm off duty. Why don't you get outta here." He pushed her away by the shoulders.

"You want me to slap your face and scream for you to take your filthy hands off me?"

Officer Falcone's mean little mouth screwed up in confusion. "No, no, no," he whispered. "Jeez, no. What's the beef, lady?"

"Frank got hurt by a guy in makeup with a stick. You carry a billy club." She pointed to his locker. "There's your makeup."

The cop chuckled. "I like your sass, babe—uh, Temple. Here, does this look like a nightstick to you?" He reached into his locker and pulled out a two-foot baton of gnarled black wood with splinters at one end.

"What's this? Where did you get it?"

"Out of the sewer at the corner of Broadway," the man boasted. "I'm not such a bad cop, you know."

Temple examined it closely. "It looks like part of a cane."

"Could be." Falcone smiled. "You and Frankie get any ideas where the matching half is, you let me know—check?"

Temple eyed him thoughtfully.

"Check," she nodded.

Forty-three

She hopped down the back steps of Paradise two at a time and rushed into the bedroom. "Guess what!"

Frank glared at her from the white brass bed. "It's almost midnight—that's what. Where have you been?"

"Lonely?"

"You were supposed to call," he grumbled, watching her pull off her sweater.

"Didn't have any change." She sat on the edge of the bed to take off her cowboy boots.

"I thought you were coming home for dinner. I was worried sick."

"I got tied up. Want me to whip up something from the refrigerator?"

"I already did. Cottage cheese, a can of pineapple, cottage cheese, two yogurts, and cottage cheese." He plucked a bottle from the bedside table and waved it at her. "And some sauce."

Temple eyed the near-empty fifth of scotch. "Quite a lot of sauce it seems." She struggled with her second boot, noticing the teddy bear on the floor, staring at the phone. "...Any calls?"

"Just Remy."

Temple became very still. "...Remy called? Did he say where he was?"

"No. It was a very short conversation." Coughlin grinned wickedly. "I think he lost interest when I answered."

"Did he leave a number?"

"I forgot to ask."

Temple threw her boot clattering across the floor. "Thanks," she muttered. "My machine took better messages after I spilled Coke into it."

"You had a call from the theater too. They wanted to know where you were. Something about a dress rehearsal."

"Yeah—I got there late." She piled Coughlin's half-dozen dishes onto the tray, rattling them as loudly as she could.

"Sounded like you were late. Where were you?" he prodded.

"You mean while you were pretending to be the man of the house? I found out who broke your ankle."

"What!" He sat up too suddenly, wincing. "Who?"

"Tell you when I get back from the kitchen."

"Temple!"

She disappeared out the door. When she returned, Frank watched patiently as she unbuttoned her sailor pants. Then, as she walked about straightening up, he eyed her bare thighs where the navy-blue wool socks she wore up over the knees didn't quite meet the tails of her shirt.

At last he grumbled, "Well?"

"Hmm?"

"My ankle...Who was it?"

"Oh. It was our friend O. M. Timm. Falcone found a piece

of the cane he used to trip you. Once we match it with the other half, he's all yours."

"That little butterball?" Coughlin scowled. "That's embarrassing."

"It's logical, though. He thinks there's gold hidden in the Saloon. You're about to comb the place from top to bottom with an engineer. A plus B means he'd better subtract Frank C. for a while."

"It's consistent," Frank admitted.

"He also provided his own excuse for abandoning us. It's pretty clever when you think about it."

He watched her take off her shirt and pick up the long flannel nightgown. "I still don't see how hurting me helps him, though. It's not his bar."

"Not yet. But if you got scared, you might sell out to Cornerstone." She knelt on the bed in her panties and knee socks. "Do you realize what that would mean?"

He shook his head.

"I think Timm is in league with Cornerstone."

Coughlin stared at the exquisitely shaped breasts rising and falling tantalizingly in front of him. "Wow," he breathed.

"Wow is right." She stuck her arms into the nightie and lifted it above her head.

Quickly, Coughlin reached up and pulled it away from her. "Not yet . . . Please."

"Huh?" Temple blinked. "Oh. Have you been paying attention to anything I just said?"

"Sure. And I think you're absolutely right. I also like looking at you."

"Well, from now on you'll just have to be satisfied with my swimsuit and lingerie ads, like the rest of the boys. We broke up, remember?"

"Then what am I doing here?"

"I'm a sucker for helpless animals." She patted his plaster cast.

He patted her naked thigh.

Temple pushed his hand away and examined him skeptically. "You know, you don't do a very thorough job of breaking up, Coughlin."

The man sighed. "Well, it's kind of like suicide. You can only do it right once. How much more thorough do you want me to be?"

Temple paused to consider. "I'll let you know." She crossed the room and picked up her spare quilt.

"I'm sorry about Remy. All I did was answer the phone."

"It really doesn't matter," she mumbled.

Coughlin measured her as she approached the bed. "What are you planning to do tomorrow?"

"I'm in a play. Hadn't you heard?"

"I mean during the day, Sherlock."

Temple shrugged. "Hadn't thought about it yet. I'll figure it out upstairs."

"Do me a favor and stay away from Timm, okay?"

Temple leaned over the bed and kissed him lightly on the forehead. "You get your rest and leave it to me." She headed for the stairs.

"Hey, lady. Want your nightgown?" He dangled it in the air.

"Oh." Temple returned to the bed and reached for the gown. "Thanks."

Coughlin grabbed her tightly by the wrist. "You're welcome . . . stay awhile." With a sudden tug, he dragged her down on top of him.

"Frank!" She struggled to break free. "No, Frank, I have to go upstairs and—"

Her protests were drowned by whiskied kisses.

"You are such a brat!" she gasped at last.

"I love you too . . ." He rolled her onto her back, pinning her under his weight.

"Stop it!" She squirmed as he pressed her legs apart. "Frank! You're drunk."

"Mmmm."

"And you have a broken ankle!"

"So be gentle with me."

His hands were roaming all over her now, holding her roughly, impossible to ignore.

"You . . . beast! Can't we talk about this?"

"No," he mumbled with his eyes closed.

With the barest flick of his wrist, Coughlin tore her panties away.

She took the opening to roll quickly onto her stomach.

Instantly, he pinned her scissoring legs.

"Oh . . . you!" She scrambled up on all fours, clad only in her long knee socks, looking wildly over her shoulder.

But he was on her now, one forearm cinched snugly under her tummy, pulling himself inside her.

"Frank . . ." she gasped weakly.

When she realized he was past answering, she sank her flushed face forward onto the mattress. Again and again, the sheet rubbed and heated and burned her cheek until it was bright flaming pink.

Even as her face was flooded with pleasure, she hid her smile deep in the pillow where he couldn't see it.

MONDAY

Forty-four

If she refused to open her eyes, Frank would still be watching her doze in her dream, and the phone would not be ringing, ringing . . .

A draft of cold air nagged her bare back where he belonged. The telephone jangled, incessant, insistent.

Temple slid one hand across the mattress—not even warm.

One eye open. Big hand on the one, little hand on the six. What in the world . . . ?

"Umm . . . 'lo?"

"That's Temple, is it?"

". . . Think so. Who's this?"

"Oh, it's the most terrible thing! Can I speak with Francis?"

". . . Dora?"

"Yes, dearie. Quickly now, quickly!"

"Let me find him . . ." Temple slid out of bed, stretching contentedly. The transparent plastic wrist tag with Frank's name inside was there on the dresser next to her own torn panties. But his crutches were gone.

Pulling a terry robe off the ballet bar, she padded into her bathroom. No one was there, except the rumpled girl in the mirror. Then she noticed his clothes were missing, and his travel bag too.

The cold sky was still pitch black as she ran up the steps calling "Frank! Telephone!" But the living room and kitchen were dark and empty. Her ravisher was gone.

Temple picked up the upstairs extension. "Dora? Afraid I've mislaid him."

"Now how can that be? He was callin' from your place all last night lookin' for ye."

"Ahh . . . Did you try the cottage?"

"Well, of course I did. Damn the man!"

"Dora, are you all right?"

"Oh, me darlin', it's been such a night, such a night! There I am, dreamin' with the angels, when this terrible crash an' shatterin' o'glass sits me bolt upright in bed. It come from out back, where my room is, ye know. So what else could I do, with my Michael dead to the world with the sleepin' pills an' all? I found me one o'his old guns and—"

"Not one of those antiques?"

"And why not? They worked well enough in the old days. We always keep one loaded because o' the Africans, don't ye know. So I went out alone, ye see, just a poor old woman creepin' along in me overcoat, and what do I find but a window pane missin' next door."

"You mean the Saloon?"

"There was somebody in there all right, bumpin' around the bar with a flashlight. Well, I like to died! But I knew me duty. 'Hold it!' I calls. 'Freeze or yer a dead man!'"

"Oh, Dora . . . Did he?"

"He did not! Well, they never obey anyone, do they? He just put that cursed light in me eyes an' started comin' at me. What else could I do?"

". . . What *did* you do?"

"I shot him 'o'course! Did ye think I'd invite the man to tea? He was still moanin' and wrigglin' on the floor when I run out to call Francis."

"Dora, did you . . . did you get a look at him?"

"Now, how could I, with the flashlight blindin' me?"

"But Dora! What if it was Pat? Or . . ."

"Merciful heaven! It never occurred to me." A rising wail keened down the wire. "I only butted in 'cause I thought sure no one was livin' there no more to defend the place. Why would our boys be breakin' into their own Saloon?"

"Easy now, Dora. Have you called the cops?"

"Oh, my word, I couldn't face 'em alone. That's for Francis to do. Where *can* the boy be?"

"I don't . . . Did you try Casey's apartment?"

"Casey's! Now why didn't I think o'that?"

"He might be there."

"But o'course! Yes. I must be callin' and—Oh, my heavens, Casey's phone's disconnected. I can't . . . I'm not settin' foot in there on my lonesome, so that hooligan can jump out and strangle me!" The old lady began whimpering pathetically.

"Dora, calm down. Do you want me to come up?"

"Oh, Temple, would ye be mindin' that? It'd make a body feel safer, havin' a hand to hold when the coppers start givin' me the third degree."

"You just stay where you are. I'm on my way."

"Ah, it's the lucky woman that has you for a daughter, dearie. But will ye meet me in front o'the Coughlins' instead? I don't want to be wakin' old Michael."

"I'll be there right away."

Temple threw on jeans and a sweatshirt, grabbed her down coat, and rushed to the door.

There, taped on the knob, she found a note in Frank's scrawl: *"Please don't be mad. It was the only way to stop missing you . . ."*

Forty-five

Feeble dawn light filtered down the street as Temple rapped on the door of Coughlin's Saloon. After a moment, someone threw off the latch and pulled it open.

Leaning forlornly on his crutches, Frank couldn't have looked more surprised.

"Good morning, Coughlin."

"You've got to be kidding."

"Where did you go? I missed you this morning."

"I was trying to get some sleep upstairs here." He eyed her curiously as she brushed past him, then he hopped in behind her before relocking the door.

"Uh, there's been some trouble here."

"I know."

"You know?"

"Dora just called me." Temple glanced around the empty room, but couldn't see anyone.

"Dora?"

"She heard a break-in over here. She thinks she shot a prowler. I was worried to death maybe you . . ."

"Stopped a bullet?" Coughlin limped around behind the bar. "No, but someone did."

When Temple moved to follow him, he blocked her with his crutch. "There's a dead man back here, Temple."

She peered around Frank's waist. "Him!"

The body lying face up was drained of color, but hardly any blood was visible on the sawdust-covered floor. In its hand was a heavy flashlight that might have looked like a gun in the dark. Lying there lifeless in his natty three-piece suit, O. M. Timm looked for all the world like a beached baby whale.

Temple felt a little dizzy. "I've never seen a corpse before. For real, I mean."

Frank looked up, wounded. "Yes, you have."

"I . . . Oh, Frank, I'm sorry. I still don't think of—"

"Neither do I."

The body was surrounded by scattered business cards and dollar bills spilled from the overturned cash box.

Temple unbuttoned her coat. "What do you suppose he was up to?"

"No damned good. I'd say from that rosewood box he wanted a nice private look behind the bar, where Pat wouldn't let him poke around the other day."

"Do you think he had any idea where the gold is?"

Coughlin shrugged. "If he did, it was the worst idea he ever had in his life. Let's look around before the cops show up." He bent over the body, and without disturbing its position, carefully began searching the pockets of Timm's suit.

Temple fingered the business cards on the floor, stacked them together, and put them back in the righted rosewood box.

"Nothing here," Frank mumbled, turning to a black tool kit Temple recognized from her visits to Timm's office. He pulled out a hammer, a crowbar, some smaller tools . . .

There was one more card under Timm's hip, just out of reach of his pasty hand. Gingerly, she pulled it away, trying to avoid any contact with the body.

Suddenly, Frank straightened up, pulled his good leg back, and kicked Timm in the stomach so hard that Temple cried out. Dropping his crutches, he kicked the corpse again, and again, and again . . .

Temple vaulted over the body and wrapped her arms tightly around him. "Frank! What is it?"

"Slime . . ." Teetering on his cast, he continued lashing out

as Temple tried to pull him away. Then his whole weight
drooped in her arms, and he let out a terrible cry deeper than
any she'd ever heard.

"You'll hurt yourself, Frank."

"It's worth it." His eyes were lit with pain. "This . . . maggot
killed my brother."

"What!"

"Look in the bag."

Temple rummaged briefly. There, glinting in the early
morning sun, were the jagged, toothy blades of a set of pinking
shears. "*He* sent those notes?"

"Looks that way, doesn't it?"

"You figure he's the one who . . ."

"Probably."

Temple sat on a barstool, dazed. "But why, Frank? He was
nuts about landmarks. He and Casey were natural allies."

"Were they? I'm not assuming anything anymore. Who
cares how he juggled his conscience? There's the evidence.
It's clear enough to me."

A barrage of blows thundered on the front door.

"Cops," Temple muttered. "Want me to let them in?"

He nodded imperceptibly.

But the face in the doorway was Dora Driscoll's, her white
hair flying, her blue eyes wide with anxiety. "Oh, Francis!"
she wailed. "Saints be praised yer here!"

She rushed across the room, then froze when she saw the
corpse on the floor. "Is he . . . ?"

"He certainly is," Frank nodded.

The old woman looked more closely, then her face flushed
furiously. "Timm! *Blast* the man! How *dare* he . . ."

Frank wrapped an arm around Dora's trembling shoulders.
"Do you know what you've done? You've shot the guy who
killed Casey."

"Have I!" Her bright eyes lit up with harsh delight. "Oh,
what a treacherous little so-and-so, wormin' his way into our
midst with his fancy ideas just to be doin' the dirty work for
them Cornerstones. I could kiss the bullet that did it."

"Uh . . . Wait a second." Temple was staring at the lifeless
face on the floor. "If he was working for Cornerstone, why
would he get in his own way by starting a landmarks crusade?"

Frank thought a bit, then shrugged. "Maybe he didn't sell

out to them until that trip to Saratoga. That's when he broke my leg. And then bowed out at the hospital."

"But he killed Casey a week before that?"

"Well, the evidence is right there . . ." Coughlin's face screwed up in confusion. "You're right—it's all tangled up."

A siren warbled spastically in the distance.

An answering wail echoed from Dora's lips. "Oh, Francis! They're comin' to take me away! Ye mustn't let them put me in jail!"

"Easy now, easy." He squeezed her shoulder affectionately. "It'll be a nuisance, but nobody's going to jail."

"I swear it was an accident! It's the man's own fault—ye can see that, can't ye?"

"Of course I can. And so will the police. They'll call it justifiable homicide. We just have to go through the paperwork first."

The old woman's eyes searched his face anxiously. "At least if they send me up the river, I'll have the comfort o'knowin' I solved yer problems."

Temple shook her head. "Not really, I'm afraid. Timm was our only link to Cornerstone. With him gone, we're even farther away than we were yesterday."

"It's even worse than that," Frank muttered. "After all our poking around, they probably know *exactly* what we're up to by now. First Dolan, then Falcone, and now Timm: Who *knows* who else we've talked to that might be taking their orders— or even giving them. We're in a hell of an exposed position."

He rubbed his unshaven beard. "I want a promise, Temple: No more sleuthing until I'm back on two feet. This bar's no good to me if I lose you."

"Okay by me," she shrugged helplessly. "I'm all out of leads anyway."

Frank looked visibly relieved. "That goes for Mickey and you, too, Dora. You'll have to lie low until this investigation blows over."

The old woman nodded dumbly.

He turned back to Temple. "You'd better make yourself scarce now."

"Shouldn't I stay here with you?"

"You have a show tonight, remember? If you're here when the cops come, you'll be hung up for hours."

"Will I see you tonight?"

His glance held a mixture of hope and wariness. "You mean at the show, or the cast party, or..." Temple let his question hang in the air until he mumbled: "I'll have to let you know from the stationhouse."

"Call my machine."

The sirens were louder now, growling down the street behind the bar. Frank nodded: "You're still, uh...speaking to me? After last night?"

"Well, I'm not going to press charges. But hold out your hand." When the man offered it warily, Temple licked the first two fingers of her right hand, and slapped his wrist lightly. "Case dismissed." She tossed him a smile, nodded encouragement to the quivering old woman, and fled happily out the door.

As she started up the block, two blue and white patrol cars whizzed by, braking to a halt outside Coughlin's Saloon. Lifting a hand to shield her eyes from the rays of the morning sun, Temple noticed the little white card she'd pulled from underneath O. M. Timm's hip, still clutched in her fingers:

JOSIAH PLUMB

Numismatic Investments

3 East 57th Street
New York City

By private appointment.

Forty-six

Shortly after ten, Temple rang the bell beside the heavy steel door in the office building at Three East Fifty-seventh. She'd spent two hours drinking tea in a local coffee shop, diligently practicing her lines as she waited for the business day to begin.

Getting off the elevator at the ninth floor, she'd found the door with the small sign J. PLUMB was locked.

She rang again.

This time a disembodied voice squawked through the brown plastic intercom. *"Can I help you?"*

With a tiny whirring noise, the closed circuit camera mounted above Plumb's door tilted, focusing its lens down on Temple.

"Yes . . . I'm, ah . . . interested in quiet investments."

"What sort of investments?"

"The same as Kevin Coughlin's."

The brown plastic box emitted only static. Temple squinted up into the camera. "I said Kevin Coughlin . . . Isn't the name familiar?"

"Can't say it is, miss."

"Can you say it isn't?"

"Can't say."

Temple pulled the glove off her right hand and worried the ring finger of her left. "You're a very discreet man, Mr. Plumb. I like that."

"Discretion is necessary in my business."

"I should hope so. May I come in?"

The camera looked her up and down, whirring as though it disapproved of her dirty jeans and sweatshirt. She hadn't dressed for an electronic once-over.

"I'm sorry. I can't help you."

Temple removed her left glove. "I think you can, Mr. Plumb—though I'm glad you insist otherwise. You see, I'm *Mrs.* Coughlin." She'd spun her birthstone ring around so only a plain gold band showed. Now she waved it under the camera's eye. "I thought you should know my husband passed away last week. They tell me I have to settle his estate, and I know he had dealings with you. Of course, if you have no interest in the estate, I'm sure I can take my business elsewhe—"

Abruptly, the red light atop the camera clicked off. With a jarring buzz, the door automatically unlocked. Temple pushed through into a maroon-carpeted showroom lined with mahogany and glass cases displaying hundreds of twinkling coins: Krugerrands, Canadians, and commemoratives, bearing inscriptions in English, Arabic, and even Greek. On the floor in one corner was a massive safe.

Behind a central case waited Josiah Plumb, a spindly, elongated man with the air of a distracted English professor. He wore a rumpled black suit, white shirt, and no tie. Pince-nez glasses were perched precariously on his beaklike nose. His sandy hair was sparse across the dome of his head but stuck up in back like unkempt plumage.

"Forgive me, Mrs. Coughlin. With the world becoming so uncivilized, precautions are necessary . . ." Josiah Plumb stepped behind her to secure the door.

"No need to apologize. I'd have left instantly if you'd acted any other way." She let him take her coat off her shoulders.

He eyed her blue jeans skeptically. "It's just that, well, you don't exactly look bereaved."

"Ah . . . Well, Casey never went in for that kind of formality."

"Certainly, certainly." His long, delicate fingers played nervously on the glass display case. "You said you were interested in . . . investments?"

"That's right. But I'd like to be sure you were up to date on my husband's affairs. When did you see him last?"

"Just before Christmas, I believe. Everyone needs extra money at that time of year, don't they? He's been coming in with his coins two or three times annually ever since his father died in '77 or so. Naturally, I could tell by the way he's been selling off his collection that times have been hard on the poor man, but I never guessed he was ill."

"It was terribly sudden."

"What a shame. I've survived two Coughlins now, you know. Of course, I didn't know Kieran as well as I did Casey."

"I never met him at all."

"He was a very brusque man, old Kieran—not easy to get to know. He must have been hard on his children too. I understand that in spite of his rather unique resources, he made his younger son pay for his own education. He used to boast it would build the boy's character to have to fend for himself."

"It did," Temple muttered.

"Excuse me?"

"Oh, nothing. Mr. Plumb, I've decided I'd like to continue my husband's relationship with you. But he never confided his business affairs to me. I don't know what arrangement he had with you, but you can presume my requirements will be the same."

Plumb's tongue streaked across his upper lip. "Cash it is, then. That's always been the sole requirement."

"And the reason for discretion, I assume."

"Indeed..." He mirrored her conspiratorial smile. "You wouldn't have any coins with you today? I wasn't expecting you, of course."

"No, no. In fact, I was wondering if you could tell me which parts of the collection you have been dealing with."

Josiah Plumb's head twitched alertly, like a bird of prey on its roost. She'd asked a good one.

"You mean there are pieces besides the Paquet double eagles?"

"Well, uh...that was all he told you about?"

"And his father as well. Tell me, what *else* do you have?"

"I'm afraid I never paid much attention to Casey's coins. Could you show me one of these eagle things, so I'll know them from the others?"

"Certainly. In fact, I've been holding one he sold me for a collector." Plumb dialed the combination of his vault and pulled it open with a grunt. From a small drawer within, he extracted a twenty-dollar gold piece in a glassine-covered square of cardboard. Hesitantly, he dropped the hefty coin into her hand. Its weight was substantial—almost comforting.

Stamped in gold was the left profile of Liberty, wearing a crown with her name on it. Thirteen six-pointed stars circled the coin's perimeter, broken at the bottom by the date: 1861.

Temple's heart began to race. Civil War gold—President U.S. Grant's bribe money?

On the back, a heraldic eagle spread its wings under tall letters spelling UNITED STATES OF AMERICA and thirteen more stars. In its beak, the bird clutched a ribbon reading *E Pluribus Unum*. Beneath it, the tiny letter *S* indicated the coin had been struck at the San Francisco mint.

"It's called a double eagle," Josiah Plumb intoned, "because it was twice the value of a ten-dollar eagle. It's the largest coin ever issued by the U.S. Mint."

"Is it rare?"

"Oh, very. This particular issue was a redesign by A. C. Paquet—and it was withdrawn from circulation soon after striking. So few of them exist that most price guides don't even list it."

"I've never seen anything like it. This is the only thing Casey ever sold you?"

"And many more of the same. I've always wondered about

the source of such an unusual cache, but he never volunteered . . . Ah, I don't suppose you'd know?"

Temple gave Josiah Plumb the first genuine look she'd managed since ringing his bell. "He never told me either."

"Of course." Plumb was disappointed, but he took it well.

"So what's one of these worth?"

"Generally, double eagles bring a hundred dollars over the melt price—that is, metal value alone if the coin was melted. But the extreme rarity of this particular issue makes it far more valuable. Let me check my auction book . . .

"Yes, here it is. In 1980, at a Stack's auction, an almost uncirculated specimen like this one sold for fifty-seven hundred dollars."

Temple whistled softly. "And you've bought how many from, uh, my husband and his father?"

"Several dozen, I'd say. Most in the last few years, of course. We're in a difficult economy, and everybody needs a little extra to get by."

"Always cash?"

"Your husband insisted. I hope I'm not tattling on him, er . . . posthumously."

"No, no. Is this arrangement legal?"

Josiah Plumb smiled obsequiously. "Special services are often performed for special customers. If I don't do it, someone else will."

"What about Uncle Sam?"

"Uncle doesn't have enough eyes to watch. And if he does notice, the penalties are quite minor."

Temple hoisted her coat with a smile. "I like your terms, Mr. Plumb. I see no reason why we can't continue to deal on the same basis."

"Wonderful." The spindly man adjusted his pince-nez glasses. "I can expect to see you again, Mrs. Coughlin?"

She liked the sound of that.

Forty-seven

Following her last afternoon rehearsal, Temple beeped her answering machine from a phone booth at the Emerald.

This is Temple Kent. My normal message is not available right now. But you can leave yours at the tone.

BEEP. "Logan calling. Where are you at ten A.M.? You're making me very nervous, peaches. I've just been told our producer is . . . indisposed. But the show must go on. I wanted to be sure you hadn't forgotten our emergency rehearsal at two. Your call tonight is for six-thirty. If you're there on time— both times—I promise never to bother you again."

BEEP. "Shelby. Ever hear the one about the priest and the prostitute? Gimme a buzz at the studio and I'll tell ya the punch line. Six-four-and-even. Over-and-out."

BEEP. "Coughlin. We're still at the cop shop with a Lieutenant Florian. No word yet. If you want to check in, his direct line is 399-9315."

BEEP. "Shelby again. C'mon, girl, time's a-wastin'."

Temple checked her watch: 5:15 P.M.

First she dialed the number Frank had left. A brusque voice told her Judge Coughlin was tied up "in conference," and advised her to call back later.

Next, she tried Shelby, holding the line for seven minutes while various operators at WSAV's switchboard tried to track down the unfamiliar name.

"'Lo?" he mumbled at last.

"Hi. What are you so jolly about?"

"Stories without endin's," he mumbled morosely. "You know, your ol' buddy O. M. Timm got air-conditioned last night?"

"Uh . . . yeah."

"Cops won't say a word about it. I got the news without the truth. Meanwhile, Cat Lady's so worried about me, she's in gettin' rolled on the carpet by the big boss at this very moment. So that's the *coup de grace* on my chances."

"Are you sure?"

"She flounced in there ten minutes ago with three buttons of her blouse undone. Five minutes ago, Henry told his secretary to hold all his calls and pulled down the shades. What do you figure? Just when I'm hot on a story that could snag the gig too. Don't it just bust your balloon?"

"I'm really sorry, Jimmy... What's this about the priest and the working girl?"

"Oh, yeah. Saturday night, I'm hidin' in the van, like I told you, when Father Dolan slips out of the parish house in street clothes about nine-thirty. He's lookin' real sneaky, T-Kay—collar up, hat down—so I tail his cab up Eighth Avenue and on up Central Park. He gets out at Eighty-eighth Street, and heads into one of those fallin'-apart old brownstones near Columbus."

"Residential?"

"You got it. A couple minutes later I spot him in the window of the ground-floor front apartment. I hung out till the lights went off around eleven. He never came out."

"Huh. Maybe he's got a civilian apartment. Did you check the name on the buzzer?"

"Sure did. All it said was SUPER."

"As in superintendent? I don't get it."

"Neither did I until I asked around a little. The guy who owns the deli next door tells me SUPER is an over-the-hill hooker—who's still pretty super. Seems some nice priest got her the job to take her off the streets."

"That figures. Father Dolan does social work with all kinds of losers."

"And stays overnight with 'em? This is a Catholic priest, darlin'. You figure he was playin' hide-the-salami?"

"Ah... Well, the flesh is weak, I suppose. What did you do then?"

"I went dancin' at Neverland."

"Aww, Shelby..."

"It was midnight, T-Kay. What else was I gonna see? Oh, yeah. Guess who owns the brownstone?"

"Owns...? Not Cornerstone?"

"Ah, skunk juice! Sometimes ya plain ruin all my fun. Well, that's it: one of those C/E symbols is stamped right there in the entryway. Funny thing, huh?"

"Shelby, please tell me you're such a good reporter you remember the address."

"Nope. But I wrote it down. . . . One-oh-one West Eighty-eighth Street."

Temple scribbled the numbers on her hand.

"Sorry I didn't come up with anythin' better, dar—Holy jumpin' toads! I gotta hang up, T-Kay."

"What's the hurry?"

"Carlotta Robertson's comin' through, and I *know* her husband ain't expectin' her."

"So?"

"So somebody's gotta warn the boss before she—"

"Quick, Jimmy! Look under your desk!"

"Look under . . . why?"

"I think you dropped a dime."

"Uh, there's nothin' . . . I don't get it."

"God is smiling on you, nitwit. Mind your own business."

"I dunno, T-Kay . . ."

"Oh, stop being such a damned Southern gentleman. The Cat Lady's got her claws out for you. First law of the jungle is, She who lives by the fuck shall die by the fuck."

"Well . . . Heh, too late now."

"Jimmy? Are you going to have a crew at the show tonight?"

"Probably, unless the Cat Lady's finished her audition and won already. Why?"

"I think you can promise your boss a big story."

"Somethin' besides the show?"

"Can't say just now. It's not a scoop yet."

"T-Kay . . ."

"Bye, Shelby."

Temple tried the police station again, and this time they gave her Coughlin.

"Hi. What's the verdict?"

"I think they're convinced this sweet little old lady isn't the next Lizzie Borden."

"How's she taking it?"

"Are you kidding? She's beating the lieutenant at gin rummy. How are you?"

"I'm all right. Why?"

"Thought you might be nervous about tonight."

"I'm too busy to be nervous. Jimmy Shelby found you a present."

"A what?"

"Information. He tailed Father Dolan out of the neighborhood last night to an apartment building up on West Eighty-eighth Street. Dolan stayed all night. It's owned by Cornerstone."

"Cornerstone!"

"Name keeps popping up, doesn't it? I'm going to run up there and look it over."

"Temple . . . Didn't Casey follow Dolan up there the night he was killed? Maybe you'd better wait until I can come with you."

"It's broad daylight, Frank. Besides, who knows when they'll let you two out of jail?"

"I don't like it, Temple."

"I'll just look at the mailboxes. You going to make it tonight?"

"We'll make it if *you* will."

"See you backstage."

". . . Hey, Temple?"

"Yeah?"

"Don't give your understudy her big break, okay?"

He hung up before she could answer.

Forty-eight

The West Eighties are a crosshatch of partially gentrified blocks, where expensively renovated brownstones rub shoulders with verminous hulks. Cornerstone's building was ratty.

Temple waited in the cramped foyer, pretending to write a note to a friend until a mangy resident slunk out the door. Before it could swing shut, she slipped inside and rang the bell marked SUPER. The door was opened by a saucer-eyed little boy who looked so much like a picture postcard she had an urge to stamp and mail him.

"Well, good afternoon, sir. Is your mommy home?"

"Mommy sleeping."

"I see. Well, is the man of the house here?"

The little boy began sucking his fingers and shook his head.

"Was he here visiting Mommy yesterday? At breakfast?"

The child's face lit up. "Daddy!"

"*Daddy . . . ?* Do you see Daddy every day?"

"Saturday!" The boy was grinning from ear to ear.

"But not last Saturday."

The boy began nodding vehemently. "Every Saturday!"

Just then a frumpy woman came up behind him. "Eddie, who's there?"

"Hello, ma'am," Temple offered her hand. "I'm doing some social work in the neighborhood and—"

The woman slapped the boy's face without even looking. "We don't socialize, lady."

She slammed the door in Temple's face.

Of course!

The explanations were hooking up in Temple's mind so fast she couldn't balance them all. Hurrying to get to Frank, she barely noticed the evening crowd jostling her along Columbus.

A few minutes later, though, caught in a pack of jackals all yipping for the same taxis, she realized she'd stumbled into rush hour. She was so late already, there was no choice but the subway—for all its putrid atmosphere, still the fastest ride in town.

The downtown platform was thronged with weary workers impatient for the AA train. The only ones enjoying themselves were two black kids, creating a nuisance by bounce-passing a basketball uncomfortably close to the prettiest woman. They lingered by Temple, nearly dribbling the ball on her toes a few times until she irritably kicked it over to the newsstand.

Grinning mischievously, the boys shrugged their farewell and set off in pursuit, nearly bowling over a large old woman who ducked behind a support column for safety.

Temple heard a low rumble and leaned out over the tracks. A headlight was veering into the station at top speed. As the crowd edged forward, jockeying for position, she realized her toes had crossed the yellow danger line.

She pressed back against the wall of determined commuters . . . and then she felt hands in the small of her back. Someone was pushing her forward—hard!

Shoved off balance, she toppled onto the tracks!

Temple scrambled to her knees in the puddle between the rails, trapped in the headlight of the hurtling monster, heart pumping so panicky her breath stuck in her throat.

An ear-splitting screech of brakes echoed through the tunnel like a thousand chalks on the blackboard.

No time to leap to the platform. Already, she saw the face of the trainman contorting in anguish, pity, apology . . .

Temple dove face-down into the foul foot-deep trench, flattening herself into the muck between the rails as the sparking fury roared toward her, its noise so stunning . . .

Until everything slowed . . . and clanked to a stop.

Temple gagged in the vile little womb, trembling all over as her audience began screaming for her.

Forty-nine

She was still in a daze as a patrolman helped her out of his squad car and steered her, limping, toward the stage door of the Emerald.

She was filthy, soaked, and shivering. One of her boots was missing its heel, her jeans were ripped at the knee, and her sweatshirt would never recover.

Just inside the door, a stagehand grinned at her fondly. "One helluva entrance, Miss Kent. Love your look."

Temple turned her slime-streaked face to the man. ". . . What?"

"Just a joke."

"Oh . . . My ears aren't working right." Cupping her hands beside her head, she tried massaging away the ghost of the subway.

"There you are!" William VanderPoel's voice came echoing down the corridor behind her. "I *knew* you'd be back by showtime. I just won a hundred dollars from Logan..."

Temple turned unsteadily, her eyes welling up with tears as she caught sight of the old patrician beaming at her like a proud father. He looked like one of the men in his own elegant advertisements—fat pearls glowing on his crisp cuffs. Only men his age looked so good in a tux.

VanderPoel's face clouded as she buried herself into his pleated chest, trembling silently. Wrapping his arms around her, he squinted at the cop. "What's going on here, mister?"

"Lady had an accident, sir. Pushed onto the subway tracks. She's lucky to be alive."

The tycoon frowned, then lowered his mouth to Temple's ear. "We're going to the hospital, young lady. Right now."

"Logan would kill me..."

"Fuck Logan."

Temple surfaced with a brittle smile. "Is Frank here?"

"I haven't seen him yet. Do you want to go home?"

Temple shook her head. "The show must go on."

"We can survive without you."

"Real flattering, Van."

"I just meant—"

Temple nodded, brushing her fingers across his lips. "Shower," she mumbled, drifting off down the hall.

She was wrapped in a white terry robe, gingerly brushing powder onto her scraped knees, when Van poked his head into her private dressing room.

"Are you sure about this?"

Temple nodded. "Just nervous."

He sat on the stool beside her. "You're playing a beautiful, unrehearsed, slightly screwball young lady. Just be yourself, and you'll do fine."

"Myself wouldn't be caught dead in a spot like this," she muttered edgily. "I wish I was more rehearsed at seeming unrehearsed."

The stagehand looked in the door. "Five minutes, Miss Kent."

Her eyes flickered fearfully at Van's in the mirror.

"Temple, do you remember what I told you the first night we met?"

"Ahh . . . to stay aware of my effect on the room, do absolutely nothing to change it, and just think: 'Thank you.'"

"That's right. Let your nerves show—it's endearing. Now this time you're out in the ocean on a surfboard, and the biggest wave you've ever seen is coming. All you've got to do is stand up and keep your balance. Instinct will do the rest."

Temple nodded, lifting her sheer silver dress. It was barely the size of a large neckerchief. "You'd better let me get indecent."

"Break a leg," he winked.

"I nearly did."

As Van turned to leave, two models paused in the doorway.

"How come she get her own room, and I have to share with six people?" groused Nina Vartell.

"Yeah, what's she got that we haven't got?"

The old tycoon smiled grimly. "Guts," he said.

"Good evening, ladies and gentlemen, and welcome to *A Comedy of Errors*."

William VanderPoel was perfectly at home in the spotlight—certainly more at ease than Temple, who was giving birth to butterflies in the wings. Molineux's slapstick chorus line had just slunk offstage looking nothing at all like Rockettes.

"Our comedy tonight highlights the serious business of landmark preservation. And so, landmarks are the backdrop of our set . . ."

The curtain rose, revealing a twinkling, back-lit slice of the New York skyline.

"The backdrop you are looking at represents the threatened structures on this very block. Structures your contributions will help to save. My name is William VanderPoel, and my company, VanderPoel Cosmetics, helped organize tonight's events . . ."

Temple tried to run over her lines one last time—and was petrified to realize she was drawing a complete blank.

"In a moment, my place onstage will be taken by the beautiful Temple Kent—and our show will begin. But just now, stop and consider a city which obliterates its past instead of learning from it. A city with no foundation and an uncertain future. A city without light . . ."

The spotlight on VanderPoel dimmed. Then the twinkling

lights of the street silhouette were blotted out, one by one, until the audience was left sitting in total darkness.

"Everyone on this stage tonight will be donating his time," the disembodied voice continued. "I beg you, if you can donate more than the cost of your seat, please stop at the box office during intermission or after the show, where receipts will be offered for your tax-deductible contributions. We need your help to keep the Great White Way shining brightly. Where else could you see something like . . . this?"

Logan hovered behind Temple in the darkness, resting an encouraging hand on her shoulder.

"I thought those were *my* lines," she hissed nervously.

"Oh, didn't I tell you? We changed your lines—all of them—they're on cue cards in the prompter pit."

"You changed my lines!?!"

"Don't worry. We planned it this way." The director placed his hand in the small of her back, and whispered ". . . five, four, three two, one—go!"

Temple stumbled the requisite number of steps to her mark in the center of the murky stage.

A microphone swinging down from the rafters clonked her on the nose.

"Ow!" Her amplified yelp came out very loud. Titters bubbled from the invisible audience.

Suddenly the spots and footlights slammed on, blazing everything impossibly white. Somewhere beyond the dazzling glare, the full house applauded warmly. Temple, squinting at them under her hand, realized Redford was right: The one in the spotlight *is* blind.

"Well, hey, everybody." She got that out fine. The silvery gossamer she wore shimmered brilliantly, barely concealing her curves. Beneath the flimsy dress, her knees were so stiff she felt as if she were balancing on stilts.

Temple glanced at her lines: "Evening, folks. My name is Temple Kent. I'm a model. The face in the quicksilver in the Narcissus ads. The love interest in the current Kawasaki commercials . . ."

A few kind souls applauded, and it felt good. Temple swam for her wave.

"Thanks, I needed that. But those aren't the reasons I was asked to be your hostess tonight . . ."

A wolf whistle echoed down from the balcony.

Temple grinned. "Well, yeah, there's that."

The audience laughter buoyed her higher.

"The real point is that you don't have to be an expert to appreciate landmark buildings—you just have to use your eyes. And Bill VanderPoel thought you'd rather use yours on me than on him."

She still couldn't make out any faces beyond those in the first few rows. Temple left her mark and the safety of her dummy cards, pulling the dangling microphone as close to the edge of the stage as she could.

"I feel like an airplane being refueled in flight," she ad libbed.

Again, the chuckles eddied out of the balcony and washed across the stage. She was used to it already—except for the clammy sweat that wouldn't go away. Backing off, she read from her idiot cards again.

"Without further ado, I'd like to introduce you to our first performer this evening, our globe-trotting former secretary of state, singing 'Welcome' from the hit musical *Cabaret*...."

As Temple relinquished the spotlight to the curly-haired bespectacled man, an usher led a pair of latecomers down the center aisle to the orchestra. Looking for all the world like a dutiful son out for an evening at the theater with his mother, Frank Coughlin inched into the middle of the fifth row, accompanied by a beaming Dora Driscoll.

As Temple wandered through the fashion number like a lost little lamb, it had gradually dawned on her that Logan had turned her lack of preparation at rehearsals into a running gag at her expense. Her cue cards were held upside down. She was pushed, poked, and jostled. Even Chloris stuck out her tongue behind Temple's back. And whenever the other models were at the microphone, they made jokes about her salary, her talents, and her reputation. No wonder Logan had repeatedly excused her early from rehearsals.

Temple was prancing along with a parasol, winking at Coughlin, when Nina Vartell stuck one leg out of the long chorus line and tripped her. She sprawled flat on her face.

The huge audience roared with laughter, as playful as a Saint Bernard unaware of its own strength.

She picked herself up, flushing, and read from her cue cards: "All the clothing in the show is being loaned by Manhattan firms, and the jewelry comes from the estate department at Cartier. Our Molineux models will be back after the intermission, and they'll be joined by more of the usual suspects from Suzy's column. . . . Thank you very much, ladies . . . and you, too, Nina."

The fashion models paraded offstage, with Temple leading the applause.

When the clapping died down, she continued: "As Bill VanderPoel mentioned at the start of the show, orange drinks and tax deductions are being served in the lobby. But before I let you go, there's the matter of the door prize . . ."

The audience buzzed uncertainly. Backstage, Logan waved frantically for her attention, slicing his hand across his throat.

But Temple just smiled at him and plunged on. "You mean they didn't tell you? Gee, I hope you all held onto your seat stubs . . . You!" She pointed out past the footlights. "Yes, you sir—the big guy in the fifth row . . ."

Frank Coughlin sank down deeper into his chair, hiding his face behind his hand. Dora began grinning delightedly at Temple.

"Come on, handsome. Don't be shy. Do you have your stub?"

Frank shook his head.

"No? Well, since this is my contest and I'm the prize, I get to change the rules. You don't need your stub after all—you win. C'mon backstage, and be quick about it. We only have twenty minutes."

The audience began giggling.

". . . And don't bring your mother."

Fifty

Temple was donning her coat when Frank hopped into the doorway of her dressing room.

"Going somewhere?" he asked, glancing at several scantily clad girls in the hall.

"You're coming too."

"I am?" He eyed a chorine taking off her shirt. "I don't want to miss the second act," he protested.

"It can't start without me." Temple grabbed his arm and pulled him away. "C'mon, we don't have much time."

They ducked out the stage door, up the alley, and turned left toward Eighth Avenue.

"So the police let Dora go?"

Frank nodded. "Released on her own recognizance, pending further investigation. They won't charge her for shooting a prowler, though. . . . By the way, they found the other end of that broken walking stick—in Timm's office."

He swayed along a few steps and began chuckling. "You should have seen the lieutenant's face when he got a load of that old revolver of Dora's—a Detective Special—it must have been fifty years old. He was surprised it didn't blow up in her hand. We're having champagne in Uncle Mickey's suite after the show, okay?"

Temple tugged him up the steps to the church. "We'll see."

St. Agnes was as shabby inside as it was out—dark red brick lined with dark brown wood. The cloying odor of incense hung in the air. Along one wall, several candles flickered in lonesome mourning.

Kneeling in front of the altar was Father Dolan, worrying the cross in his hands. By one knee was a silver chalice full of sacramental wine.

The cleric picked it up and gulped deeply.

Temple stopped right behind him. "Who are you praying for, Father?"

The priest's head snapped around, his face gray and lined with pain. He tried to force a smile. "Even men of God need His guidance sometimes. Can I help you?"

Temple nodded. "We've come for a confession."

"Oh? Well, whose will it be—yours? Or Frankie's?"

"Actually . . . yours." Temple sat next to him on the plain wood steps. "We understand you weren't taking down the parish Christmas tree the night Casey was killed after all."

Father Dolan blinked. "Who told you that?"

"Your son."

Dolan sank slowly on the steps. "God help me. How did you find out?"

"Does it matter?"

Frank was peering at them both intently.

Dolan wrung his hands between his knees. "That poor woman came in off the street and I had to give her shelter. And then . . . I guess I persuaded myself I'd be cruel to reject the only thing she had to offer in return. But it was just the one time—I swear . . . And everyone assumes it's only the girls who end up payin' for their mistakes."

"Temple," Coughlin frowned. "This isn't really any of our affair."

"You're not paying attention, Frank. I don't care if a priest did something too human. I'm just wondering why Dora gave him that phony alibi. . . . Father?"

The priest avoided their eyes, drinking again from the silver chalice. "She wanted to spare me the embarrassment of explaining my whereabouts to the police."

"Is that what it was? Are you sure she wasn't more interested in an alibi for herself?"

Dolan swayed as though struck by a whip.

Temple turned to Frank who was staring at her with an odd look on his face. Finally, he nodded at her to continue.

She looked down at the cowering priest and explained it gently. "You see, if you weren't really here when Dora said you were alone together, then *she's* the one without an alibi. Where was she, Father?"

The tormented man shook his head.

Coughlin prodded him rudely with the tip of one crutch. "Where *was* she?" the judge growled harshly.

"I don't know . . . I don't . . . Honestly."

Temple nudged Frank's crutch away. "Where do you *think* she was? C'mon—give us a guess."

Dolan stared up at them with anguish in his eyes.

"Confession is good for the soul, Father," Temple pressed him. "You look like you could use some."

With a sob, the priest lunged suddenly at Frank's knees—but he didn't pull the big man down. Instead he just clung there, hiding his face as he wept.

"Holy Mother, forgive me, Frankie! It never occurred to me what was going on in the beginning. I thought it was a gift from heaven, her coming forward like that. I was so grateful, it's just today I realized she was out killing Casey." Dolan choked on his grief, hugging the last Coughlin's knees as though hanging on for dear life.

Frank was staring into the church's holy darkness. He looked as though he'd just been hit in the face with a two-by-four. Suddenly, his eyes narrowed. He swung his crutch like a polo mallet, knocking the priest's silver chalice clanging across the floor, spilling wine over the marble like blood.

"But *why?!*" he groaned. "She was our friend—almost a relative."

Dolan slumped, shaking his head. "Your brother was too stubborn. He wouldn't sell the Saloon, don't you see?"

"The . . . Saloon?"

"I suppose I mighta guessed if I'd let myself think about it. I didn't want to believe it. But then, when she shot Mr. Timm this morning—I knew right away that was no accident. She did it quite on purpose, you see."

Coughlin squinted at him. "But . . ."

"Did you really believe me all this time I've been telling you I never met the real estate big shots? Well, it's Dora, man! Dora is Cornerstone!"

Frank shut his eyes and tried violently to shake the idea out of his head.

"She was blackmailing me with the boy, don't you see? With little Eddie. All she asked was that I carry her messages. Just be the middleman is all. And then, I suppose, I persuaded myself that selling was really the best way out for most of us anyway. On my soul, Frankie, I never thought it would come to this."

Frank shoved the man rudely away from him. He scowled

at Temple. "She must have been after the Emerald too. How could she *do* that behind Uncle Mickey's back?"

Temple crossed her arms. "Unless she was working for him all along."

"No!!" Frank glared at her furiously. Then he nudged the priest with his crutch. "Well? Was she?"

"I don't know." The fallen father lowered his eyes. "It wasn't my business to ask."

Coughlin sneered. "You're a real soldier of Christ, you know that, Dolan? Just following orders from on high. Well, here's another order: Tomorrow morning, you're going to find everybody you carried offers to and tell them the deal's off. Permanently. The sooner they know there's no manna coming from heaven, the sooner they'll be able to make other plans. Now I'm getting out of here before I choke on the stench of contrition. Come on, Temple." He went stumping up the aisle.

"What . . ." Dolan shuffled around, still on his knees. "What are you going to do about me?"

"You?" Frank spun around, grinning at the man scornfully. "I'm sure our God has more exquisite tortures for your soul than any court of man could dream up . . . Don't forget to say your prayers, holy man."

Frank was hobbling cautiously down the church steps when an icy patch spun him off balance. Quickly, Temple steadied him, keeping one hand on the small of his back until they reached the sidewalk.

"Thanks," he murmured, ". . . for everything. I haven't been giving you much credit, have I?"

"I didn't do much—and I sure didn't think it was going to work . . ." They headed back to the theater. Little knots of people stood out front, enjoying intermission cigarettes.

Temple stopped short of the theatergoers. "The one who does the sewing, Frank. The one who does the wash. She does all the dirty work."

"What?"

"It all fits. I should have guessed. It's so . . . womanly."

"Must be. I can't understand a word you're saying."

"The warning notes were cut with pinking shears, Frank. Those are for sewing, they aren't a man's tool. That's why they didn't make sense in Timm's bag—they weren't his! Who else could have planted them there but the person who shot him?"

He shrugged helplessly. "You're right."

"And what about the clothes pole? Who hangs her wash there? Who has the best access to the roof? For God's sake, she *owns* Casey's murder weapon!"

Coughlin leaned his head against the wall of the Saloon.

"Figure it out, Frank: She was there in the coatroom at the Frick when Casey decided to check out the priest. Once he located Dolan's little family on West Eighty-eighth Street, it was just a matter of time before he'd pressure the guy into exposing Dora as Cornerstone. She had to eliminate him."

Temple pulled her scarf tighter to keep out the frigid wind. "Then, when I went up on the roof, it was a cinch for her to lock me out there. When that didn't finish me, she gave all this grandmotherly advice that translated into how I should coax you into selling the Saloon... And what about the night I got back from Saratoga and told you about Timm digging up the deeds to the Emerald? Wasn't she there at the bar?"

Coughlin nodded. "And two nights later, she shot him ...accidentally."

"You see what I mean? Dora was there all the time ... *every* time."

Temple started suddenly. "Jesus—was she in the lieutenant's office this afternoon when I called you about Eighty-eighth Street?"

"Yeah. Why?"

"When did the cops let her go?"

"Right after that. I dunno, maybe five-thirty. She was impatient—said she had some errands to run."

Temple nodded. "Well, at six-thirty, somebody pushed me onto the subway tracks at Eighty-sixth Street."

"What!"

"Right in front of the AA train. Notice my knees?"

Coughlin leaned over, peering intently at her camouflaged bruises. "Oh, Temple..." He wrapped his arms around her and squeezed gently. "A woman who was practically my aunt... Why would she do it? Where would she get that kind of money?"

"From your uncle?"

Frank shook his head. "He's no killer. I *know* that."

"You see people on the news every night who *know* the mass murderer next door."

Grimly, Coughlin watched the Emerald's flashing marquee lights signal the end of intermission.

"What are we going to do now, Frank?"

"I don't know. There's a circumstantial case against her for killing Casey—the D.A. will have to pay attention to it—but it's pretty shaky. Who knows if that priest will testify?"

"Won't the city have to find out who's behind Cornerstone now?"

"Maybe. But even if we do tie her to them, she probably hasn't done anything illegal with those offers. We don't quite have it nailed down yet, Temple."

Coughlin hoisted himself up on his crutches as a sudden blast of wind shoved him into Temple's arms. When she caught him, he sank wearily against her chest.

Temple's eyes swept the night sky. There, bathed in emerald light, the mask of Comedy was still laughing down at them.

"We need a miracle," she sighed.

Fifty-one

The curtain fell to thunderous applause as fifty Molineux models kicked their way offstage, dancing the spangles off the Rockettes.

While her fellow performers fell into one another's arms backstage, Temple whistled nervously, scanning the squealing throng for Frank Coughlin.

Logan walked among them, his face tranquilized into uncommon composure. The sequined penguins on his tuxedo cummerbund cavorted with delight. "Don't whistle backstage, peaches. It's bad luck."

Then she spotted Frank on the pay phone near the dressing rooms, holding his free ear closed against the din. He was shaking his head, looking dumbfounded.

Before Temple could reach him, he hung up and limped toward the spiral stairs to McQueeney's apartment.

"Frank!"

He glanced over his shoulder without stopping. "Find Dora and get her up here. I'm going to try something . . . Play along with me."

"Temple!!" The director beckoned her back to the wings. She held up a finger and glanced back up the spiral stair. Coughlin had disappeared through the door at the top.

"Curtain call, Temple! Move it!"

"All right, all right." Reluctantly, she returned to the side of the stage just in time to see Dora's sea-green chiffon dress trundling up the center aisle to the box office.

"Thank you, peaches." Logan kissed her on the cheek. "You were wonderful."

Temple arched one eyebrow at him. "Helluva concept, Logan—giving me grief all night."

The little man chuckled smugly. "A textbook case of audience dynamics: Everyone sympathizes with a pretty girl in distress—if she's game."

Suddenly a group of male models hoisted Temple onto their shoulders and carried her out to center stage.

A steady cascade of applause rose to greet her as she leaned into the microphone. "May these buildings stand even longer than this evening seemed to me. Good night!"

The cheers grew as the massive curtain swept open behind her. Fifty Molineux models paraded across the stage to take their bows, each decorating the arm of one of the evening's celebrity stars.

Last in line was Nina Vartell . . . on the arm of William VanderPoel. As the pair cruised up next to Temple, the ice-blonde vamp smirked at her, then turned to dip a swanlike curtsy to the audience.

Then Temple realized Van was nudging her. Looking down, she saw the old patrician was offering her a squirt gun behind his back. He raised his eyebrows suggestively.

Grinning, Temple grabbed the weapon. When Nina rose from her curtsy, Temple fired a steady stream of water from point-blank range, soaking the French girl's face until her mascara ran down her cheeks like long black tears.

The crowd went berserk.

Even after the curtain swept regally closed, the clapping continued, building into a tidal wave.

The curtain flew open again. This time Van pushed Temple forward to make her curtsy alone.

A young girl shyly laid a bouquet of roses at her feet. More flowers flew up from the front rows of the orchestra.

Temple glanced up to see Michael McQueeney waving through his trapdoor in the ceiling, with Frank hovering behind him.

Then another bouquet floated down the aisle, a gorgeous spray so tall it obscured the man carrying it until he'd hefted it onto the stage.

"One good fan deserves another, babe." Officer Falcone beamed up at her, resplendent in his dress blues with a dozen ribbons pinned to his chest.

Temple plunged her face into the flowers, savoring the sweet aroma. Then, as the audience roared around them, she got down on her knees, bent over, and began whispering into the policeman's ear.

Fifty-two

Michael McQueeney was struggling with a champagne bottle as Temple joined Frank on the blue silk sofa, giving him a searching look. Seconds later, Dora bustled into the private apartment, a gray metal cash box tucked under her arm. The old man's cork exploded.

"Say, what a day!" Uncle Mickey cackled, catching the fizzy amber liquid in a fluted glass and raising it to them all.

Dora shook the heavy box. "And what a night."

"Night's not over yet," Frank muttered.

"Ah, the party!" Dora's eyes glimmered with excitement. She handed Temple a glass and began polishing one for herself.

"Why don't you sit down a minute, Dora? We have to talk."

McQueeney rolled his chair closer to the sofa and offered Frank a bubbling glass. "First we get oiled—*then* we talk."

Frank shook his head. "It's about Casey, Uncle Mickey. I think I know who killed him."

"Do ye now!" Dora pulled up a chintz chair, as eager as a child waiting for a bedtime story. "So ye've got the goods on that O. M. Timm, then? I never did like that fella's looks."

Frank avoided the old lady's piercing stare. "It wasn't Timm."

"But those pinkin' shears ye found—don't they prove he's the devil as sent them threats to yer dear brother and you kids?"

Temple dug her elbow into Coughlin's side. "Threats? What makes you think we got any threats?"

Dora pulled the dripping champagne bottle from its silver bucket and filled everyone's glasses carefully. "Didn't ye tell me . . ." The rest of the big woman's sentence dangled in midair beside the dripping bottle of bubbly.

"Tell you what?" Frank stared across at the lady in sea-green chiffon.

Dora shook her head. "Ah, well. Me memory's slippin' on me at last, I'm afraid." The corners of her mouth twitched up and down.

Frank put down his champagne, untasted. "I'm afraid I have some bad news for you, Uncle Mickey. Dora and Father Dolan alibied each other for the night Casey died. But they were lying."

"That so?" McQueeney scratched the tip of his nose. "So it was Dolan all the time?"

"Not Dolan. I know where he was. Where were you that night, Dora?"

The old woman's mouth opened and closed, but she didn't make a sound.

"Say, what's goin' on here?" McQueeney growled.

Dora replaced the champagne in the silver bucket. "Are you implyin' somethin', Francis?"

"You bet I am."

The old woman smiled winningly. "Don't be foolin' with an old lady, Francis. Why would I be harmin' the dear lad? I'd have no cause to do a thing like that."

"You would if you were working with Cornerstone."

McQueeney's eyes narrowed. "What are ya talkin' about, boy?"

"We just got it straight from Father Dolan. You know those option checks he's been offering around? He says they come from Dora. She's been selling us out all along."

"Cripes, that's the most cockamamie notion I ever heard." The old man's frail white hands bounced on the rubber wheels of his chair. "I don't know, Francis, I wouldn't believe a man who spends his life preachin' fairy-tales . . ."

"Dolan's the Cornerstone contact, Uncle. He didn't find those checks in the collection box."

McQueeney glanced at Dora, sizing up the situation. "Listen to me, Francis Coughlin: Even if she does have this angle ya say, that don't make her no killer. Casey died by accident. The police say so, and *I'm* sayin' so."

"Maybe." Frank shot him a cunning smile. "But even if it *was* an accident, we still have to find Cornerstone. Dora has all the answers. Just look at her."

The old lady bit her lip as they turned to her, but the leering smile never wavered.

"It's a neat little frame," Frank grinned, "and she fits it perfectly. Unless she decides to tell us who's *really* been after us. . . ."

The babble of voices filtered up through the floorboards as a crowd of gangster-revival buffs streamed into the theater below them for the midnight show. Michael McQueeney rolled over to the trapdoor in front of his desk and swung it open.

"Cagney tonight," the old man muttered. "One of my favorites." He continued staring down into the hole until the reflected light on his face dimmed, and the movie music stirred the expectant crowd. Then he shut the trap with a weary sigh.

"Ya got it all wrong, Francis," the gravelly voice whispered. "*I'm* Cornerstone . . ."

Uncle Mickey poured himself another glass of champagne. "Or did ya guess that much already? Ah, I thought so. You're a clever kid to figure it out."

Frank nodded slowly. "Clever me. So you were selling out the whole block at the same time you were taking credit for protecting the Emerald . . . from yourself?"

"*Buyin'* it out, Francis—not sellin' it out. There's a hell of a difference. Well, there's no point arguin' about it. We needed the block that's all. Had to have it to make my plan work. But Francis, boy, use your senses. If we waited all these years, why hurt Casey now when the whole city's watchin' us?"

When Frank didn't reply, Temple cut in. "What about the other people on the block? How are they going to feel when they find out you've conned them into selling?"

"Conned? I'm talking real money here, kid. There's nothin' phony about it. I figure our friends and neighbors'll be grateful I'm givin' 'em the dough to start fresh somewhere else..."

"If you think they're so happy about the offers, why couldn't you be open about them in the first place?"

"Cripes, Francis, ya got an honest woman here." The old man sipped slowly, allowing the champagne bubbles to tickle his nose. "Ya see, Temple, if you're out in the open, all sorts of fellas on the make are gonna take potshots at your plans. So bein' devious is how business is done. It's the whole fun of the game."

Frank shook his head. "Let me get this straight, Uncle Mickey. Timm was in on the deal all along?"

"Hell, no—not till he started smellin' money. The cause of that little complication is Miss Temple Kent, here."

Temple blinked. "Me?"

"Ya tipped the fella I been tryin' to buy up the Saloon since forever. Once he got diggin' around, he knew I was up to somethin'." McQueeney chuckled. "'Course, he got it all wrong..."

"What do you mean?"

The old man snickered into his handkerchief. "Timm comes to me with some story about lost gold... Well, I don't believe a word of it, but this joker thinks I'm just playin' dumb. He decides I had Casey put away so I could get my mitts on this imaginary gold—and he threatens to spill the news to you if I don't cut him in on it."

"Wait a second," Temple interrupted. "Did he call you the night he got back from Saratoga?"

"Some night last week. Thursday, I think. So I'm in a spot, ya see, because even if this guy's story is screwy as a three-dollar bill, once Francis starts dreamin' about gold and suspectin' my motives, no way will he sell me the bar and get on with his career."

McQueeney adjusted his magenta glasses. "So, okay, I got to string the fella along. If he wants to buy this gold story, I'm willin' to cut him in on half a fairy-tale." He wiped his lips. "So this is the deal: He keeps his yap shut—I buy the Saloon from ya—and we split up the gold, fifty-fifty. If he ever finds it. But that busted ankle was his own idea, Francis. I had nothin' to do with that."

"Glad to hear it," Coughlin muttered.

"Oh, yeah—and I give him my solemn word I'll protect the Saloon from those evil Cornerstones." McQueeney snickered. "The sap never figured it was Cornerstone he was dealin' with all the time."

"Innocent as a lamb lyin' down in the lion's paws," Dora marveled affectionately. "Isn't my Michael a devil, now?"

McQueeney was tickled pink. "See what I mean about fun and games, Temple? Only then the fella gets itchy and says he wants to find the gold now. I tell him this is no time to be stirrin' up trouble, but he comes around snoopin' anyway. When I heard Dora shot him, well . . . he asked for it, didn't he?"

The old woman nodded. "The little busybody was beggin' for it from the start. Messin' with a block where he don't belong. Throwin' his fancy cocktail parties. And then double-dealin' behind Michael's back!"

"Still," McQueeney sighed, "ya mighta left him alone. He wasn't gonna find anything anyway."

"Oh, don't be daft, Michael! Ye had to shut him up someday. I been thankin' the Lord all day for deliverin' him to us on a silver platter."

The old lady chortled. "Oh, dearie, the way I put it over on these two lambs, doin' the helpless-old-lady act. Ye should have seen Francis, here, warnin' me not to mess with Cornerstone. And then, downtown, playin' cards with the lieutenant all afternoon while me own personal judge is makin' excuses for me to the coppers!"

Uncle Mickey fixed his shrewd eyes on his protégé. "Listen, Francis, there's no point in makin' a federal case about this. Dora shot a prowler, and ya won't be able to prove any different. Ya can blow my Cornerstone cover, I guess, but Dolan and the rest will be sellin' to me just the same. It's plain good business."

"Not for me, Uncle Mickey—not ever."

"Why not? Use yer noodle, boy. How long before that Saloon has ya bankrupt? My next offer won't be as handsome, ya know."

"I don't give a damn about your deals," Coughlin scowled.

"Now don't be such a sore loser, fella. Ya got to learn to take yer lumps and move on. Ya did good, but ya ain't tricky enough to play in the major leagues yet. Go back to bein' a judge, Francis. The good people need ya."

Coughlin's gold-flecked eye glinted dangerously. "She stole a brother from me, Uncle Mickey! And I want her to pay for it!"

"Can ye prove it?" Dora beamed at him smugly.

"Well . . . no."

The old man made a sour face. "She knows I don't stand for killin', boy. Don't be so full of revenge ya start grabbin' at straws. Casey's death wasn't our doin' . . ."

He lifted the dripping bottle of champagne from its bucket. "You're upset, Francis. Have yerself another glass of the bubbly. And then it's time we got down to the racket next door."

"Not so fast, Uncle Mickey." Coughlin rose to his feet and began prowling the room. "See, I don't have to prove that Dora killed Casey. I can send her to jail for the other murder."

"Ya mean Timm? I already told ya—"

"Not Timm, Uncle Mickey." Coughlin limped around behind the old people's chairs. "That was an old, old gun she used last night, but the police ran a check anyway—and guess what? I just got off the phone with the boys downtown and they tell me the bullets they pulled out of Timm match up to a very old crime. A killing that's never been solved. . . . You know what that means, don't you?"

Coughlin leaned down between the elderly couple and clamped his hand on Dora's shoulder. "I'm charging her with the murder of Arnold Rothstein."

Fifty-three

Uncle Mickey laughed and laughed.

"Oh, Francis, I'm mighty impressed! That's as tricky a move as I ever seen. Ya might make a major leaguer after all."

Temple snapped out of her astonishment. "You mean they never found the gun back in 1928?"

"Oh, they found it all right," Frank nodded. "But the police property clerk destroys guns after fifty years. Either they take them out on barges and dump them into the sea, or they melt them down in a furnace. The records say the Rothstein gun was destroyed. You can imagine their surprise when it turned up this morning. . . . Where did you get it, Dora?"

Her bright blue eyes danced with amusement. "Why, from Inspector Johnny Coughlin, o'course."

The old man's chuckles wheezed to rest. "It was part of the deal, ya see? He pulled a switch at headquarters and gave it back to me the day he kicked me out of the country. Why do ya think they dropped him from the force?"

"And you kept it? That was a big mistake, Uncle Mickey. You're going to have a tough time explaining why Dora had it."

McQueeney waved the idea away. "Francis, if the coppers spent fifty years refusin' to solve the Rothstein case, what makes ya think they'll change their minds now?"

"You forget, Uncle—I'm an officer of the court. I can arrest her this instant. There's no statute of limitations on murder, you know. One of you is coming downtown with me tonight. Which one is it going to be?"

The old man put a shaky hand on Dora's knee. "Y'aint convictin' anyone, Francis. But if ya got to make a nuisance, take me. She can't handle it."

"Don't be so foolish, Michael McQueeney!" Dora rose to her feet and reached for her coat. "None of those brave men could do Mr. Rothstein in, so I did—and a good deed it was. Right clever, too, else they'd have jailed me long ago."

Temple's eyes flickered. "It was your lipstick on the cigarettes in that hotel room."

"That it was," the lady said proudly. "Mr. Rothstein was in the hole so deep he was near to China." Dora settled into her rocking chair and began fingering the hem of her sea-green chiffon dress. "He started callin' in his loans—includin' the one to my Michael that bought us this place. He actually wanted us to sell the Emerald to settle the debt."

"Not a chance," McQueeney muttered.

"Then the man turned nasty, threatenin' to have the Vice frame me for a loose woman. Me, who he was givin' the eye for years! So Michael, bein' as smart as he is, sees the picture clear right away. Everyone knows Mr. Rothstein's been welshin' on his debts—particularly to George McManus, who is very loudly unhappy about it. So rubbin' out Mr. Rothstein cancels two old scores with one bullet, see?"

McQueeney muttered hoarsely, "I figured how I'd end up with my Emerald free and clear . . . that thief, McManus, would take the fall . . . and maybe I'd even get the Saloon he stole from me."

"Ah, 'twas a lovely plan." Dora patted the man's knee affectionately before picking up her mending basket. "I'm watchin' a McManus poker game in the Park Central one night, when Michael tips us his cousin Johnny Coughlin is sendin' over a raidin' party. Well, ye shoulda seen all them brave gangsters scatterin' like scared rabbits—with me sittin' on McManus's coat the whole while. Then I call Mr. Rothstein at Lindy's, askin' if he'd like to come to the hotel so I can give him some interest on our loan—personal." Dora winked at the younger couple. "O'course, I tell him to say he's meetin' McManus so my Michael won't find out . . .

"But sure enough, Michael bursts in on us pretendin' to be crazy with jealousy—and poor Mr. Rothstein never sees the stubby little gun I'm pullin'. Then it's simple enough to walk out, leavin' McManus's coat hangin' in the closet there . . ." The old woman's bright blue eyes leapt merrily. "Oh, me, what a lovely thing to get away with for so many years."

Coughlin rose slowly to his feet.

"Now hold on here!" McQueeney snapped. "*I* pulled the trigger, Francis, not her."

"Oh, stop yer boastin', old man." Dora turned her macabre smile on the other two. "He's as fine and gallant a gentleman as ye think he is—and I'm the one keeps his good name clean. Don't ye believe a word he says." She wrapped her strong arms around his shoulders.

McQueeney shook her off. "If anyone dies in jail, it's me, Francis." He slapped his useless legs. "I've been half-dead for years."

"Hush now, Michael. He's not like his grandfather. He'll not be happy with less than the truth. It's not Mr. Rothstein's killer the boy wants. It's Casey's."

Uncle Mickey craned his head at her desperately. "Are ya loony, woman? How do we give him Casey's killer when it was an accident?"

"Ah, it wasn't no accident, ye sweet old goat." Dora turned her unnatural smile on Frank as though eager to win a school prize. "It was me that hurt Casey—and Michael had nothin' to do with it."

"But ya *didn't!*" Uncle Mickey insisted.

The old woman beamed at him. "Yes . . . I . . . *did*. I had to get your bar back, didn't I? And ye can't wait forever. I knew ye wouldn't do it for yerself—so I did it for ye. As a gift!"

McQueeney stared at the radiant woman, his face getting grayer and grayer. "Ah, she's makin' it all up, can't ya see? She's tryin' to take a bum rap for me."

"Now, stop yer nonsense." Dora shook a finger at him. "I saw it comin' for days. First Casey ignores my warnin'. Then this landmarks meetin'. And him about to pull Francis and his girl into it too. I had to move quick, ye see?" She paused to thread a needle carefully with sea-green thread. "Old Glum was comin' loose anyway. He only needed a little push. And didn't it work now? A neater trick ye never did see . . ."

Michael McQueeney's wrinkled old face rested on a steeple of frail white fingers, his eyes shut tight. "I been afraid of this," he murmured finally. "I been prayin' all along it was really an accident." When he looked up, his old eyes were damp with tears. "Is this all true, woman?"

"O'course it's true! It had to be done, and ye know it. The man was too stubborn to deal with, and gettin' too near the truth. Well, I say it's about time a Coughlin saw the truth the way we been livin' it for all these years."

Dora turned to Frank. "Yer old grandpa ruined us, Francis, plain as if he'd sentenced us to hell. We had the whole city fooled until Johnny Coughlin started puttin' two and two together. He let McManus off . . . sent my Michael away . . . and winded up with the Saloon that's rightly ours." She jabbed her needle into the loose hem of her chiffon dress.

"Dora, Dora . . ." McQueeney sighed, his features wrenched with pain. "It don't do to pick at old wounds. I told ya once, Inspector John was bein' as true as he knew how. The man lost his job when he coulda been a hero."

"I don't care, Michael. You was family. He stole our child-bearin' years together as plain as a thief in the night." The old lady's hands were trembling.

"My dream was tendin' a family for you, Michael Mc-Queeney. Now I'm too old to give ye the posterity ye deserve— but I'm damned if I'll let you die without seein' yer immortality guaranteed. And if I have to give my life bringin' it about, well, that's no more than any woman risks givin' birth." Her flushed face remained intent on her sewing.

McQueeney wheeled his chair around, resting his hand on her old familiar knee. "I'm afraid our plans are gonna have to be changed, old girl."

Dora sat up, keenly alert in her straight-backed chair, as the old man turned to Frank.

"I'll tell ya why yer brother died, Francis—and how I get the blame. Then I'm askin' ya one last time to send me up the river if anyone's goin'."

Dora began shaking her head back and forth as McQueeney continued: "She's like this for a couple years now, thinkin' on the past and all we lost there. I had to get her away from this block, this theater, these memories—understand? But not without leavin' somethin' behind to say we been here . . .

"Ya remember I told ya how dreams keep an old man young, kid? Well, I been dreamin'—but not of a buildin', Francis. Oh no . . ." McQueeney's eyes clouded behind his magenta lenses.

"A park is what's behind it all. An Emerald Isle right here in the middle of Manhattan. I want to knock down all the Yankee crap on this block, savin' my Emerald, and plant the whole thing with sod from County Cork." The old man reached for his handkerchief. "And there'd be a sign: 'This park is for the people of the neighborhood, from a man who cared. No politicians allowed.'"

He smothered his wheezing laughter. "What a joke on the system!"

Dora stirred. "Ah, the people will put up a statue to ye, Michael—the man who made a green instead of an ugly old tower. You'd have the one thing no McManus or Rothstein ever had: respect."

"Only Casey got in the way," Frank muttered quietly.

McQueeney shrugged. "He was born in the way, Francis. But I never planned to hurt the fella—never. Only Dora wants me to have this park, see, and she doesn't understand killin' ain't the way I operate. I told her we'd have to 'take care of' Casey." He shook his head. "She just heard me wrong, ya see?"

"I heard yer heart," Dora scoffed. "Casey Coughlin was cheatin' you o'yer destiny, same as his grandfather before him."

McQueeney nodded sadly. "But it's lost in the end anyway."

Dora looked from one miserable face to the next. Her smile crumpled uncertainly, broken by their eyes, until she was weeping soundlessly.

McQueeney wrapped his frail arms around her. His sad eyes pleaded with the young ones. "We're both practical fellas, Francis. We know how the world runs and why. The truth of what goes on here depends on where ya sit. I see a fifty-year-old crime nobody wants solved . . . a load of real estate rumors nobody pins down . . . a dead prowler who got too nosy . . . and a terrible, terrible mistake. It's too late for the dead, Francis. No court can pay back Casey for what he lost."

Frank nodded. "And what about me, Uncle Mickey? Where do I get another brother?"

"Francis, Francis . . . Yer grief is my grief—ya see that, don't ya? We got to keep this in the family. At least give me a hearing. We owe each other that much—for old time's sake."

"Old time's sake?" Coughlin shook his head. "You make a lousy hero, Uncle Mickey."

"Well, hell, I know we're a pair of crooked dice. But jail ain't the answer for her. She wouldn't last a month. Ya can see that, can't ya?"

Dora slid off her chair to kneel over the old man's useless legs, snuffling quietly against his sleeve. McQueeney began stroking her thinning hair with wrinkled fingers. "She can be in a convent tomorrow, Francis—never to be seen again. Let the old girl meet God's justice, boy. There's none here on earth."

Frank gazed at him from far away. "And you?"

Putting the old woman aside, McQueeney began rolling around the room in aimless figure eights. "I'll help ya support the Saloon, how's that? Maybe there's gold in there—maybe not. But if there ain't, you'll need yer old Uncle Mickey, right? And we'll build my park together, wrapped around our own two buildings—the two sides of the family together at last. We'll name it after Casey, how's that? Coughlin-McQueeney Memorial Green—alphabetical, see?"

Frank regarded the old man silently.

"Think of the future, Francis—not the past. Ask yer pretty girlfriend there. She'll set ya straight."

Coughlin's clouded eyes slid over to Temple. He studied her moodily. Not asking, just . . . waiting.

Temple held his gaze while she spoke softly. "Why don't you pretend your own grandson is watching you . . . right now."

Gradually, Coughlin's face cleared. He smiled before dropping his eyes.

"Uncle Mickey, I owe you so much. You remember that night I shoplifted, when you beat me up? You taught me a hell of a lesson."

"Yeah," the old man chuckled, scratching his nose. "Don't get caught."

A tiny grin flitted over the young judge's face. "Well, that's one lesson you should have learned better yourself. No, the main thing I learned was that the man in power sets the example. I didn't stop stealing because it was wrong. I went straight because you were bigger than I. Well, Uncle Mickey . . ." Frank rose to his feet. "I'm bigger than you now."

McQueeney's chair stopped dead still by the old gun collection. After spinning around, he folded his hands sadly across the blanket covering his lap. "You're certainly quite the fella now, Francis. What'll ya do with all this power? It's a big responsibility."

Frank wandered to the trapdoor and lifted it open with his crutch. He stood staring down with his back to them as muffled dialogue rose from the theater below.

Finally, he turned around. "Afraid you pounded too much sense into me when you gave me that beating, Uncle Mickey." He pulled a card from his wallet, walked over to Dora, and began reading in a voice as firm as it was reluctant:

"You have the right to remain silent. You have the right to an attorn—"

"Ya have the right to stick up yer hands!" Uncle Mickey's command was backed up with the pearl-handled revolver he'd plucked from the display case. "Stick 'em up. Go on, tug on yer earlobes like you're fixin' yer earrings. You too, kid."

Frank and Temple reluctantly assumed the ridiculous position. "I'm proud of ya, Francis, I really am. I wasn't sure if ya had the guts. I taught ya well, boy—though you're maybe a little too unsuspectin' . . ." He wheeled back to the desk. "Sorry, fella. Ya could have had me—I deserve it a hundred times over—but I can't let ya lock away Dora on my account."

Lifting the cash box from his desk, McQueeney waved it at Dora. "Aer Lingus has a late flight to Shannon, girl. You go straight to the airport. I'll hold 'em here till you're safe away."

Dora frowned. "I'll not have ye rottin' in some old jail cell, Michael McQueeney. You go back to Ireland yerself, and let cousin Colleen care for ye. I'll take what's comin' to us."

"Ya want to listen to me once? They ain't convictin' me. I'll see ya by Easter. Now beat it."

Dora moved over to the old man and took the cash box from him. In the moment of silence, gunfire drifted up through the open trap. She bent to his ear. "Let's *both* take that night flight, Michael."

McQueeney waved his gun. "Somebody has to stay and hold these kids here."

"Not necessarily." The bright blue eyes glittered. "Not if . . ."
Uncle Mickey started frowning.

"Ye know we're in trouble as long as they live," Dora insisted, hugging his shoulders. "Do it now, Michael. Do it for both of us. The movie will cover the noise."

McQueeney glared at her sharply. "There's been enough killin' around here."

"Has there, now?" Clamping one thick arm across his lap, Dora wrenched the gun from the old man's feeble grasp. As they struggled, Temple grabbed the empty champagne bottle and slipped it into the sofa cushions next to her.

Dora waved the shiny pistol at Frank and Temple. "Yer a soft old goat, Michael—but somebody's got to do the dirty work. Remember what ye taught me our first night together? Once ye start there's no turnin' back?" She giggled naughtily. "We're no use apart, old man. I learned that a lifetime ago." Dora held the gun awkwardly in front of her, cocking it carefully with both thumbs.

The chill of goosebumps crawled over Temple's skin as she tensed herself for one last leap, but Coughlin's hand checked her firmly. He was speaking in a casual voice: "Will he love you the same tomorrow, Dora?"

"Eh?" She looked up from the gun uncertainly.

"Uncle Mickey fell in love with a chorus girl. What if you're making him ashamed of you now?"

Dora glanced down at the man in the wheelchair, just as McQueeney grabbed for the gun in her hands. She yanked it away, scolding him maternally. "Be sensible, Michael. There's no—"

A slam from the back of the room startled them all. Scrambling out of the dumbwaiter was Officer Falcone, a .38 police pistol in his hand.

Fifty-four

"Drop it, lady! I'm in charge now."

Dora spun around, facing him unsteadily. As the cop swaggered across the room, he leveled his gun at Michael McQueeney's skull. Carefully, Dora put the pearl-handled revolver down on the desk.

Temple hopped to her feet. "You cut it pretty fine, Officer Falcone."

"Down, babe," he snapped.

Temple blinked. "What?"

Falcone pivoted, waving his gun at her menacingly. "Park your butt—now!"

"Anything you say, Officer." Temple dropped back to the sofa. ". . . Scrotum."

Dora Driscoll began chuckling. "Takin' the night off from the warehouse, are ye?"

"I'm takin' the rest of my life off, lady. The little actress here guaranteed me a promotion if I came up that dumbwaiter and listened awhile. And the things I heard . . ." The cop shook his head in mock disapproval. "Now the only question left is, Who gives me the bigger promotion—the department . . . or Cornerstone?"

Coughlin stirred uneasily beside Temple. "Jesus Christ. Now we've got trouble."

Dora's eyes were shining. "Well, I think we can make ye the better offer, lad. Now, would ye mind pointin' yer gun at those two there? That Francis makes me terrible nervous."

Obligingly, Falcone swung around and aimed at Coughlin's navel. "What kinda offer are we talkin' about, lady? Somethin' worth quittin' the force?"

Dora whispered into Michael McQueeney's ear, and the old man grinned in spite of himself.

"Tell me somethin', young fella," Dora bubbled cheerfully. "Did ye ever have it in mind to own a saloon?"

"What!" Coughlin's gold-flecked eyes flashed. He was steaming so furiously that Falcone moved back a step.

"It's an old tradition of the house," the woman continued. "Get rid of the owner, retire from the police, and spend the rest o'yer days drinkin' his liquor."

The cop's eyes darted at her skeptically. "How does that work?"

"With these two gone, Michael will inherit the Saloon. Then he'll deed it over to ye—for a dollar. Think o'the theater crowd, man. Ye'd be hostin' a party o'chorus girls every night o'the week."

Officer Falcone gave Temple a mean grin. "Sounds pretty good—check?"

"There's some as think there's gold in there, too, ye know." The old lady winked. "Think of it, Michael. This way, we won't have to run off a'tall. We sit right here and build ourselves that park after all."

"No . . . no . . . no. Not with the blood of family on my hands."

"It's a little too late for that, Michael McQueeney. Ah, Falcone, yer a lifesaver."

She moved around behind McQueeney's metal chair, resting her hands on its grips, and began pulling him backward. "Now, ye keep these two quiet till we're off to the party, lad. And then take 'em wherever ye will—as long as they don't come back."

"It's too late, Dora. People will have missed Frank and me. They'll come looking any time."

"Now, there yer probably right. We'll have to be hurryin', Michael." She continued dragging the wheelchair away, leaning down to coo into the ear of her wrinkled old man. "Do ye think there'd be time to change me dress, Michael, or should I—"

Dora staggered. Suddenly she fell down behind the chair, screaming in terror.

"*AHHH! MICH . . .*" Plunging through the open trapdoor in the floor, her muffled shriek snapped off abruptly, on the other side of the hole. Then a yell of surprise was followed by a series of horrified shouts, echoing around the dark theater.

Michael McQueeney spun his chair around, confused.

Officer Falcone stared at the spot where Dora had vanished, not yet comprehending.

Temple swung the champagne bottle hard, cracking the revolver from the stunned cop's hand before he knew it. When she plucked it from the floor, he smiled weakly and raised his hands.

Frank was already by the wheelchair with the pearl-handled gun in his hand.

But Michael McQueeney didn't even notice. He was leaning over his knees, staring down into the palace of dreams.

On the giant screen below, Jimmy Cagney stood all alone like a king atop a blazing oil storage tank. "I made it, Ma!" the young hoodlum cried through the furious flames. "Top o' the world!"

Uncle Mickey stared wistfully into his past, as the world in front of him exploded.

"I'll be along soon, old girl." The gravelly whisper was almost inaudible. "Don't I always come back to ya in the end . . . ?"

Fifty-five

" . . . So, summin' up this WSAV special bulletin, police tonight linked three supposedly accidental deaths in the theater district, uncoverin' two murders and a complex real estate swindle that threatened potential city landmarks. Behind it all, a sweet little ol' perpetrator with a taste for murderous mayhem, Dora Driscoll. Her duped benefactor, Emerald Theater owner Michael McQueeney, has reportedly gone into seclusion, grievin' over the shockin' news of her betrayal. This is Jimmy Shelby, reportin' live from the steps of the Emerald, returnin' you now to our regular program . . ."

Pat flicked off the late newsbreak, and leaned on the dark mahogany bar. "Now there's a bit o'news I never wanted to hear. Imagine Dora turnin' on Casey and Mickey that way! Why, she could barely run the Emerald, let alone a place like this." The bartender shook his head and surveyed the room.

Coughlin's Saloon surged with a swankiness it hadn't known in years. Surprised yelps and shrieks of delight punctuated the merry babble of the *Comedy of Errors* cast party.

"It just don't make no sense," the burly barman continued. "Unless the old girl was plain addled, that is. What coulda made her do it?"

"Love," Temple murmured.

Pat cocked his head as Frank glanced at her curiously. "Well, it didn't say nothin' about love on the TV there. I'm thinkin' that wasn't the most thorough police briefin' I ever heard. D'ye think there's more to it?"

"It was thorough enough for me." Frank caught the other man's eye and held it. "Casey's killer paid with her life. The rest is . . . history."

Pat nodded slowly. "Well, that's true, right enough . . ."

He glanced down the bar to where three older men in working clothes nursed their beers while they stared at the milling models. "Oh, Frankie. Some of the regular boys is wonderin' what the rates are tonight. Considerin' Mr. VanderPoel is pickin' up the tab for the party and all."

Frank glanced down the bar and back. "Those guys all look like uncles of the chorus line to me. No charge."

"Now, there's a decision!" Pat grinned. "I always knew ye had executive talent . . . boss."

"Temple!"

She swiveled on her barstool. Tina Molineux was bearing down on her like a luxury liner under full steam.

"Hello, Frank. Listen, dear, Annabel tells me this Lewis Tedesco has been calling you about becoming a James Bond girl."

"Not anymore. I never even called him back."

"It's just as well, believe me. That's him—over there in the satin jacket." In a dark corner of the dining room, Lewis Tedesco was leading Nina Vartell into the men's room.

"That hustler was trying to make himself a scam sandwich," Tina was saying.

"A *what?*"

"He was promising you to the Bond people, and promising

the Bond people to you, trying to find a percentage for himself in the middle. He doesn't represent anyone."

The bugle in the men's room blared loudly.

Pat snatched a bottle of beer out of the way just as a tipsy Chloris Ames tap-danced down the length of the bar. She hopped to the floor in front of Logan and tapped out a ringing solo on the hollow footrail with her metal cleats. The penguins circling the director's cummerbund jiggled back and forth in time to her taps.

Chloris skipped away with Tina Molineux in hot pursuit. Temple watched them disappear into the throng, where a local fireman and the young heir to a European cognac fortune were carrying Consuela Forberg across the room on their shoulders. Marla, Judy, and the other mimes filtered through the crowd distributing party favors.

"Why, hi, Judge Coughlin! Feeling better?" A balding, gangly man clapped Frank on the back, nearly knocking him off his crutches. In a lower voice, the mayor of the City of New York continued: "I appreciate your letting us handle that reporter's briefing, Frank. I hope you don't mind if his story seemed . . . incomplete."

Coughlin shrugged. "The right people got what they deserved."

"Exactly. You know, the public doesn't want us wasting city funds poking around in ancient history."

"I suppose. But it sure would be fun to see who'd start squirming if we did."

The mayor rolled his eyes theatrically. "You have an odd sense of humor, young man."

Coughlin smiled noncommittally.

"Don't get me wrong—I like it. You have a great future in this city, Frank. It's great to have you on the team. Meanwhile, we'll see what we can do about landmarking this building, okay?" His Honor winked, moving off without waiting for a reply.

"Now, isn't he a lovely man," Pat purred sweetly. "Imagine him helpin' us out o'the goodness of his heart."

Coughlin gave him a wry smile. "It's a mixed blessing, you know. Father Dolan was right about one thing: this whole block needed Cornerstone's money. Even Coughlin's Saloon."

"Maybe your luck is about to change." Temple put her arm around him.

Frank shook his head. "This family's luck died with Casey. I don't know how he did it all those years—if he was cheating the IRS or spinning straw into gold—but it was some kind of magic that's beyond me. If only he'd left us a clue."

Temple smiled. "What would you do if you found the gold?"

"What Uncle Mickey should have been doing—taking care of the neighborhood. Those old Tammany bosses had the right idea, you know, helping the little man get his foot on the first rung of the ladder. They just took too much advantage, that's all. Wouldn't it be nice if a guy could pour out his troubles to the man behind the neighborhood bar, and find a miracle on his doorstep the next morning?" Coughlin chuckled. "Don't you think Pat would make a good Santa Claus?"

Temple leaned over and planted a big kiss on Frank's cheek. "I have a surprise for—"

"May I have your attention, please!" Across the room, Bill VanderPoel was on his feet, tapping his glass with a spoon. "Excuse me, but I have several announcements to make! I've just heard from the box office, and I'm told we not only reached our goal tonight, we surpassed it." The news was greeted by riotous applause.

"I'm not finished yet! I have also been informed that Michael McQueeney, owner of the marvelous theater next door, has made a most magnanimous gesture. He's decided to make one last pilgrimage back to the land of his fathers, and he wants to leave his theater in good hands. In other words . . . with the Upper Times Square Landmarks League. He's also promised a substantial contribution to our endowment. Mr. McQueeney's health does not permit him to be with us tonight, but I know we all wish him godspeed."

More applause crackled around the room.

"Thank you . . . thank you. What this all means is we now have enough money to fund a preservation survey of the entire Upper Times Square area. No more giant toasters! Right, Mr. Mayor?"

Laughter rippled through the crowd.

"Now a last, unfortunate note. Ogden Timm, the producer of tonight's extravaganza, died this morning. I'm sure you'll be reading the unhappy details of this morning's events in the papers, but for now, I'd like to offer a toast in his memory. . . . To O. M. Timm!"

Van raised his glass and took a swallow.

Temple felt a tentative tap on her elbow. She turned to find her cousin wrapped in a voluptuous mink.

"Oh, Pamela, you came!"

"I wouldn't have missed it for anything. I even got Dick Cavett's autograph." Pamela's eyes swept over Frank as though she were trying to memorize him.

"Oh, this is my friend, Frank Coughlin . . . My cousin Pamela."

Frank smiled. "Glad to meet you."

"And how. Temple, I wish I could stay, but Paul's idea of baby-sitting is teaching the kid to mix martinis."

Temple laughed. "You can tell me: Was I really awful?"

"Not at all. But stay away from *A Streetcar Named Desire*."

"I promise. Call me tomorrow?"

Pamela sized up Coughlin one last time. "You better believe it."

The women hugged warmly before the young mother vanished into the crowd.

"Nice lady," Frank observed.

"Mmm. Happy too." Temple stifled a yawn. "I didn't realize I was so wiped out."

He slid his arm around her waist and whispered into her ear. "Why don't we escape upstairs, then? We could save ourselves a trip downtown tonight. I've got eggs for breakfast and—"

"Frank." Temple pulled away from him. "I know I've been, well, disappointing you lately, but . . . something's bothering me."

"I know—independence. Well, I'll untie you right after breakfast. Scout's honor."

"No, no, it's . . ."

Temple's eyes widened as an attractive redhead cruised up to them and kissed Coughlin smack on the cheek. It was the woman she'd seen doing the dishes at his house several nights ago.

Temple glared at them irritably. "It's *this!*"

"This?" A half smile flitted over his face. "Oh, my other redhead." He put aside his crutches, wrapped his arms around the woman's waist, and squeezed affectionately.

"I'll thank ye to take yer grubby paws off me wife, young man, before I rearrange yer face and turn ye handsome!"

Temple whirled around and stared at Pat. "*Your* wife?"

"The beautiful Mrs. Duggan herself. I know it's hard to imagine so pretty a creature livin' with the likes o'me, but redheads have no sense a'tall. Kathleen Kelly Duggan, this pretty little thing is the lady of the Coughlin house—two or three times a week, that is."

"Then you're Temple! I've heard so much about you." Kathleen Duggan squeezed the girl's hand fondly. "That's right, I remember you from the hospital and—Why look at you! What's wrong now?"

Temple's eyes were swimming with happiness. She turned to Frank, wrapping her arms around his neck, and hugged him fiercely. "God," she whispered. "I am such an idiot."

Kathleen Duggan chuckled contentedly. "Now, how many drinks ahead of me are you three scalawags?"

"Forty-seven," Frank said gravely. "Apiece. Ready for number forty-eight, Temple?"

"Well . . ." She twined her fingers among his. "I'm kinda ready to retire. You know . . . upstairs?"

Coughlin's eyes fell into hers. "Oh. Umm . . . Pat? Think you can get rid of these people later?"

The bartender handed him his crutches. "Anythin' ye like . . . boss."

When Temple and Frank reached the back stairs, she paused on the first step. "You know, some people say sex is the ultimate language."

"Could be. So?"

She nuzzled his ear.

"Talk to me."

Fifty-six

It was long past midnight when Temple crept barefoot down the creaky back steps of the old mansion. The gas jets still sputtered cosily in the deserted Saloon. The only sound in the room was the soft clink of coins as the brawny man behind the bar packed rows of quarters into orange paper tubes.

Pat looked up in surprise as Temple padded in wearing Frank's shirt.

"Are ye bored with him already, then? I can't say as I blame ye. They don't make men like they did in my day."

"Mind your manners now, Patrick." Sitting across from him at the bar, Kathleen Duggan didn't even look up from her knitting.

"But the poor girl's all alone," the barman protested. "Himself must have fallen asleep on the little lamb."

"Hardly." Temple smiled. "Himself wants more champagne."

"Well, there's a good sign. Bottom shelf of the cooler. Ah . . . would there be somethin' to celebrate, Red?"

Temple crossed the planked floor behind the bar and knelt for a chilled magnum of Cristal Brut.

"He doesn't know it yet—but I think we're going to be living together."

"Oh, what a rotten shame!" Pat slapped a roll of quarters down on the corner.

Temple's head snapped up. "Why?"

"Me and the missus and some o'the lads have been runnin' a pool, wagerin' when ye'd set up housekeepin' together. I didn't figure it to happen until St. Patrick's Day. Now, let's just see who was down for this week . . ." He licked his thumb and began flicking through a small notebook.

"I was." Kathleen looked up and scrutinized the younger woman carefully. "How do you feel about it?"

Temple thought a moment. "I never realized how much

energy you waste by hesitating all the time. I'm so flooded with it now I . . . I can feel myself better."

Kathleen nodded. "That'll do. Patrick—my winnings, please."

He fished a handful of bills out of a cigar box.

Kathleen waved them at Temple. "You aren't going to change your mind, are you?"

"Not anytime soon."

"Well, that's what happily-ever-after is all about." She stuffed the money into her purse. "Remember, all you two have to do to make it true is believe in it."

Temple smiled. "That's a hundred and ten percent right."

"Well, that's fine. Now come on, you big side of mutton. It's time you had the privilege of walking a beautiful woman home." She grabbed her husband's arm so sharply he fumbled a roll of quarters. The orange tube tumbled off the counter and bounced off the brass footrail with a solid clink.

"Comin', my sweet. Soon as I put the bar to bed for the night."

"Never mind that," Kathleen chided. "The lady of the house will see to it."

Temple locked up after them, then padded back to the bar and stooped for the roll of quarters. The orange tube had split, and a row of twinkling coins had spilled onto the floor.

Coins.

Temple got down on her knees. Right under her nose, the footrail gleamed in the soft amber light, a long brass tube stretching off into the shadows.

She grabbed one of the quarters and tapped the railing. Once again, it clinked solidly.

Then she hurried to the other end of the rail, where Chloris Ames had tap-danced her solo during the cast party. Here it rang with a hollow echo.

"Where's my champagne?" Coughlin stomped into the room, swaying precariously on his crutches. He halted in his tracks when he saw Temple kneeling on the floor.

"Temple? We have scrub ladies who do the floors in the morning. What are you doing?"

"Prospecting." Running behind the bar, she fetched a hammer, screwdriver, and flashlight. At the solid end of the footrail she applied the screwdriver to the brass cap that plugged it, and began banging away.

Coughlin watched her curiously. "Have you cleared this demolition with the landmarks commission?"

The cap clattered to the floor. Without answering him, Temple snapped on the flashlight and peered into the footrail. There, circled by thirteen six-pointed stars, the left profile of Liberty was resting on its golden head.

The footrail of Coughlin's Saloon was lined with Paquet double eagles. President U. S. Grant's uncollected bribe money had fallen into the hands of an honest politician at last.

Fifty-seven

Coughlin was combing her hair with his hands, brushing it off her forehead. "Aren't you being a little . . . personal?" he teased.

Temple paused. "In this bed you can't help it. Want me to stop?"

"Are you kidding?"

Frank's boyhood bed in the middle room was a narrow single—perfect for a Little Leaguer. For a couple of lovers, though, it was overly cosy.

Some time later, he pulled her up into his arms.

"You taste like spring rain." Temple cuddled closer. "Move over."

"Over where? I can't levitate."

She raised one knee, resting it across his stomach. "How could you sleep like this?"

"Well, I didn't have company in those days."

Temple pulled the covers up over them. "Do you still want some now?"

"Hmmmm?"

"Company . . . all the time . . . We passed the audition, didn't we?"

Frank lifted his head in wonder. Then he lay back and gazed at the ceiling. "I thought I made you feel threatened."

"I used to think you were out to steal my freedom."

"And now you don't?"

Temple shook her head. "Being with you is a different kind of freedom. Free to try what I'm afraid of, instead of running away. I feel more free with you than when I'm alone."

". . . I wish Casey had lived to see this." He kissed her lightly on her eyelids. "I warn you, we may be thoroughly happy."

"Let's start now." She tossed back the covers and straddled him carefully.

They were still pressing together, driving themselves deeper into the heart of the night, when Temple leaned down, her long titian hair forming a curtain around their faces.

"Frank . . . ? There's just one thing . . . about . . . living together."

"Mmmmm . . . What, angel?"

Temple waited for him to open his eyes . . . and then she giggled. "My place or yours?"

Several of the historical characters in this novel actually lived—
Jim Fisk, Helen "Josie" Mansfield Reade, George McManus,
Inspector John Coughlin, and the notorious gambler, Arnold
Rothstein. In most respects their stories are accurately repre-
sented—except where they touch on the fictional Coughlin
family and its saloon.

All references to the Coughlin family descendants and to
Coughlin's Saloon are entirely fictitious.

The murder of Arnold Rothstein has never been solved . . .

From Ballantine

       TA-43